The Onyx Crown

A Tale of Ancient Africa

Alan Hurst

Dedication

To Mom, for the many years of love and encouragement.

Contents

List of Characters

Sania
Chaos. One of the three Khuselas destined to restore Tribe of Toloron to Numerian throne. Former *Dukka-Vinyo* girl.

Jorann
Calm. Former slave boy. One of the three Khuselas. Commands an army of the Kumazi

Gesemni
Conflict. Companion to royal siblings of East Rhydor. One of the three Khuselas. Current owner of the Emi Sword. Often called Gesi.

K'Nan
Legendary Paladin of Numeria. Searching for the Khuselas and the Heir to begin the Toloron restoration.

Zoe
Young princess of East Rhydor. Companioned by Gesemni. Prospective bride of the usurper Crown Prince, Azzolari Azu.

Zadeemo
Young prince of East Rhydor. Companioned by Gesemni. Former student of the First Knight.

Jorell Boro
Known as the First Knight. Hero of the Coastal Wars and Protector of the Prince of East Rhydor.

Daphni	Prophetess and Tribal Leader of the Kumazi.
Mistress Jayda	Owner of kumaze-we *Dukka-Vinyo*. Former caretaker of Sania.
Mr. Mohann	Manager of kumaze-we *Dukka-Vinyo*. Former caretaker of Sania, who escorts her to
Magistrate Dioni	Official who frequents Mistress Jayda's *Dukka-Vinyo*. Object of incessant Sania pranks.
Darious	Avaremba of the First Prince of East Rhydor. Foster father of Gesemni.
Lord Jasonne	Tribal leader. Former loyal retainer of Lord Toloron. Member of Numerian conclave
Saddique/ Rushdi	Members of Gilded Fisherman's clan.
Semri/Semarion	Trusted twin retainers of K'Nan.
Reverent Mordu	Numerian tribal leader. Religious zealot. Mortal enemy of King Toloron. Executor of the Kula Selawa.
Lord Mutuofu	Numerian tribal leader. Enemy of Lord Jashu Jasonne. Spy for Lord Okon.

Lady Ilayna	Widow of Azu the Despot. Mother of defeated Azinna Azu and current "usurper" heir Azzolari Azu
Regent Okon	Former officer of Toloron turned traitor. Protector of the usurper heir. Currently most powerful man in Numeria.
Azzolari Azu	Usurper heir, brought back from exile by Lord Okon to restore Azu line to rule.
Toloron	Deceased all-powerful conqueror of Numeria. Defeater of Victo Ngeppu, Azu the Despot and Azinna Azu. "Chief of Chiefs", or Mekuwa Waku.
Aiiesha	Deceased former queen of King Toloron
Azoni Azu	The Despot. Former Numerian tribal warlord and would-be conqueror. Defeated by then Lord Toloron
Azinna Azu	Son of the Despotic Azoni Azu and older brother of Azzolari the usurper crown prince. Defeated by Toloron
Victo Ngeppu	Numerian tribal warlord. Made an ill-advised bid to conquer the other tribes and provinces. Defeated by Toloron.

The
Onyx
Crown

Alan Hurst

Fate of the Hunters

I was beginning to get used to the cold, thought K'Nan.

As he looked down from the jagged cliffs, the warm winter winds seemed to swirl in every direction. Below him, hundreds of *Win-Daji*, or hunters, were clustered together at the town exit gates, horses and camels burdened to their limits with food, weapons, and valuables.

In tow were their families, generally just as burdened as their beasts with any household items too valuable to be left behind during the temperate winter season.

The families may all have been the same, so identical were the members of most of them. The wife, the stout, no-nonsense matriarch with the perpetually grim expression, followed by the *Halanbi* (firstborn son), who was expected to carry a weapon, as well as the *Win-Daji*, generally tall and thin from wilderness trapping or training thereof, wearing an imperious look and far too eager to begin the journey.

In direct contrast to this look would be that of the *Halandi*, (other son, literally 'one who would not inherit'), and his expression of resignation to that of being a servant for the foreseeable future.

In general, the Halandi had quite a few responsibilities, but most of them were related to administration of the family and properties, considered secondary and even shameful to the *Win-Daji*, so when in the presence of the Halanbi and their fathers and father's attendmen, there was very little that the Halandi could not feel inferior about.

Any of the other remaining were daughters of the *Win-Daji* and their servants. As it was through their marriages and breeding that the Hunting Groups created alliances and ultimately advanced through the ranks, the daughters were of great importance.

Nonetheless, they kept a discreet distance from these hunters, and the rest of the men as protocol required. It was not unusual to see a daughter of the *Win-Daji* or the wife of one of the Halandi beaten while being accused with flirting with men from some of the other groups.

At the gates stood several of the town's bravest and most dependable border guards, checking credentials and questioning families to help them decide whether or not they should join this year's Equinox Hunt.

The Equinox Hunt was the once-every-ten-moon foray into the *chakkha*, or jungle, made by only the most celebrated hunters of the Nabii tribe of Numeria. Its primary purpose was to keep the beast population to manageable levels and stop them from foraging into the grasslands but had long ago become a reliable way to create fortunes for some Nabii tribesmen (called merely 'the *Win-Daji*'), and their families.

Although wealth and riches beyond all imagination could be found beyond the gates of the chief Nabii citadel, Abir City, if the *Win-Daji* knew where to look, for most families it was more likely that they would return to the gates destitute, starving, and missing several family members.

K'Nan knew this as well as anyone. He knew he was looking at mostly dead men. *Damn men are such fools*, he thought. Most of these hunters were already successful enough to provide for their families, own property, perhaps even bribe for themselves a minor position on the council. Success is never satisfying, and in fact, it spurs on the hunger drive for more success.

This time, he thought, *things just may turn out differently for them.* Why he had decided to lead the Hunt this year was a puzzle even to himself.

He knew better than to rely on the nonsensical rumors that had been trickling out of the wilderness for the last year and a half. Tales of mythical beasts and fearsome fighters attacking the

Numerian migrants seemed just that, more myth than reality, except...

Except he'd also dreamt of them for the last several moons of his life. He could probably count the number of peaceful nights he'd slept in that time quite easily if he stopped to think about it. There damned sure hadn't been many.

How could he sleep? The unimaginable horror of some of the things he'd seen during those dreams wasn't easy to forget—man-eating beasts, bloodthirsty warriors, and infants dying in the wilderness.

It was this last dream, the one about three infant children that spurred him toward the innermost reaches of the *chakkha*—the destination of these Equinox Hunters, the *Win-Daji*.

"Why does it bother you so much?" he said to himself. "It's just a dream like any other, and those other three are long lost now."

And yet here he was. All because of a dream.

He shook his head at himself. "When will you finally give up hope?"

The winds started blowing even more briskly now, bringing a mini-sandstorm to the town gates. Instinctively, everyone covered their eyes and faces, through conditioning more than fear.

It was apparent that they were in no danger from sand this far from the wilderness, but hiding from it was a habit both born and bred in them from childbirth. Heat can indeed kill you, but in the desert, you learn to fear the sand much more than the heat.

Luckily for the *Win-Daji*, the summer had not begun. In the summer, sandstorms morphed from deadly to catastrophic—it was widely known that the one approaching would last for many months and be one of the hottest ever recorded.

The hunter talking with the sentries now was unique enough to catch K'Nan's interest. This man was tall and pale-skinned (a rarity this far south) with a scar leading from the corner of his left eye to his left ear, a love-kiss from a Deluthian rhino most likely, K'Nan's *imoya*, or spirit, told him.

He wore his hair in the traditional Nabii tribesman style, shaved on the sides with a thin strip of hair about two inches high down the middle. On his hip, he carried a crescent sword, very worn and very menacing, and two bows slung carelessly across his back.

Tied around his left thigh was a two-cubic-long dagger with a polished bone handle covered with notches. *This man has done some killing,* thought K'Nan, *and without a doubt not confined it to beasts.*

Whatever he was arguing with the sentries about must've been important. Gradually all of the other *Win-Daji* and Halanbi moved closer to them to listen in. Some were nodding and raising their weapons. Every now and then there'd be a little shout of encouragement from the group. Meanwhile, the guards were shaking their heads all the more emphatically.

K'Nan ended his reverie and motioned his two companions, Semri and Semarion, to follow him down the rocky path toward the gates. The steadfast twin brothers hastily complied.

They had fought and hunted with him the better part of the last five moons and were two of the only people he felt he could truly rely on, despite the fact that they were not full-blooded Numerians. So, he'd asked them to accompany him, without telling them the true reason.

What are you so worried about? He asked himself. *Aren't you K'Nan the Savage Slayer, a legend in all three territories of the savannah, defender of the Numerians, the scourge of all Panthia? How many countless men have died under your two-bladed spear, deservedly all?*

How many beasts have you saved these wretched villagers from? You've dined with tribal chieftains between both seas, shared their spoils, and bedded their daughters. How could a life as full as yours end so quickly? Have you forgotten what the prophetess told you?

And what of your life before that? What about your other identity? Will you ever be able to reclaim that?

Inside he knew none of that mattered. If he could not lead these *Win-Daji* back safely, he was as good as dead. In this region, all a man has is his reputation, and when that's gone, they may as well find a comfortably soft place to lie down and die.

As they reached the gates, the shouting began to get even louder. The families were obviously agitated about something, but the more they shouted, the more the guards looked even more resolute.

"It is much too dangerous this season," said one of the sentries in a dialect called *Tandish*, which was nothing more than an informal mix of the free warrior tongue of the Nabii and another more formal language known as the Common Tongue, or simply Numerian. "I don't care how often your people have prepared for the hunt; they don't go out without a guide."

The uproar got even more furious, and it seemed inevitable that an altercation would follow. Walking up to the sentries briskly and stepping between them and the angry *Win-Daji*, K'Nan briefly touched his forehead with his first two fingers, a gesture of salute. It was immediately returned.

"I am their guide for this hunt," he said loud enough so that all could hear.

Instantly, fifty pairs of eyes turned to him and his entourage.

Scanning the group, he saw five additional men, dressed efficiently in light-toned sabaar (cactus) armor and addax skins, the native dress of those from the outer reaches of the wilderness. All five had a sinewy build, a level of conditioning that could only come from both extreme strength and discipline.

K'Nan noticed it was the man in front of the other four who had the most magnetic presence. He sat rigid and extremely upright on his ha'mal, a strange feat in itself. A beast native to the driest reaches of the wilderness, a ha'mal is the genetic equivalent of a horse, desert steer, and camel. Very muscular beasts, it was almost impossible to saddle them, meaning the rider generally must lean forward to keep from falling off.

This man's weapons were all white, made from the densest bone, and polished to a high sheen.

K'Nan was mostly conscious of the man's eyes. They set deeper inside his skull than normal and were dark and unreadable. But there was unmistakable energy coming from them, making a person feel compelled to look away. With his black coarsely braided hair speckled with gray lending him a distinguished and severe look, he appeared more weathered than old.

There was an air of arrogance about him, his weapons, and even his ha'mal, which made him all the more interesting. The *Win-Daji* appreciated seeing confidence and pride in a man's demeanor above all else. There was a famous Numerian proverb, *Konto hakanti kunye themba*, which translated meant, "Below average spear combined with above average confidence can be invincible." This hunter seemed to embody that saying.

After a few seconds, that very same hunter stepped forward. "We are all honored that you would offer your services, warrior," he said a bit hesitantly, "but we have never met before, and you've never been employed by our group in the past. Is that correct?"

"This is correct," said K'Nan. "No *Win-Daji* have ever employed myself or my two associates, and we have never guided the Nabii through the Equinox Hunt before." Upon hearing this, a low murmur quickly spread throughout the group, and the lead hunter shook his head over and over.

"This will not do, brave sir. Although it may seem to outsiders that the Nabii would accept almost any hero from the outer territories to act as our guide, we cannot risk your life or the lives of our families. Considering your lack of experience leading these expeditions, it's most likely that you'd wind up getting us lost or even killed."

K'Nan bristled at this covertly disrespectful rejection. *When I was trampling the enemies of Lord Toloron under my spear, you were probably stuck in a sand shelter somewhere, beating your women and binging on wine, so who the hell are you to question me?*

He responded stiffly, "As the saying goes, 'will the place you live one day become a landmark or a ruin?' It seems the world-famous *Win-Daji* of the Nabii want to gain wealth and glory, yet do so without taking any risks at all, or am I mistaken?"

The hunter also seemed to sense he'd gone too far. He paused, then continued thoughtfully, "No disrespect meant, Numerian. Although we must decline your offer, we would never be so inconsiderate as to not compensate you for meeting us at the rally point. Gisad!"

He shouted toward some younger men about fifty *en-yawo* away. An *en-yawo* was a Numerian unit of distance measurement roughly the equivalent of a foot. One of them, obviously Halandi of the lead hunter, came forward with a purse and offered it to K'Nan.

Annoyed at the suggestion that he would take money for a job not completed, K'Nan quickly waved the boy away. The Halandi boy, now completely confused, looked back at him, then at the lead hunter, unsure of what to do.

The lead hunter cleared his throat.

"A true hero with principles, indeed. May we have the honor of knowing the brave hero's name, so future generations of the *Win-Daji* will know to whom they are indebted?" He said this with mock gravitas, and it seemed obvious to K'Nan that he and the other Nabii tribal leaders thought he was insane. For one, he refused payment—and hunt guides were not known for being particularly wealthy, even the busiest ones.

Secondly, he acted to them as if guiding the most dangerous hunt in the last few hundred moons was no more difficult than deciding what to have for your morning meal.

"I am K'Nan Urmandu. Perhaps you have heard my humble name once or twice during your journeys. Although it's true that I've never participated in a hunt, I've lived a large part of my life in the *chakka,* and there's nothing new I can be shown there." He hoped that was true. "I wish to lead your Hunt this year, but if there is someone who wants to formally oppose me, please let him make his presence known."

At the mention of his name, every man, woman, and child gasped. Everyone in the savannah had heard of the exploits and heroism of the fabled warrior from Urmandu—K'Nan the Savage Slayer.

In the *chakkha,* he killed an adult *alnamaa* (Black Panther) with only a spear and addaxx shield.

That was at age seven.

He was well known to be adept with a spear, flawless with his bow, and damn near unbeatable in a bare-handed fight. He'd famously trapped and killed many legendary beasts, including the wilderness chim'ra and a couple of fifty-rod gilasand dragons.

All of these things he did more for the safety of the tribesmen and settlers in the wilderness than for fame or glory. As always after he'd completed some monumental feat, he would disappear, and his name would fade into obscurity, at least for a while.

Adding to his already mythical legend, it was rumored that K'Nan could take the shape of any animal found in the chakkha, desert, or grasslands. Sometimes he could become a leopard, sometimes a large rhino—and these were all thought to be just a tiny part of his legendary abilities.

The entire hunt was amazed that he was now facing them, living and breathing. Looks of disbelief were all around him until one of the children spoke up. It was obvious he wanted to believe he was really K'Nan the Savage Slayer. "But...but K'Nan bai-hei (honorable brother) is three rods tall!!! Plus, he always travels with a sand serpent...he..."

K'Nan was amazed. All of these *Win-Daji* here, and the only one with the guts to question him was one of their slave boys. His initial annoyance quickly subsided to sympathy as his eyes took in the boy's dirty hair, ragged clothing, and bare feet, at the same time noticing his sturdy and tall build. *What a waste,* he thought.

"Son," said K'Nan patiently "have you ever actually seen a Numerian sand serpent?" The boy blinked, a bit embarrassed and afraid to look him in the eye, something K'Nan despised, realizing it was a habit born from his status as a captive.

"No," the boy admitted.

"Fearsome beasts they are, as ferocious as all the legends say. Faster than the wind, and their breath burns white and hotter than the hottest fire you've ever seen or felt. But not the biggest beasts in the world, that's for certain. No man three rods tall would be able to sit on even the strongest of them, and neither would you." He chuckled inwardly as he told the kid this. It always amused him to see how exponentially these useless legends always grew.

The boy looked around him for help, but none was forthcoming.

K'Nan...would not..." His voice trailed away. He was out of reasons to doubt, yet still persisted. K'Nan sighed. Had it been so long since he'd been around others that no one was able to recognize him by bearing or look?

"Take a look at this, boy." Reaching back over his shoulder, he slid his magnificent ivory sword out of his scabbard and pointed the handle toward the lad.

Everything stopped. Only the wind bouncing off of the grayish-red cliffs could now be heard. As they all looked at his weapon, they instantly recognized it; a silver handle engraved flawlessly in the shape of an angry pachyderm. The savage white elephant perched and waiting to strike, its eyes made from green emeralds.

Amnesia. Named such by the High King Toloron himself, the blade was given to K'Nan after the second battle of the Dunes, a battle in which they had been on opposing sides.

The entrance to the village was deathly quiet.

Eyes as wide as the plateau itself, the boy reached forward to touch the blade with his left hand. K'Nan seemed to freeze for a moment, then quickly grabbed the boy's wrist and turned it to him, staring intently for what seemed like minutes before switching his gaze to the boy's eyes, mindless of the others around him.

"So?" K'Nan said briskly, dropping the boy's wrist and unceremoniously shoving the sword back into the scabbard. "Shall we be off then? *Win-Daji* and Halanbi to the right, left, and rear, scouts to the front with me, families and servants in the midst. We'll follow the Taranzi trail due northwest before reaching the wilderness."

He hoped that no one who listened carefully to his orders might have detected a slight quiver in his tone, a sense of urgency in his words.

Turning to Semri and Semarion, he gave them several urgent instructions in one of the native dry region dialects, which none of the hunters understood. Initially appearing puzzled, they soon raced on their brown spotted stallions to form the vanguard out of view.

The *Win-Daji* and their families hurried to form up, all of them had wanted to talk more to the Slayer and find out more about him, to hear his stories, ask about his weapons and his beast, but he'd given them no chance.

The hunting party was briefly held up by the ridiculously slow crossing of an elderly man, looking at least about ninety moons of age. His hair was unkempt and filthy, his clothes soiled with excrement, and his feet bare.

Quite deliberately, he made his way toward the other side of the street. As he came into view, everyone noticed with amazement that the bag over his right shoulder had gold sequins sewn into the fabric, as well as precious gems embedded around the handle. It appeared to be expensive beyond measure.

What on Earth was this old, decrepit elder doing with such a bag?

*   *

It took about three hours for the bulk of the *Win-Daji* to steer their motley caravan through the massive iron gates, which were still manned by another thirty sentries, toward the jagged cliffs.

Altogether their party covered an area of about two hundred square en-yawo, not so large as to make it cumbersome to move, though the small children and animals slowed down their progress quite a bit.

It wasn't till midday that they made their way past all of the jagged cliffs to the only reliable avenue of travel to the outskirts of the wilderness.

As everyone stopped in the plateau to drink water and remove sand from their faces and clothes, K'Nan approached the lead party on foot. "Boy," he asked the young lad of about twelve moons, the one who'd questioned him earlier, "how would you like to ride on my left for the first part of the journey?"

Instantly, the boy jumped to his feet, his excitement lending him an impressive burst of energy. He made to run toward K'Nan but suddenly stopped and glanced back at the hunter and Halanbi of his party. They glanced at him briefly, then spoke to the boy sharply in Tandish.

Eyes downcast, he began to walk back to the party. "Is something wrong?" K'Nan asked the hunter in Tandish. "Is this boy not free to travel as he chooses, even at his age?"

The hunter glared at him. "This boy is my personal property from combat spoils since before he was five moons old. By law, I don't have to release him into anyone's custody." The hunter was respectful but firm.

"Are you afraid the child will run? Have you not been a good master, sir?" he asked the hunter, who bristled.

"A good master is still, after all, a master," was the man's only reply.

Hearing this, K'Nan's eyes blazed murderously, causing the hunter to shift his weight back almost imperceptibly.

K'Nan spoke to him again, a bit more gently this time. "Sir, I take complete responsibility for this boy as your property. I will not let him leave this party as long as you're under my charge— that I swear to you."

Eyes slightly wide, the hunter nodded once to K'Nan and once to the boy and stumbled back to his own mount. K'Nan watched, emotionless, as the boy ran over to his horse and led it to K'Nan's tha'mal.

Once the caravan began moving, the boy looked back nervously as if to see whether or not his hunter or Halanbi had changed their minds, only to see that they remained in their normal position at the head of the Hunt.

Excitedly, he turned to K'Nan. Though it didn't mean much in the plateau, once in the wilderness, any distance of greater than a hundred en-yawo would be like being on the other side of the ocean.

"Tell me, sir! What..."

"Silence," K'Nan said harshly, turning his eyes directly ahead.

Stunned, the boy wondered what he could have possibly done to anger the Slayer. Of all the dreams he'd had the most growing up in the drylands, next to his master being killed, and his master granting him his freedom, by far the next most frequent dream was him meeting the famous K'Nan and becoming a great warrior.

Now he'd finally met his idol, the man he'd heard stories about and wanted to emulate since he could remember.

Of course, the other kids in the *Win-Daji* families, the ones who were not slaves, had quickly dispelled any such notions that he would ever amount to anything. "Slaves need to know their place!"

They would yell disgusting insults at him, then begin beating him with cacti ropes, supposedly made to play with but also the preferred weapon of torture for kids of the dry lands.

In fact, from age seven to age nine, he could scarcely remember a day when he hadn't been beaten or otherwise humiliated in some way by the children of the hunt. His legs and arms were a labyrinth of scars from the cacti knots.

The boy knew they had been correct in their thinking, though. After all, only the children of the hunters were even allowed to learn weapons—how to use a bow, a spear, a knife.

Swords were never used in the wilderness and were thought to be generally inept, even in battle, until not so long ago, during the wars with the Pale Tribes, who had come over from the great blue seas with their swords, their crossbows, their fire arrows, and their steeds. Although they had been brutally beaten and sent scurrying back across the seas, thanks in no small part to the Slayer and the High King's armies, there was much that the people from the southern lands had learned from them.

The foremost idea being that the effectiveness of modern shields had rendered the spear useless in combat, and it was now necessary to get much closer to your adversary in order to deal a killing blow. Swords were a great weapon for that, and so had become the weapon of choice for the Southern Armies of the High King, if not so for the hunters.

In addition to no training in the arts of war, the boy had had no instruction in even the most basic survival techniques. Concepts of trapping, foraging, evasion, and escape from wild beasts were things he'd never been taught, although he'd taught himself some hunting.

So inside he'd always known that only through his dreams would he ever be able to experience the thrill of conquest in battle or in the hunt. He'd known this and accepted it.

Until today.

Today he'd unbelievably managed to meet K'Nan the Savage Slayer, even be favored by him—enough that he'd been asked for his accompaniment as left counselor—and just as quickly to have angered him. So went his last hope. He sighed inwardly. *Destiny, boy. You were destined to be what you are.*

The boy sighed, muttering under his breath. "I only wanted to ask you if the sword really had no memories."

* *

Although a little perturbed that the boy had disregarded his command to be silent, the boy's question brought many deeply buried memories to the forefront of his mind. Indeed, the tale of how he had been gifted the sword was legendary.

"Would you like to hear how it got the name?" He asked the boy, eyeing his ragged clothes.

A hopeful gleam appeared in the young slave's eyes. He nodded vigorously.

Taking time throughout to answer the child's questions patiently, he told the boy the story of how Amnesia got its name.

"It was all made possible by one of the most idiotic men to ever proclaim himself lord of Numeria, Victo Ngeppu...." he began.

Sometime later, as he finished the story, the details of which were known to very few people still alive, he paused for a second and looked down at his hunting skins, his simple shoes, and his calloused hands. He had fallen far in look and appearance from when he had been the most feared general on the continent.

For his part, the boy's eyes were agape with wonder. "So...it wasn't actually YOU who came up with the name, it was King Toloron himself," he breathed.

"This is so."

"Wow," said the boy. "I've heard many stories about you before, but never that one. I don't think any of the other kids knew it, either." The boy paused as if there was something else on his mind.

"Pala K'Nan...why did you choose to tell me this story right now?"

K'Nan looked up at the sky, then back down toward the boy's wrists, before saying, "I have my reasons."

After an hour, the party reached the black rocky sands that marked the entry into the savannah. As the caravan began narrowing its flanks for the final passage out of the plateau, the dark red sun's final rays blanketed the area surrounding the cliffs. Flying overhead, several swift yirna birds squawked quizzically at the group. K'Nan and his small companion rode through the thirty en-yawo exit leading into the savannah, the *Win-Daji* several paces behind.

Arrows whistled over the cliffs with incredulous speed, as if they were being hurled down by the clouds themselves. The first volley took the lead hunter in the throat, and several more decimated the entire lead party within seconds.

Chaos followed. The plateau echoed with the sounds of screaming women and children, killed by both arrows and horses as *Win-Daji* tried desperately to steer their mounts toward the cliff walls, trampling those on foot. It was only once they reached the walls that the boulders began to tumble down from the top of the cliffs.

From a height of two hundred *en-yawo*, their impact sounded like thunder hitting the earth, and those who were not crushed immediately were forever trapped beneath the boulders.

Some of the more clever ones tried to gallop to the plateau's exit but found the entrance too far away to evade the attack. They perished miserably. The last to die were the steeds and the children, the horses running wildly to and from trying to dodge the boulders, most of them breaking their legs or collapsing from fatigue.

The children, who'd been shielded in desperation by their unfortunate mothers, crying, pulled themselves up from under their human shields and were cut down.

The boy watched the scene unfolding in horror; K'Nan himself was emotionless. In the time it takes to eat a small meal, it was finished. There were only a few low moaning sounds and the sounds of the yirna birds, who gleefully rushed down to scavenge, particularly having an affinity for the entrails of the dying.

All at once, a blanket of billowing dust covered the plateau. It served to form a grim burial shroud over the remains of the last-ever Equinox Hunt.

2

Gesemni's Conflict

"Can't you hurry up a bit? Any slower and we'll miss everything!" Gesemni heard the whining voice again, just as he seemed every second of every day for seemingly the last five moons.

Five moons! He was certain he could hear her high-pitched whine in his sleep sometimes. *No matter how much she threatens me, I will not force this donkey to move any faster*, he swore to himself.

Of course, it was easy for the girl, Zoe, and her twin brother, Zadeemo, to complain about him being slow since they were riding two of the fastest ponies in the Red Sand Straits, both blood-red mares with notoriously bad tempers and hooves that hardly seemed to touch the ground.

In contrast, Gesemni's poor packhorse, which he'd taken to calling Dumb Ass, seemed to expend maximum effort just to plod two or three steps. *It's not your fault*, Gesemni thought, gritting his teeth as he half-nudged, half-dragged the reins away from a thorn patch a few *en-yawo* ahead. *I'm just going to have to learn to tell them no.*

You're daydreaming again, Gesi, he told himself. *What you are to them is an evolved species of a servant, one who must play companion to the two most insufferable and petulant children anywhere under the six moons.*

Not for the first time, he wondered why his adopted father or *muzuri*, Darious, had moved them from the coastal cities where he could first remember growing up to work in the household of the First Prince as his *avaremba*, or master of the skies.

His father's role was the most indispensable position in the household, responsible for the breeding, training, and utilization of all messenger and war falcons of the noble houses.

The First Prince's *avaremba* had under his supervision around seventy such creatures of flight, and thus was the person primarily tasked with making sure the prince could communicate with the outside world.

If that wasn't enough to make him invaluable to the prince, Darious was also a prodigious hunter and tracker. There weren't too many exploits that the First Prince enjoyed more than hunting, and he'd come to rely on Darious's uncanny ability to track some of the more exotic beasts that inhabited the chakkha of East Rhydor, the First Prince's dominion.

Just in the past few months they'd tracked several saralions, a few dozen armored mammoths, and even a flathead Derennian boar. Of course, the First Prince always took most of the glory associated with the hunting, but he graciously allowed Darious to offload some of his duties as *avaremba* to his subordinates, which gave Gesi more time to accompany him on hunts.

Gesi loved this. He'd always hated the fortress where they lived, the monolithic Caledon, with its fourteen hundred men-at-arms and six thousand commonfolk all crammed within towering black walls completely encircled by ten moats—and beyond that the dense wildwoods, which meant freedom and adventure to his young wandering mind.

He could scarcely remember a time since they'd arrived—with only the clothes they wore and some letters of reference from some mysterious former master—when he hadn't wished they could get away from the foul smell of horse feces and rotten food that interminably choked the air within its walls.

Caledon once had enjoyed a reputation for being the cross-roads of culture and learning a hundred moons before, primarily during the reign of the seven kings, but since those enlightened rulers' descendants had been deposed, its condition and prestige steadily deteriorated, and these days it was less than a shadow of what it had been back then.

Of course, as retainers of the First Prince, he and Darious did enjoy a certain amount of prestige in and around the fortress. Once the many bakers, cooks, and vendors within the fortress walls had learned who his foster father was, they'd wasted no time in offering him free food and rich pastries. It seemed to him as if they thought doing a favor for the son of the First Prince's *avaremba* was akin to them serving the First Prince directly.

However, his *muzuri* had raised him well. He'd taught him to realize that in the times during and immediately following war, the commonfolk suffered more than anyone, and so he had determined never to accept gifts from the townspeople because it always ended up costing their families.

For this reason, among many, most of the commonfolk seemed to like him. Although he had a haughty personality—"He seems an arrogant little chap," remarked more than one of them from time to time—more likely than not those who met Gesi came away with rather a kind impression of the young lad.

Still, he spent less time than he would have liked among the commoners in the fortress because Zoe and Zadeemo were the children of the First Prince, and children of royal blood never *ever* became friends with or "fraternized" with commoners.

Naturally, they never let him forget that he himself was a commoner. As if he actually needed more of a reminder than the obvious—that his clothing and shoes were always weathered, while the two of them dressed exquisitely for the most trivial occasions, even for a hunt. In addition, his looks, though handsome, were much more serious and sterner than his age would normally indicate.

Contrastingly, the twins possessed the type of looks that you would expect to see from two of the noblest children in the empire.

Then there was Zoe herself. She had that rare quality of having just the right combination of arrogance and beauty, which turned the heads of all those who saw her, smiling adults and envious children alike.

Gesi felt uncomfortable around her; he just never seemed to be able to do anything that pleased her. Why that was so important to him, he couldn't fathom, but it was. To make matters more complicated, she seemed to sense his discomfiture in her presence and usually sought to do whatever she could to magnify it.

Today she was thronged in pale green, which served to enhance her dark brown eyes and long black braided hair, tied back neatly with a jade clip.

Right now, those dark brown eyes carried a look of impatience and disgust. "Gesi," she warned him, "I'm telling father if we miss the final kill because of your stupid animal. If you had any respect for our royal house whatsoever, you'd be flogging him right now." Stubbornly, Gesi looked into her eyes and, despite himself, refused to blink. "Arrggh!" She cried in one final fit of disgust. "Zadeemo, let's leave him." Ever the more silent one, though Gesi thought perhaps the more intelligent, Zadeemo shrugged indifferently and spurred his mare toward the noise ahead. In a few seconds, they were well out of sight.

He allowed himself a brief smile of satisfaction. *Had to happen sooner or later*, he told himself. *It's time they learned to take no for an answer.* Three minutes later, though, as he approached the shouts and laughter of the hunting party, he began to wish he'd done otherwise.

It was apparent from the elated looks of the group that they'd caught their main quarry, a Kushite female leopard. "Father! Gesi caused us to miss everything," Zoe whined, sniffling pitifully. *When Zoe cries*, he reflected wryly; *you could almost imagine helpless baby cubs weeping in the savannah*. Nearly every head turned in his direction in unison.

A man of some considerable experience in warfare and politics, as well as quite a womanizer in his youth, the First Prince was utterly inept at fatherhood, and—his wife having died in childbirth after delivering the twins—had always spoiled his children, particularly Zoe. Normally he would've been moved by her impressive emotional display, but flushed with the success of the hunt, he said, "Zoe, not now, my dear. We'll discuss this later this evening."

Darious, however, was a lot more sympathetic. "Gesi," he sternly reproached, "you know how important this hunt was to the young master and mistress, and you're supposed to be accompanying them. How could you let them down in this way?"

Though not his birth father, a reprimand from Darious was one of the few things that could shame Gesi. Never a night went by where Gesi didn't include his gratitude for his *muzuri* in his prayers—for finding him as a young child and raising him as his own.

Countless times, he'd thought to himself, *I'd probably be dead or worse if not for him.* However, it sure did seem to him that his foster father sometimes went out of his way to take the twins' side instead of his.

"I'm sorry, Darious." Boiling inside, he lowered his head. He didn't mind apologizing to Darious, but he also knew how much those insufferable brats were enjoying this. "Be that as it seems," Darious replied, "I don't think I was the one hurt by your reticence this morning, child...."

"Zoe, Zadeemo...please forgive my slowness. It won't happen again." Inside, though, he was cursing their ancestors as he forced a remorseful expression to his face. A few seconds passed without either of them saying anything.

"Hmmph," Zoe said. "I can forgive his taking liberties only so much—"

"I know," said Gesemni. "You're about to say you're going to ask his Grace to replace me as your royal companion, right?"

Both children stared at him in stunned silence. They had indeed been discussing this before they complained to their father, but there's no way Gesemni could have known that.

"Eavesdropper," Zoe sniffed disdainfully, turned her nose away from both of them, and sauntered away without another glance. Zadeemo, his usual stoic yet arrogant self, did likewise. They both followed their father's personal troupe toward the camp entrance, where there would certainly be feasts of roasted lamb, milkwine, flakken with honey, and spiced meat pies.

After that, the First Prince would begin rewarding the members of the party who had distinguished themselves, perhaps with a couple of fine desert saber pelts, ivory tusks, or some gold trinkets from his own treasury.

Given all this, of course they couldn't be bothered with any further conversation or "fraternization" with the family help.

He and Darious looked after them for a few moments, then glanced at each other and smiled. Both of them found a couple of grazpalm stumps to sit down on. "Gesi," Darious asked him, eyes twinkling, "what really happened with those twins? Let me guess, Zoe couldn't decide what to wear?"

"No." *Not this particular time*, he thought.

"Surely Zadeemo wasn't the reason then? Do you know why she complained to the First Prince?"

He shrugged. "They weren't lying. I could've gone a bit faster. Dumb Ass was tired, in any case. I got tired of pushing him."

"This is the wrong kingdom and time to be an animal lover, Gesi. They are beasts, not people."

Well, that was something the two of them would never agree on. He decided to change the subject.

"Darious," he asked, "why do you always side with them?"

Darious raised his eyes. "What?"

"Zoe and Zadeemo. I don't ever remember you defending me when they complain to the prince. And that happens all the time." He paused, then said, "I remember an incident almost two moons ago—Zadeemo and I were practicing swords with the First Knight, with Zoe looking on and jeering.

We had a pretty good battle, but I won, as always. The First Knight then gave us a pair of matching knight figurines that he'd carved himself some time before. He said he wanted us to have them because we'd been learning our swordplay well."

"But when Zoe saw the figurines, she became furious. Said treasures from a knight shouldn't go to a peasant boy..." Gesi crossed his arms angrily on the stump, recalling the incident. "When you came by to pick me up, the twins had rehearsed their plan to cheat me out of it. Their version of events was that we'd both won the figurines from the First Knight, and I had promised mine to Zoe, but then reneged."

He shrugged. "If she had just asked me for the figurine, I would've given it to her without a second thought. But they always scheme.... In any case, you immediately made me give it 'back' to Zoe." He paused again, suddenly not feeling like that incident was such a big deal anymore. Why had it upset him so much back then?

"It just seems strange that you didn't even want to hear my side of the story, that's all."

Darious looked at him sympathetically. "Gesi, I already knew your side of the story."

Gesi looked up at him doubtfully. "You did? But I never—"

"Of course, I did. I know how protective you feel about Zoe also, then and now. You would never do anything to hurt her. That's why I was shocked to hear about your disagreement today."

Not knowing what his guardian was referring to exactly, he probed a bit, embarrassed. "*Muzuri*...I'm not sure what you think..."

"It's okay, son. There's nothing wrong with falling for a princess, even at your extremely young age. I had a crush on one myself, quite some time ago. As long as you remember this—she feels that you are beneath her lineage, so there's not going be much of a future for you two." He smiled at him, then winked, making Gesi laugh.

After another pause, Darious sighed. "Gesi, I know it seems like I always side with your companions over you, but you should know that secretly I always side with you." The crickets and menke birds chirping in the background accentuated the silence that hung in the air between them as he spoke.

"I do this to make sure that there won't be any lingering disputes between you three. Gesi, you love conflict. It's what you do best. It's even who you really are....." Darious hesitated a bit, afraid that with that last sentence he had said too much.

"That said, you're not ready to take on the world, yet. I keep you and the twins on good terms to protect you." He leaned close to Gesi's ear and whispered intently.

"Gesi, there is a reason why you're never wrong when you disagree with them. It's not that you're better than them or smarter than they are. You have certain talents...when it comes to knowing people's thoughts..."

Huh? Gesi thought.

This puzzled him, but also scared him, as he'd several times wondered the same thing but had always concluded that he was imagining things. Also, what did Darious mean when he told him that he 'is' conflict?

"Please remember you have to be very caref—"

"Master Darious!" One of the First Prince's personal guards appeared. Even in the forest, they were required to wear their traditional citadel attire, and his bright white tunic with its diamond accented armor made a sharp contrast to what existed in the thick natural forests that surrounded them. The *Unassailables*, they were called, presumably because they couldn't be bested, were the group of six guards who protected the First Prince.

But for some reason, they had never seemed to Gesi what he always thought knights to be. They'd always seemed a lot more preoccupied with protecting their own reputations than protecting their prince.

Like now, for example. The First Prince still insisted on never taking more than one personal guard with them on a hunt, so using one as a messenger meant he was unprotected.

If he had been one of the Unassailables, he'd have insisted that the prince send another messenger. This particular guard, Pala Nolo (Pala short for Paladin), should've known better.

"You're wanted by the First Prince, immediately," he said. Darious nodded.

"Go and enjoy the celebration, Gesi. And don't be so hard on the twins, they can't help how and to whom they were born." Darious firmly placed his arm around Gesi's shoulders, and together they walked out of the forest.

The next morning, he woke up excited. Staring into the almost extinguished candle he'd lit the night before, he'd thought long and hard on how to best mend the argument he'd had with the twins, as well as making sure that they got along well going forward.

Clearly, it was essential to Darious that he treats Zoe and her brother well, and looking within, he knew it was important to himself also. He'd gone to sleep with a smile on his face, not even noticing the normal unsettling sounds of the Lifeless Ones running the red hyenas through the streets to clean up the garbage and sewage, another reason why he really detested the *khalqaddi*.

The Lifeless Ones, despised as they were, were migrating into Numeria in large numbers—accepting employment no one else wanted, saving their money, and forming their own close-knit communities within the various citadels. They were despised by other poor Numerians mainly for those reasons.

Walking out to the forum in front of the First Prince's residence, where he waited for them every morning, he was mildly shocked to see that they were there waiting for him this time.

This has to be bad, he thought, but looking closer, he saw signs of friendliness on the face of both brother and sister.

"Hello, Gesi," said Zoe. "I trust you slept well last night?" Zadeemo nodded, which was almost like a speech for him. At that, Gesi broke out into a sudden sweat. Still, he felt he had to go through with what he'd decided the previous night.

"Zoe...Zadeemo. I slept well, thanks." He paused. "I actually wanted to apologize to you guys...for causing you to miss the kill yesterday morning." Now it was their eyebrows being visibly raised. *Okay*, thought Gesi, *now let's lay it on real thick.*

"I really didn't think that we would be that late, but I should have trusted your judgment. After all, you guys have been through a lot more of these hunting expeditions than I have, so I should have known you would be right on target with the schedule." *And by the way*, he thought, *thanks for forcing me to wait for you before we left. Otherwise, we really would have been on time.*

He gave his most contrite look, followed up by an apologetic smile, and then glanced back up at them. "I'll definitely make it up to you guys, don't worry." Zoe looked at Zadeemo hesitantly, then surprisingly grabbed Gesi's hand.

"Never mind all of these stupid apologies. We're still as close as we've always been. A couple of cross words thrown either way could never change that." Gesi didn't quite know whether or not to believe Zoe, but he felt as if he were floating three *en-yawo* above the earth right now, finally being seen by Zoe as a real person, not a footstool or an errand boy.

"After all, you're basically the only commoner friend we have. Right, Zadeemo?"

*   *

For the next few days, the three of them did virtually everything together, including games, horse riding, and spear training with the First Knight, who seemed to be getting sterner and tougher on them with every lesson. The First Knight, whose given name was Jorell Boro, was famed throughout the fourteen provinces as one of the best living warriors of all time. He'd made his name fighting for the upstart Regent Okon in his war of usurpation against the High King Toloron.

After Toloron was defeated, the regent rewarded Boro with the titles of First Knight of the Crown, Protector of the House of the First Prince, and the moniker "the Bloodless Death," because supposedly his bladed spear could kill a person so quickly and with such precision that they would be dead before any blood was even visible.

Okon, along with the ruling conclave, also granted a treaty to Pala Jorell's home kingdom of East Rhydor, including a guarantee that no Numerian troops would invade as long as the East Rhydor king or his son, the prince, were in power.

The First Prince had asked Pala Jorell to begin instructing Zadeemo in the ways of knighthood, and also Gesemni himself, most likely reasoning that Zadeemo would need a sparring partner when the First Prince was absent.

The First Knight had been reluctant to train a "commoner" in the higher arts of warfare but, at the insistence of both the First Prince and Zadeemo, had relented. Still, one could tell he took great pains to make sure that Zadeemo understood some of the finer points of the moves he instructed, while not deigning to help Gesi.

Luckily for Gesi, he had tremendous aptitude and seemingly a womb-borne comprehension of instinctual combat. As such, he rarely needed the extra tutoring that Zadeemo couldn't seem to do without.

On this day, the two of them were instructed for quite some time on hand-spear counters, an ancient method of grappling that involved an unarmed warrior wresting the control of spears and other long objects away from their adversary. It was an extremely rough and unpolished method of fighting, and the First Knight took the better part of the morning explaining it to them.

Finally, the paladin suggested they work the puzzling elements out with a few rounds of sparring. Boro handed him a bladed spear and marked out a circle four *en-yawo* in diameter with his carving knife. Zadeemo was given a pair of lyocell gloves, which felt like silk but were made from the toughest fibers in existence. These were to be used to protect his hands from blade cuts.

Gesi shifted nervously. Always when they'd fought before they'd both been armed. Oddly, there's a certain amount of safety involved when two weapons compete against each other. But with Zadeemo being unarmed, Gesi felt he'd have to be very careful. He was also very conscious of Zoe sitting on her tilbury, watching them both amusedly.

"Engage!" The First Knight's voice rang out through the square as the boys stepped into the circle. Zadeemo immediately lowered his stance, thrusting the heel of his boot inside Gesi's left calf to disrupt his balance, simultaneously snatching at the bladed spear handle.

Shuffle-stepping to counter, Gesi twisted the blade ninety degrees, forcing Zadeemo to withdraw his hands. He knew he was supposed to be nothing more than a punching target for Zadeemo, but in situations like this, his stubborn, competitive *imoya* always got in the way of things, and yes...he also wanted to show off a bit in front of Zoe.

Surprisingly, Zadeemo must've anticipated his counter because he nimbly moved to his left, crashing his knee into Gesi's right thigh and causing him to grimace. Ducking underneath the spear, Zadeemo swung his right elbow fiercely into Gesi's solar plexus. The few servants and townspeople who were looking on cheered loudly, including Zoe.

At that second, he felt like he was going to black out. Zadeemo may have been slower than a stuck rhino, but he had strength far beyond what most twelve-year-olds could muster.

Instinctively, he twisted his bladed spear to block the next grasping move he felt was coming, slid his left knee under Zadeemo's right, and reverse-swung the spear in a sweeping arc toward Zadeemo's chest. The cheering stopped, followed by a deathly silence as Zadeemo crashed down to the dirt awkwardly.

Everyone was staring at Gesi. Some looked angry, some fearful, some puzzled. Even he didn't know how he'd won.

Still out of breath, he knelt down to help Zadeemo up. "Zadeemo, wow! That was a great—"

WHAP! WHAP! WHAP! Before Gesi knew what happened, he'd been grabbed by the back of his collar and struck three times on the cheek. He fell over Zadeemo and looked up to see the First Knight, his face twisted into an ugly glowering mask.

"Don't touch him, boy." He crouched next to Zadeemo. "Young master, are you all right?"

Knocking his hand away, Zadeemo looking around in embarrassment. "Yeah." He jumped up quickly and dusted off his young warrior's tunic and bamboo armor.

"Ready to go again, Gesi?"

It took Gesi a few seconds to fully realize where he was. A trickle of blood ran down his mouth and dripped onto his collar, and as he felt it, a look of hate appeared in his eyes. Not thinking clearly, he grasped the spear until his knuckles turned red and leaped to his feet, thinking only to attack. He swung the spear upward toward Pala Jorell's right shoulder.

"Gesi, no!" Screamed Zoe from her tilbury.

Surprised, the First Knight used a simple counter-step to the right and lunged to catch the spear with his left hand, reaching instinctively for his feared scimitar.

Somehow knowing the counter almost before it was completed, Gesi quickly stepped back and withdrew the spear toward his own chest.

Most fighters would have instinctively tried to thrust with or move the spear either to the left or right and would have been easily disarmed by Pala Jorell. However, when Gesi instead withdrew the spear, he forced the First Knight to remove his left hand completely or risk cutting all five of his fingers off. It was a profound countermove, and all those in the square who saw it gasped in surprise.

This principle of "Retreat to Attack" was one of the highest levels of bladed-spear combat, and the First Knight would've been on guard against it had he been facing a seasoned fighter instead of a mere peasant boy.

Stunned, Gesi looked at the spear he was still holding. Neither he nor anyone else could believe that he had actually forced the world-renowned First Knight of the East Rhydor back into a defensive posture within just a couple of moves. It had almost seemed as if he was inside Pala Jorell's head, and, thinking back to his conversation with Darious, Gesi wondered if that could possibly be true.

Coldly, the famed spearman moved forward, compelling him to take several steps back.

"Boy," Pala Jorell demanded, "who taught you that counter?"

He was at a loss for words. Given the First Knight's current emotional state, saying "I knew what you were going to do" could reasonably bring about his premature demise.

"Wh-what do you mean who taught me...? All I did was pull..."

"I saw precisely what you did!" Jorell spat.

As he took off his helmet, his dark brown locks fell chest-height. At his visible anger, several villagers who'd been watching discreetly remembered other tasks that were past due for completion. They scampered away, with only a sympathetic glance in his direction.

The First Knight grabbed him by the front of his brown tunic in a vice-like grip.

"Stop it!" A voice called out from the other side of the courtyard. It was Zoe. Gesi would never be sick of hearing her voice again.

"Pala Jorell, unhand him. He's royal companion to a prince and princess of the blood. You do not have the authority to discipline him."

That seemed to stop the First Knight in his tracks. He loosened his grip, grabbed the bladed spear from Gesi's hand, and tossed it on the ground. "Quite right, milady. Please forgive me. Please consider your lesson ended for today, young master."

He turned to walk away, then glanced back at Gesi. "We'll continue our discussion later, boy." His eyes were full of foreboding as he spat at the ground.

Turning toward Gesi, Zadeemo said, "Well fought, Gesi." Though it was said somewhat grudgingly, Gesi could tell he meant it. He knew that Zadeemo had always considered Gesi lesser than he simply because he'd always been led to believe that a commoner could never be better than a person of noble blood, no matter how good his training or aptitude.

However, Gesi, his peasant companion, had just lasted two moves with the First Prince's number one warrior, and that was something that neither Zadeemo (nor apparently the First Knight himself) could overlook.

"Well fought, Zadeemo. That second move of yours was really something. My counter was just a matter of luck, we both know that." He didn't feel as if he was putting Zadeemo on as he said this.

"Do we?" Zadeemo paused for a second, shook his head, and then walked away. He'd obviously used up his lexeme total for the day.

"Gesemni, come over here." He looked over to where Zoe was sitting up in her tilbury, looking as refined as ever in her sapphire-colored dress with ivory sleeves. Trying his best to seem nonchalant, he made his way across the straw-bricked square, readying himself for the grudging acknowledgement and respect that she would finally give him after his performance against the First Knight.

"Gesi...?" She crooked her finger to him and beckoned him closer.

"Yes...milady." *What does it hurt to be extra courteous,* he thought to himself as he leaned closer, figuring she deserved the title now that she'd decided to praise him.

Enticingly, she whispered into his ear. "The next time you presume to physically harm my brother, I will personally see to it that you are beaten." With that, she raised her hand to the tilbury porters and said, "Let's go."

As the tilbury carried her around the corner, the sunset reflected off the jeweled beads in her hair, teasing him until she was out of sight.

*   *

The next morning, he felt the person or persons outside his door well before he heard the knock. Why this early? He expected it to be his father or perhaps their maid, Baako. But Baako would almost never wake him up this early, except before a hunt, and there was no hunt today, of that he was certain.

Hastily, he slid out of bed. *A couple of hours missed here or there, what's the big deal?* He thought grumpily to himself, although he'd never been a heavy sleeper in any case and had easily managed to be functional on days when he'd had no sleep at all the night before. It had always been a great mystery to him, particularly since the twins were forever complaining about being sleep-deprived. That and the small matter of him never being sick. Not one day in his entire life. Good bloodlines, Darious had always told him, and left it at that.

He opened the door and peered out to see Zadeemo there, looking wide awake and dressed in hunting garb. "Have you forgotten?" he said. "We're going to look for a Red Mandrill today." Red Mandrills were the rarest of the rare primates in the forests surrounding the fortress.

Most commonfolk didn't dare hunt them because they'd been set aside by royalty as sacred animals. But their fur was said to have potent healing properties when placed around wounds, so the boldest of the hunters (and the nobility), hunted them by the dozens when there were rumored to be sightings.

Perhaps he was still a bit groggy, but he couldn't remember them making any appointments to hunt this morning.

"I don't think..."

"Gesi...do you seriously want to keep Zoe waiting?"

"Zoe is outside?"

'Zoe wouldn't be caught dead in this part of the *khalqaddi*,' he'd always told himself, as he headed to his quarters every night since becoming their companion. Hurriedly, he turned back into his room and groped around for his tunic, boots, a couple of utility knives and the spear Darious had given him for hunting. Quickly, he blew out the candles illuminating his room and closed the door behind him, following Zadeemo down the single flight of stairs leading from his and Darious's quarters into the street.

Zoe was there indeed, astride her mare, but dressed as a boy and heavily cloaked, as to try and disguise herself. *Silly girl*, he thought wryly. *Your horse gives you away as nobility to anyone with even a fraction of a rhino's wit.* Playing along, he approached her and nodded coolly.

"Hi."

"Hi. Ready to go?"

"Sure, it's just that I can't rem—"

"Remember that we were going to hunt a Red Mandrill? Hmm...I guess maybe we thought we told you but never did. My apologies, Gesi. You, um...don't mind going, do you?"

Since when did they care what he minded?

"...Oh no, not at all...I'm supposed to accompany you guys everywhere, I just thought maybe you'd want me to tell Darious..." At this point, he was actually trying to stall their departure for as long as he possibly could. There was something unsettling about how the morning was unfolding.

"Darious doesn't need to know every time we go hunting. Besides, this time we wanted to do it without guides." Eyes twinkling, she leaned in closer to him. "We brought some things along we don't want Darious or our own guides to know about. Zadeemo, show Gesi."

Reaching onto his saddle, Zadeemo partially unwrapped the cloth covering a bundle slung across the back. It only took Gesemni a brief second to recognize the jet-black handle protruding from the similarly jet-black scabbard.

It was one of the most valuable treasures in the First Prince's collection and an heirloom of considerable fame and mystique throughout the entirety of the fourteen provinces.

The Emi Sword.

When Gesi first saw it casually draped over the back of Zadeemo's red mare like a simple commoner's hunting knife, every hair on the back of his neck stood up. He realized now, maybe for the first time, that not only were his two royal companions dim-witted at best and lacking foresight at worst, they were also reckless.

For a treasure such as this, half of the bandits and marauders in the kingdom would gladly slit their young throats and leave them buried in the savannah, royal birth or no. The First Prince himself would quite assuredly send both of the twins to a long exile on the southern coast if he suspected them of having stolen his heirloom.

What was with these two?

He cleared his throat, wondering how to make them see without angering them. "What if something happens...?"

"Oh c'mon, Gesi, not you, too. I was sure you would be a lot more willing than Zadeemo when it came to something like this. I spent an hour last night convincing him to bring it along. If we bring this sword we have nothing to fear. Don't you agree?"

He couldn't disagree. From what he'd heard, the Emi Sword would cut through the most thickly armored beast as if it were made from clay.

"You know, Gesi...I think I know what the problem with you is." It was Zoe, of course.

"All this time you've been wanting everyone in the citadel to believe you're a knight in peasant's clothing, but do you know what the truth is? You're *nemaah*." Gesemni stiffened.

There were many things you could call a person, some with less consequences than others, but one thing you definitely could never call someone was *nemaah*, the spineless fish that inhabited the Great River and provided the bulk of food for those people of the upper river region. Zoe calling Gesi *nemaah* was the highest caliber of insult.

Jaw set, Gesi became somewhat aware of his fist clenching and unclenching repeatedly.

The sound of a carriage rounding the corner snapped him out of his trance and caused all of them to look up. "Let's go," said Zoe, hopping on the back of her mare and signaling Zadeemo to follow. Looking to Gesi, the corners of Zadeemo's lips curved slightly, forming a mocking smile. As his horse followed Zoe's around the corner, Gesi watched. Then with scarcely a sound, he walked to where Dumb Ass was tethered, saddled him quickly, and set off in their direction, headed due south away from the fortress.

After twenty minutes of riding, he picked up their trail and could see them in the distance, maybe about two hundred en-yawo ahead. He also saw something that they couldn't—a couple of wild hyenas stalking them, maybe about a hundred en-yawo away.

He couldn't tell if they were part of a larger pack, as the forested hyenas tended to travel in, or if they were the only two, but it didn't really matter. From the manginess of their hides, and the way they were not intimidated by the size of the mares they seemed to be stalking, it was obvious they were starving and were looking for an opening to pounce.

For the millionth time, he wondered what he'd done wrong in his previous life to be burdened with these two and their incredible stupidity.

That may not have been fair, he thought to himself. One day Zadeemo would probably make a fine warrior, and Zoe would find herself married to some provincial prince or sheikah, if not higher. *A person doesn't have to be great in everything they do to be great,* he thought.

He just wished they would stick to the things they were good at.

As the twins prepared to round a hilly clearing, the hyenas seemed to sense an opening. In unison, they broke into a run and started closing the distance on the pair.

Soon they were one hundred en-yawo closer, then eighty...seventy en-yawo. Sensing something, Zoe turned her head around briefly as they continued forward and let out an ear-piercing scream. Zadeemo jumped in his saddle, whipped his horse around and paled. Upon seeing the hyenas, the horses reared onto their hind legs and raced off for the hill.

Though rudely ejected from their horses, the twins appeared okay...for the moment. Scrambling up immediately, they pulled their spears from their shoulder packs just in time to see the hyenas pull up to a circling speed, now about thirty en-yawo away, snarling.

It was indeed a chilling sight.

Whish! Whish! Two arrows left Gesi's bow and whistled through the thick morning air, almost synchronously striking both beasts precisely in their necks. They never had a chance. Soundlessly, they each died where they were hit.

Quickly, he rode to the twins to make sure they were all right. As he got closer, he could see Zoe's hands shaking uncontrollably. There was a faraway look to her eyes when she finally saw him. Her eyes widened, and Gesi felt as though she were seeing him—really him, and not just some peasant—for the first time.

"Are you both okay?" Gesi asked.

While Zadeemo shrugged, Zoe seemed to be inexplicably tongue-tied all of a sudden.

"Thank you, Gesemni. That was really... Aah..."

Thanks? He shook his head. The other day she scolded him for being slow, but today she thanks him for the same thing. He did not understand her at all.

Dismounting from Dumb Ass, he slowly walked over, searching the horizon with his hands shading his eyes. "It appears your two mares went in that direction. Probably take us the next hour or so to catch up to them unless they somehow get un-spooked and turn back. Especially since we're not all mounted anymore."

Zoe frowned. "No," she said, "actually it'll be quite easy to get them to come back. Zadeemo, call them."

Taking a red whistle from his pocket, Zadeemo blew it. The noise startled the magpies resting on the tops of all the surrounding trees, and they flew away at once, but in the distance, they could see their red mares sheepishly trotting back to them.

"I wonder why you couldn't use it to stop them from abandoning you in the first place?" he asked them. They were not amused.

As he helped Zoe up on the red mare, he asked, "So which direction do we go to now?"

Zoe was quick to reply. "Back to the fortress."

"Back to the citadel?" He was floored. *She must be distraught*, he thought.

Zadeemo looked quizzically at her. Zoe hung her head briefly, then looked up in defiance.

"I'm never hunting again," she said.

"Never?" They both asked her.

She shrugged.

"Why should I? I'm going to be a lady of rank one day, perhaps even a queen. Not a soldier. This is a waste of my time."

She glanced at Gesi softly and said, "Gesi? Zadeemo and I owe you an apology. Well, I do at least..." She paused as if she wanted to say more, then decided against it and turned the mare around, heading back toward the citadel, the sun now almost directly overhead and warning them to take shelter, or suffer consequences—another reminder of the impending approach of the Great Summer.

"Wait!" he shouted. She and Zadeemo both pulled on the reins.

He quickly trotted over to Zadeemo's mare and gave it a once over. "What happened to the sword? The bundle... WHERE'S THE EMI SWORD?"

Silence.

All at once the three of them started desperately checking each other's saddles. Then their bundles. Then their shoulder bags.

"You idiot!!!" Gesi shouted at Zadeemo.

"What? What happened?" The twins both ran to him. Gesi was shaking with anger, holding Zadeemo's shoulder bag up for both of them to see.

"This is what happened," he said through barely open lips. "Didn't anyone ever teach either of you how to tie a blasted shoulder bag properly?" Even as the words escaped, he knew the answer.

Of course no one had, he sneered inwardly. *Why would the exalted children of a third-rate prince ever need to tie their own bags?*

The twins were predictably contrite yet unrepentant. They continued to search.

Not finding any clues, they each steered their horses around a different perimeter—while following the direction of where the red mares initially fled to escape the hyenas.

No luck.

Almost frantic now, the twins dismounted and started walking the area on foot, extremely slowly. The search turned up nothing. Cursing inwardly, Gesi looked around until he found a smallish Kegelia tree, sometimes called the sausage tree. Undoing his outerwear and then his belt, he grabbed hold of the base firmly and climbed to the top with minimal effort.

Locating a semi-sturdy branch, he slid forward until he had a good vantage point. Taking a very deliberate path, he shielded his eyes and slowly scanned a 360-degree path around their current location, from the tree to about ninety en-yawo away, the farthest range of unobstructed view he had.

After about two minutes, he grimaced, leaped off the branch to swing from it with his hands, and then jumped to the ground.

Deflated, he put back on his things then walked over to the twins. "I don't see anything," he wearily said.

"Me either," admitted Zoe. "Zadeemo?" Zadeemo shook his head. "Okay, so what now?" She asked.

Gesi frowned. "I'm pretty sure I'm not the best person to answer that question, but I do have some advice."

"What's that?" They both wanted to know what he had in mind.

"When we get home, forget about the sword. Forget you ever saw it, or it ever even existed. If someone asks you about it, feign ignorance. If you walk past the place where it was once kept, feign blindness. But never, EVER, admit that you took it."

He paused for effect. "Trust me on this; your father will not forgive you."

Crestfallen, Zadeemo and Zoe looked at each other. They appeared to want to say something, but the words wouldn't come out.

He turned away and mounted his horse. "Let's go."

As they rode back, he simmered. *More lousy luck and bad timing. Seemed like for the first time she was actually able to be friendly to me, and now what?*

They hadn't ridden far when a large commotion a few hundred en-yawo down caused them to come to a halt. To their horror, several young men had been rounded up, interrogated, and beaten. Worse yet, they were being made to suffer the *shadim shahar.* Their cries could be heard throughout the valley.

Not able to bear the tragic scene, Zoe buried her face in her hands and wept quietly. Zadeemo stared impassively. Gesi asked them both, "What's going on?"

Zadeemo shrugged.

"It's the *Kula Selawa,*" sobbed Zoe. "The sedition trials. Don't you know about anything that's going on around you?"

No, he thought. *I've been too busy playing babysitter to both of you*. He shook his head.

"They're trying to catch the Toloron loyalists." With each word she spoke, she seemed able to control herself a bit more.

What Toloron loyalists? He thought incredulously. *The guy died about a hundred moons ago.*

Why do the powerful never need a good reason for killing the weak? He had wondered about this many times but naturally couldn't express this thought in his present company.

"Let's go." He sighed.

Thankfully, the trip back didn't seem so long. After leaving the twins, Gesi sat down on his bed and decided to get back a couple of hours of sleep that the twins had deprived of him.

Still, he couldn't shake the feeling that he hadn't heard the last of this incident, and he only hoped that Zoe would be okay, if and when the First Prince ever found out what she had done.

3

The First Demise

Gesi was abruptly awakened from sleep by the sound of many horses outside their house. Startled, he briefly wondered if he had been dreaming, until he next heard the sound of boots coming up his stairs, about six to eight men, it seemed.

He quickly jumped out of bed and groped around for his things, thinking that Darious was probably sending for him to join this morning's falcon breaking.

However, before he could get his boots on, the door exploded from the blow of a flat axe, and he was yanked roughly toward the door by three of them. Intending to resist, he pulled free one of his arms and was struck immediately in the back of the head by a spear handle. He never saw it coming.

He had no idea how long he'd been unconscious, yet even more disquieting was that he had no idea where he was. What he did know was that he'd never been in as dark a place. Holding out his hands in front of him, he couldn't see a single finger. The surrounding smells told him a great deal, in any case. It was a smell of dampness and mildew; the air seemed choked with it. There was no doubt; he was somewhere below ground.

A cold panic gripped him as he wondered if he'd somehow been buried alive. Jumping up, he ran forward a couple of steps, and WHAP!

His forehead smacked against something cold and hard. Reaching up with his hands, he no longer had any questions about his current location. He was a prisoner.

He trailed his fingers carefully around the perimeter of the cell. It appeared that his area of enclosure was about four by six *en-yawo*, a tiny space. The floors were made of dirt, and the walls stone except for the one that contained the bars. There was nowhere to sit and no privy to make use of.

On a whim, he jumped straight up, stretching his hand toward the roof of the cell. With a dull thud, the top of his head slammed into the ceiling, probably only about a rod overhead. In anguish, he tried to find a place against the wall to steady himself but collapsed into unconsciousness once more before he could reach it.

* *

A bucket of fetid, smelly water splashing over his head jarred him awake. Half coughing and half choking, he wiped the water from his eyes and sat up on the floor. Standing outside of the cell and holding candles were four of the prince's guards.

The leader of them, a bald, disgusting, short runt of a man, whom Gesi had seen on several occasions (and had always secretly called "Witless"), sneered in Gesi's direction and took a step toward the cell.

"That woke the stinking little savage up. Thanks, Polde." He squinted his eyes.

"Okay, then, boy, so let's have it." They all waited expectantly.

Gesi almost rolled his eyes but thought better of it. "Have what?"

"Don't play games with us, boy. The sword. We know you've got it."

Accursed Qandisa! Gesi immediately thought. How had they found out?

Had Zoe and Zadeemo been overheard discussing the sword?

Had someone seen the three of them together? Were they being held captive also?

The First Prince was away right now, so there was no one to stop these brutes from forcing the twins to confess. Anger immediately swelled up with him.

"If you dare hurt Zoe, I'll make you pay for it...you and the rest of these clowns as well!" he shouted with as much bravado as he could muster, considering he had no idea whose urine he was currently wearing.

That brought a huge explosion of laughter throughout the dungeon. Witless and the others were doubled over, and all of the candles were shaking precariously on their holders. It went on for quite some time, until Witless raised his hand.

"Boy," he chuckled, "your *muzuri* (adoptive father) may be the 'ottest thing to the First Prince since the Great Summer, but it's obvious tha' you dun come from his seed." His thick upper *Kumaz-we* accent, and the fact that he had barely any usable teeth, made him impossible to understand.

Gesemni found it more and more challenging to understand him.

"You think we would 'arm the prince's own young? We're asking YOU about the sword, and we won't ask too many more times." All Gesi could make out was that he was likely wrong in thinking the twins were in danger.

"Listen, Wit...umm, sir," he began. "I'm pretty sure Zoe and Zadeemo can straighten out any misunderstandings we seem to have." Politeness was definitely the way to go with these morons. "I'm twelve and have nothing to gain by taking the Emi Sword or any other weapon belonging to his Highness."

He stood up a bit straighter now and looked them all in the eye, something Darious had taught him, trying to gain back some of their respect. "I think maybe someone's been intentionally misleading you."

"Misleading us, huh? Why you lee-al... We never said it was the Emi Sword! Trying to pull a fast one on the First Prince?"

He grabbed a key from his belt, hurriedly opened the cell, and shouted to his guards, "Hold him, boys." As Gesi was quickly caught by both arms, Witless turned his spear around and jabbed it into his midsection.

The pain was so sharp and intense that Gesi couldn't even think, let alone breathe.

"We're asking you again, boy. Where's the sword?"

Shaking his head, he wondered how they expected him to speak if he couldn't breathe.

"Where's the sword?"

Another blow with the spear. If it were not for the guards holding him up, there's no way he could've stood on his own power.

"Listen, boy," said Polde, "the prince is coming back from fal-con-en soon. We'd like to have this whole nasty situation tidied up by the time he gets back. So if you let us know where you stashed the sword, it'll be our little secret. Once the prince gets back, though...we can't protect you. Understand?"

"Sure, sure," he grunted. "You guys are doing such a great job protecting me already. If you think about it, Polde, you already know where I hid the sword."

Witless and Polde moved closer. As Gesi fully knew, they had no intention of letting him off the hook once the prince returned. The retrieval of the prince's prized heirloom, as well as the capture of the "thief" would be good at least for one or two nights liberty from the prince, if not an outright promotion.

"Where? Where is it, lad?" whispered Polde.

"It's under your bed at home, of course," Gesemni replied matter-of-factly. "I trusted it to your wife to keep it nice and safe for me. That is assuming I can make it back there sometime soon." He felt the blow from Polde before he saw it, flush against his jaw and full of force. As the guards continued to hold Gesi, Polde rained slaps upon him until he couldn't even feel his face or the blows anymore.

"Enough!" said one of the other guards. "By Qandisa's triangle, Polde. He's just a kid."

"He's a thief and a le'al bastard," Polde replied.

"Throw 'im back in the cell," said Witless. "He belongs to the prince now."

Gesemni was barely conscious as sometime later an entirely different group of men came to drag him upstairs, he supposed for an audience with the First Prince, though he was in too much pain to know for certain or care.

His tunic was a bloody mess, and when they brought him around the exit leading from the dungeons to the main hall of the prince's residence, he glanced into the mirror. In shock, his first thoughts went to Zoe and what she would think of him now.

Not even he recognized the swollen, bloody mess of a face staring back at him. He was sure he'd be scarred for life—not even all the gold in the famous Lord Jashu Jasonne's treasury could heal his face.

They led him through a set of great doors to the prince's reception hall. He could vaguely make out the faces of a few of his former friends and some of the staff who'd been kind to him in the past. Now they wanted nothing to do with him, glancing away quickly and pretending they didn't see the physical state he was in.

Finally, he was dumped abruptly at the foot of the stairs. Using his hands to raise himself, he struggled to get to his feet. He didn't want to give them the satisfaction of seeing him on the ground.

"Stay on your knees, boy!" A booming voice from the top of the stairs thundered down on him. Looking up, he saw the First Knight standing in a simple tunic and light armor next to the First Prince, looking stern but concerned at the same time.

"Silence, Pala Jorell," said the prince. Sternly, he turned toward the guards.

"Why has this boy been beaten so? Captain of the Guard, I'd like to have an explanation at once."

From somewhere to the left of the gathering, Witless came forward. "My lord, the prison guards did their best to protect this young man, as did the palace guard. Unfortunately, word spread that this was the young fellow who stole the First Prince's treasured sword, and, well, even amongst those scum, there are loyal subjects who would kill for you."

He shook his head sorrowfully. "It was all we could do just to stop them from tearing this young man apart."

"Hmmm..."

It was a very timely flatter. The First Prince nodded approvingly, seemingly pleased that he had loyal subjects even in his own palace dungeon. In his mind, Gesi was ready to explode, but he was careful not to show anger in front of the First Prince.

"Gesi, I hope now you can see the consequences of what you've done." He looked around the audience room. "Your father, Darious, is one of my most trusted men, very invaluable to me and my own father, His Grace the Regent. Were it not so, no doubt you would already have been tortured to find out the sword's whereabouts, then summarily beheaded."

Again the kindly look. "Your father should be returning to court very soon; he had to tend to the falcons before he could do so. Is there anything you'd like to tell us about the sword before he gets here?"

"Your Highness, I have no idea where the sword is. I think if you talk to Zoe and Zadeemo, all this can be cleared up."

"Yes," he said dryly, clearly having no more patience. "I intend to do that right this moment. Pala Jorell, are my son and daughter waiting outside?"

"They are, my lord. I brought them here myself, anticipating the boy would try and use them to save his neck." The First Knight looked smugly down at him.

"Bring in the young master and young mistress!"

Wondering what nonsense they were going to come up with this time, Gesi sat in silence.

Several moments later, one of the auxiliary entrances opened and the twins were both led in to kneel before their father. After doing so, the First Prince took Zoe by the hand and said to her gently, "My dear, Gesemni is here."

He pointed down the stairs and bid her follow his gaze. Zoe took one look at him and screamed, an extremely high-pitched piteous wail that shocked all in the courtroom. He felt even worse when he saw the way she looked at him.

"Why did you have to hurt him?" she cried, sobbing uncontrollably.

He went into the clouds when he realized that she was actually standing up for him, until she said next, "He didn't mean to steal and lose the sword. He just wanted to use it for the hunt!"

Still sobbing, she ran to her dad and buried her face into his chest.

It felt like a stone fortress had just collapsed on Gesi without warning. The twins had used him as a scapegoat. He shouldn't have been surprised, but he was.

"Hold on!" Gesi shouted. Seventy pairs of eyes turned from the crying girl to him, expecting that her tears had moved him to make a full confession.

"They're lying! They're lying to you! It was them who took the sword and then lost it in the woods just south of here, I swear it!"

Complete silence.

"It's true," he said again, "they wanted to go hunting Red Mandrills and forced me to go along. Zoe, tell them! Zadeemo!"

"Why you little..." With astonishing speed, the First Knight came down the stairs and grabbed Gesi. "You dare accuse the children of the Royal House of stealing from their own father? Boy! Are you insane?"

He looked up at the First Prince. "My lord, I submit that this boy is condemned by his own words. By your father's laws, the penalty for slander against any member of the royal family is instant death." Everyone in the audience hall gasped. Gesi was after all a boy, and the son of the First Prince's *avaremba*.

Even some of the other Unassailables seemed to feel Pala Jorell had gone too far. Some winced disapprovingly.

Gauging all of this, the First Prince made his decision. "Out of respect for your foster father, Gesemni, you will be spared the death sentence for this heinous crime." He looked at the First Knight.

"However, Pala Jorell is correct that you must be punished for your slanderous words, and the punishment must be severe. It is the judgment of myself, Iyasu Solla, First Prince of the Province of East Rhydor, second of the lineage of my brother Chief Rhoboron, lawful ruler of this province, that you be given fifteen lashes with the whip and then sold into bondage to the Irruvian pirates of the Upper Great River. That is my judgment."

As Gesi was seized and tied to one of the pillars in the audience hall, there was more wailing from Zoe. The commotion in the Great Hall was deafening, jeers from those who supported the First Prince's decision, and outcry from those who thought it inhumane. The guard in charge of administering the floggings straightened out his whip and began.

Just think of something else, Gesemni, he told himself. *Think of someplace far away that you and Darious escape to, away from these liars and these* nemaah. *It'll be over soon.*

But there was no place he could think of far enough away for him to ignore the lashes. It took every ounce of strength and will-power he could muster to not cry out as the painful ordeal he was being subjected to seemed to stretch for an eternity. Then, just as the guard flogging him prepared to say "two," sounds of several people shrieking in agony came from the east end of the room.

"Let him go!"

A loud voice, belying boundless strength, cut through all of the discord, and hearing it, Gesi exhaled deeply with relief. Darious was here. Everything would finally be all right. No one would bully him anymore. A man appeared menacingly in front of Darious.

"*Avaremba*," he sneered, "you are interfering with a legal pu—"

He silenced as Darious's spear took him in the throat, causing an immense amount of blood to spray into the air. Darious ran toward the First Prince.

"My lord, this boy—"

As the First Knight thrust his spear at Darious, the First Prince yelled, "Do not fight! We can discuss another punishment for the boy." It was futile. Pala Jorell had already aimed a second blow at Darious, this time going straight for his lower abdomen. Everyone gasped. An attack like that was meant to kill.

However, before he could finish his attack, Darious neatly sidestepped the spear, circled left around the First Knight's exposed right flank, and drove his spear directly through his ribcage.

There was complete silence in the hall. The First Knight, Jorell Boro, legendary warrior of the fourteen provinces, stood there dumbly looking at the spear that had just skewered him. Then he sank to his knees, an expression of disbelief on his face. He died on his knees.

"Kill him!" The First Prince shouted, pointing angrily at Darious. However, his command came much too slowly. Gesi watched in wonder as Darious vaulted up the stairs to the prince's chair and grabbed him. *Where did Darious learn to move and fight like that?*

"Stay back!" the former royal *avaremba* warned. No one moved. Darious steered the First Prince slowly down the stairs, his favorite hunting knife menacingly at the prince's throat, to where Gesi was still tied. Sorrow filled Darious's face as he cut his ropes and pulled him gently away from the pillar, pushing the First Prince down to his knees at the same time.

"Gesemni." He reached into his pocket and pulled out a black cloth, then used it to wipe Gesi's forehead. "I'm sorry I couldn't take better care of you, my boy." A trickle of perspiration ran down his temple. "I hope you remember all of the things I've taught you. Do you?" Darious stared intently into his eyes.

Gesi nodded.

"Okay. Well done." He smiled grimly. "In that case, here are your final two instructions." He leaned close and whispered in Gesi's ear, "Seek the man, Nank, who will lead you to your destiny beneath the Great River." Ignoring the quizzical expression on Gesemni's face, he spoke again. "Instruction two; look towards a part of you."

Leaving the prince where he knelt, Darious grabbed Gesi by the collar and half pushed him, half threw him out the door.

"Never forget where you came from," he warned. "Run."

As Gesi started to run toward the bridges leading out of the citadel, he gave a quick glance back and saw waves of guards and soldiers running at Darious—and being continually pierced by his spear. A spear that seemed to bring death to all who encountered it, even as more and more of the First Prince's soldiers began to close the noose around him.

4

Jorann's Calm

It took a very long time before the screams ended.

After witnessing the brutal ambush and destruction of the *Win-Daji*, the boy who'd once been their captive stared far beyond the clearing, where they'd just viewed the carnage. All at once, as nausea overtook him, he half-jumped, half-fell from his horse and ran to the edge of the grass, each blade about seven rods high and incredibly stiff.

Lurching forward, he lost his morning meal and most likely the one from the prior night also. Finally empty and trembling, he clambered shakily to his feet. K'Nan stood sternly in front of him, eyes disapproving.

Before the boy knew what was happening, K'Nan's hand flew out and slapped him. Stunned, his eyes blurred for a second, and he felt he might pass out from the blow. K'Nan caught him by his ragged tunic, noticed the tears forming, and slapped him again. The boy couldn't figure out what he'd done wrong.

"Are you worth it?" The legendary warrior shouted at him. "All those deaths. Are you worth it?" The boy felt the man searching his eyes intently. He seemed to be looking for something, anything that could justify all of the destruction and death he'd just implemented.

"Pala K'Nan...whatever I've done to displease you..."

"Displease me? You're worried about displeasing me?"

He paused for a second and then looked into the boy's eyes. "Tell me something, boy. Do you think you're a slave?"

"Yes, I was s-sold—"

WHAP!! This time the boy was knocked through the air by the force of the blow. His mind whirled in many different directions as he tried desperately to realize what he'd done wrong. Not that he'd never been beaten before without reason, but this man was different from his former masters. This was K'Nan the Savage Slayer.

Through his extreme disappointment and despair, he felt tears bristle at the corner of his eyes again and unconsciously put up a hand to brush them away.

"You had best stop crying immediately."

K'Nan leaned forward menacingly. Calmly, the boy rose and, eyes downcast, looked toward him.

"What I think I am does not matter, Pala K'Nan." Jaw clenched, he paused. "I do recall it was you who asked me to accompany you, though, not the other way around. Maybe you should think about that before you hit me again."

He somehow found the courage to look up from the deep black soil into the face of K'Nan, Son of Loffri, but where he'd expected to find anger and contempt, he saw only satisfaction. Satisfaction and compassion.

"Are you not angry with me?" the boy asked hesitantly.

"Angry?" K'Nan seemed taken aback. "You couldn't be more wrong, boy, you've just given me life once more."

For the briefest of moments, K'Nan stared wistfully beyond the blades. He then slowly led the boy back onto a small rocky patch of land that contrasted with the otherwise lush surroundings of the savannah.

"Look around you," the old soldier commanded. The boy looked up. Standing in front of them in two perfect rows were twenty men. The word "menacing" would have done a grave injustice were it used to describe them. These men were all tall and bulging with muscles prominent on every square inch of their lean frames.

Their dark complexions both glistened under the reflection of the red sun, yet also seemed to blend in with the black rocky soil on which they now stood stiffly at attention. The boy had no idea who these fearsome men were. What was certain was this: they were not to be trifled with.

As emotionless as they seemed at first glance, there was a barely contained excitement in their eyes. He wondered what could make these men, who had just committed cold-blooded mass murder, so excited so soon after.

His further thoughts on this were interrupted, however, when K'Nan reached over to grab his left wrist and held it up to the group of soldiers. A great roar immediately rose from the ranks of the men.

"*Shohamu Taiji! Shohamu Taiji!*" shouted the group of warriors over and over. The boy was stunned. All of the soldiers continued cheering wildly for a few moments, then quickly they all kneeled before him in perfect synchronization.

At this point, his uncertainty and shock made him very nervous. Taking a hesitant step away from the men, he looked at K'Nan. "Sir," he held up his wrist, "I don't exactly know how this mark—"

"You are never to call me 'sir' again," replied K'Nan sternly. Thinking he was about to be punished again, the boy stiffened, but K'Nan continued.

"And you shall no longer call yourself 'boy' or a 'slave' or 'servant.' Do not show any deference whatsoever to anyone beneath you. I will explain the mark to you soon, but was that reaction you just saw one of soldiers to a slave?"

K'Nan's expression hardened. "For you were not born, nor have you ever been, any of those three things—whether you knew it or not."

He wanted to shout that he got it. That he understood you should never accept whatever unfortunate fate the gods chose to burden you with. '*Why are you belaboring this sad point,*' the boy thought?

Pala K'Nan, for his part, seemed to want to explain further, then hesitated and turned back to the men, informing the soldiers that they would make camp. The sun was now too low on the horizon to attempt to navigate the savannah. Staring at it, the boy wondered if the Great Summer was really going to be as deadly as people claimed.

"Come with me, young lad."

He followed Pala K'Nan up a steep hill that had an even clearer vantage point of the place where the *Win-Daji* had just met their grisly end. It seemed as if Pala K'Nan wanted him to remember it on purpose.

He motioned the boy to sit, and they both gazed off into the distance for some time, watching the pirna birds, hyenas, and jackals forage through the remains. Although the boy had no love for any of the adults nor most of the children who had just been slaughtered, he knew that there were also a lot of innocent young babies and other servants who'd met their end there. He wasn't really sure how he felt about that, and so he wasn't entirely sure how he felt about K'Nan, either.

He seemed to be neither chivalrous nor callous, fish nor fowl. So as much as the boy wanted, almost needed someone whom he could look up to and respect, during this loneliest period of his life, he wasn't about to trust anyone. Not yet.

Once they'd taken in the ghastly scene for quite long enough, K'Nan finally spoke. "I wanted you to see this so that you could remember that they're all truly dead, and so then is your identity as a slave boy. Now, tell me how you came to be a slave of the *Win-Daji* and what you've been doing amongst them for the past seven moons."

"How did you know how long I've been with them?" he asked, then just shook his head. It was becoming evident to him that Pala K'Nan knew more about his origins than he himself.

"I'll explain everything later, but first I need to know the answer to those particular questions," replied K'Nan, pulling on his water skins and giving him a drink. "I'm an excellent listener."

Feeling he could perhaps exorcise some of the inner demons that he'd been carrying in his heart, the boy obeyed.

"I don't actually know my name or even my age...." With that, he began his story.

"I was told by one of the other children in a village of the Nabii that the *patral maja,* the chief father, had not been my first owner, but that I had been sold to him by a soldier who had gotten into some trouble when I was younger."

"Apparently the soldier had raised me from infancy but had somehow gotten into a nasty altercation with authorities of the great Lord Okon and had been forced to flee. To evade them more easily, the soldier decided I must be sold. The soldier who sold me is one of many who I swore to one day get revenge on in this life."

His eyes turned cold recollecting his long list of self-appointed enemies.

"Most likely he had no choice," K'Nan said. "My guess is he either planned to come back for you at a later time and failed to locate you, or was killed. He would not have abandoned you."

Not so eager to give up on his hatred, the boy shrugged. "I'm not sure exactly what I did to upset the *patral maja* and Halanbi, but life as a servant to them was definitely hell."

Speaking about his experience in past tense seemed surreal to him. Was he truly free? Regardless of K'Nan's directives, what if someone showed up to claim him? A relative of the *Win-Daji*, perhaps?

"I was made to do the most degrading of chores and whipped often. I was never fed well but became an expert at snatching crumbs in the middle of the night. The family decided that under no circumstances should I ever be taught to use a weapon, which was disappointing because I was fascinated with weapons.

However, I taught myself to hunt and surprisingly seemed to have a natural talent for it. Before long, I was capturing my own game and eating as well as any of the *patral's* family.

"When the Simic found out what I'd learned, I was scourged and thrown into a pit with very little food and water for two weeks. They wanted to make sure that I'd been taught a thorough lesson, and I had. After I was released, I never again attempted to hunt without permission. At this point, I was still not yet five."

"The days and nights after that passed pretty uneventfully. I was allowed eventually to live in the actual household and was given the duties of cleaning and feeding all of the animals.

I suppose by then I'd gained their trust and they were sure that I would no longer run away. Even so, I had bad days still and worse days. I even tried to..." He paused for a while thinking about how hopeless his life had seemed, then sighed and shook his head.

"The only thing that would calm me and convince me to keep going was this same mark on my wrist that you just showed to your men. I never knew why but looking at it and touching it always consoled me. It was like a reminder of some kind that I was not born a slave, and maybe I did have some sort of important role to play in this world."

He looked again at his wrist, at this black mark that somehow stood out boldly from his obsidian skin, now knowing that Pala K'Nan knew what the symbol meant and also knowing that he himself would soon know. The anticipation made him almost fearful, but excited.

Pala K'Nan nodded. "You do have a role. These men are your soldiers, not mine." The renowned warrior hesitated, then, ignoring the boy's incredulous look, continued.

"For quite some time now, I've been following a prophecy that has to do with your birth and also the future security of Numeria. Because of that prophecy, my intention was actually to lead the Equinox hunt."

From the Kumazi (sands),
From the savannah,
From the chakkha (jungle),
The never-lost will again be found,
To lead the restorer back to his throne.

"That mark on your wrist is the only reliable source of your true identity in this world. Yet only a handful of people are supposed to know that you truly exist. If anyone were to stumble on the truth, just as I did, you would have been executed, and the prophecy could never have been fulfilled. That's why the *Win-Daji* and all of their people had to be killed, to prevent anyone else from ever knowing."

A wave of remorse washed over him as he realized for certain that he was solely responsible for the cold-blooded massacre that had just occurred.

After everything that had happened to the boy since this morning, this did not strike him as being particularly impossible, yet his face and features still projected his sense of disbelief. What exactly was Pala K'Nan saying? Convinced now that he was not born a slave, but who was he?

"Trust me when I tell you that the Nabii tribesmen were wretched people—if for no other reason than they hunted and killed animals for profit. When they wake up in hell, they won't even know how they got there. You've hopefully shed your last tear over their lot." Jorann nodded.

"Before I tell you a little bit about yourself and where you truly come from," K'Nan continued, "I think we'd best give you a name. You were probably gifted one at birth, but not even the soldier responsible for your protection would know what it is, and I'm sure he had given you another."

"I wonder what name was chosen for me?" he thought aloud to K'Nan. He assumed that it was something powerful and mysterious.

"As he's nowhere to be found, and probably not even alive, we may never know what your true name is. And so from this day forth, you shall be named Jorann. In the ancient Ashantic dialects of the coast, it means 'unleashed.'"

"Indeed, young master, you have been freed from a life of bondage to take revenge on the enemies of the rightful ruler of Numeria. Tell me?........What do you think of this name?"

Though ecstatic, Jorann, as he was now named, was ever the pragmatist. "Thank you for the honor you do me, Pala K'Nan. However, a name and destiny like that sound very...umm...difficult to live up to. Who exactly am I...was I?"

The early evening winds swirled through the savannah, creating a peaceful moment of meditation for both of them. Around them, the sounds were changing as light gave way to darkness and the nocturne creatures stirred from their habitats to join the extraneous activities of their surroundings.

Suddenly a flurry of action snapped him from his reverie. "Be on your guard!" barked K'Nan. In his hands, a long black spear with a golden haft and blade magically appeared, and without warning, he thrust the spear at Jorann.

Jorann clumsily moved to step back and slipped on a jagged stone beneath his back right foot. Unsteady, he barely managed to right himself.

K'Nan looked puzzled—and disappointed. "Logically, with your gifts, you should have been able to react to and counter that."

Jorann didn't know how to respond. He felt like a disappointment. "Maybe, I'm just not—"

"Silence!" K'Nan shouted, again swinging the spear, this time in a crescent trajectory towards his front left leg. Again Jorann saw the spear coming but couldn't move quickly enough to avoid. Fortunately for him, K'Nan pulled it back once more. If not, his left shinbone would have been smashed for sure, crippling him.

Jorann, despite knowing who K'Nan was, was more frightened than he had ever been. Clumsily, he reached for his hunting knife wedged in his waistband, but no sooner did his fingers touch it than the spear swept around again. In horror, Jorann felt his legs completely go out from under him, as his eyes suddenly focused on clouds located where his head used to be.

He tried to tuck his knees in, but K'Nan again struck with the spear and two quick jabs forced him to straighten his legs completely.

He was standing on both of his hands, completely still.

He saw from his topsy-turvy position that K'Nan was closely monitoring his breathing and his body posture, seemingly trying to figure out something. Jorann felt his right foot begin to drop a bit too much, and knew he was going to fall forward back onto his feet. But, after yet another spear thrust from K'Nan, he was again upright, stiff, but relaxed.

"Stay there for a while," a calmer sounding K'Nan said to him. Jorann heard a melodious sound coming from the direction where his voice had just been. K'Nan had taken a sitting position in the dirt and was now playing a mini-version of the ancient *udu* instrument, which resembles a cross between a flute and a jug.

For whatever reason, Jorann now felt as if he were perfectly comfortable; as if he had gone his entire life walking on his hands. He was initially disturbed by the feeling that blood was rushing to his face, but it didn't bother him at all now.

"Stop thinking." The music paused for a second. "Focus only on your hands. Try and feel the earth's energy through the tips of your fingers."

No sooner had K'Nan said this than Jorann indeed felt an enormous surge of power into his fingers, then hands, then his body—all the way up to his toes. He suddenly felt as if he could stay in this position forever if he had to.

What sort of witchcraft was K'Nan using on him? He wondered.

"You are wrong." Again the music stopped. "The power is not being given to you, it is within you. The position you are in now is merely forcing you to channel it into the area just below your waistline. It is from here that all inner power derives."

The music again began to play. Jorann now began to realize that the music was a distraction. It helped his mind relax and not think of things that would upset his equilibrium. Every time K'Nan sensed his balance faltering, he began playing the music.

"Touch your navel with your left hand," K'Nan casually instructed.

Won't I fall? Thought Jorann. Thinking this, he did indeed feel himself begin to tilt to the left, but the spear struck out again like a bolt of lightning. His shoulder and ribcage were struck, instantly forcing him to remain upright but also making him gasp in pain.

It was around then when he realized the upside-down position must have expelled all of the air from his lungs—his gasp caused him to cough.

K'Nan scoffed at him. "I know you're thinking right now, 'But...but...I thought you're supposed to be my subordinate!' This is true, but first and foremost I'm your tutor. Now stabilize your breathing and STOP THINKING." He did not yell, but the effect was just the same.

Jorann did stabilize his breathing in seconds, and soon after moved his left hand down to his navel.

"Very good, young Lord Jorann." He sat back down and paid no attention to the funny looking boy who was standing on one hand with a wide open mouth and bugged eyes. Instead, he began playing the song again.

A few minutes passed this way, and he saw Jorann was now extremely relaxed. The music paused.

"Not long ago, you heard those warriors shouting 'Shohamu Taiji.' Do you understand what this means in Tandish?" Jorann thought for a minute, then shook his head.

"And what about the *Onyx Crown*? Have you ever heard of it?"

Jorann nodded impatiently. Anyone over the age of three moons had heard the legend. The Onyx Crown was the absolute symbol of power for the High King Toloron, worn by him during his reign as lawful sovereign of the fourteen provinces.

He told K'Nan, "It's pretty well known that Toloron commissioned the four corners of the earth to make him a crown that would symbolize his absolute rule over Numeria."

K'Nan nodded. "The Supreme Chieftain had just consolidated the Azinna armies into his own and continued his war against the Islanders, eventually winning that war and another against the Ngeppu of the coastal regions." He smiled, remembering. "At that point, everyone was pretty sure he was unconquerable under the heavens."

But of course he must not have been, Jorann thought.

"So he thought it was acceptable to take total power and wear a crown? Even though crowns are forbidden to wear by mortals of Numeria? Wasn't he angering the gods by doing that?"

"Another way to look at it would be that he must have been favored in the eyes of the gods, or he could even have been semi-divine himself."

Jorann frowned, not buying that at all. "So what did he do next?"

"Lord Toloron next assumed the title of High King and commissioned several royal gemologists and metallurgists to create a crown that would boldly and accurately symbolize the power he wielded over the fourteen provinces."

The most successful members of Numerian families were usually the heads of tribes, some small, some numbering tens of thousands. Toloron was only the second tribal leader ever to claim complete control over the fourteen provinces and, as such, proclaimed himself a king, just as Azu the Despot did before him. The distinction was that Azu made his claim before he could completely subdue all of the tribes.

"Obviously," he told K'Nan, "someone brought the crown to Toloron, and he was impressed."

Impatiently, K'Nan waved his hand. "Yes. The first man arrived several weeks later with an elaborately ornate crown of gold, diamonds, and ivory.

"'These are the three treasures abundant in your kingdom, your grace,' that man said solemnly. The crown was magnificent, and so shimmering it could hardly be gazed upon in daytime.

"Toloron was indeed pleased but told the man that the crown would 'only' be kept as one of the kingdom's great treasures. He did not think it fit for a symbol of the House of Toloron. He rewarded the jeweler with three hundred coins of silver and sent him away."

"Wow," he said to K'Nan. "I suppose Lord Toloron had extravagant tastes then, if even that crown was not sufficient."

"It is the gravest of insults to refer to him as simply 'Lord Toloron,' young master." K'Nan corrected, then replied, "Yes and no. A second man arrived a few days later with a curious crown, a series of strips carved as sharp spikes, made from the precious mineral tereniuum. Stronger than iron, it was long ago used to make the royal armaments but was so scarce by then that very few people had ever seen it.'"

"'Explain this,' said King Toloron in wonder. 'Your Highness,' said the retainer, 'this crown was forged from the last few deposits of tereniuum found in the Mines of Frost."

"As you know, those mines were widely thought to be depleted long ago, but using the funds given by his grace, we were able to convince a few locals to go in and forage enough for us to weld this tereniuum crown for the royal house."

"Almost indestructible, yet light, remarkable to behold, but without sheen or polish, I believe this crown symbolizes the blood and sweat shed by your grace during your conquest of the fourteen.'"

Breathlessly, Jorann asked, "So he accepted the crown?" To him, the story was happening all over again, as if he had been there many years ago.

Despite himself, K'Nan seemed to be relishing his role as the storyteller. "Yes and no," the old paladin said again.

"The king nodded and smiled slightly in approval. Rising from his throne, he began to descend the steps to accept the crown with both hands.

"At that point, we all heard a man's scream," K'Nan said.

Jorann hadn't expected this. "What scream?" he asked. K'Nan didn't answer. He stared at Jorann's posture for a second, then nodded slightly.

"Switch hands." He told him.

This time Jorann knew better than to question him. Without a second thought, he brought his right hand down into the dirt and, without pausing, brought his left hand into his midsection.

"What happened next?" He calmly asked. K'Nan chuckled, then continued the story.

"'YOUR GRACE! YOUR GRACE!' Everyone in the hall froze, startled at this sudden interruption. A ragged scarecrow of a man was trying to force his way through to the steps of the audience room."

"What?" he asked K'Nan in shock. "Who was he? Did he get the king's attention? Did he give him another crown?"

"Yes," K'Nan told him, "and no.

"Several of King Toloron's guards were showing remarkable restraint in holding him back, as it was considered a crime against the crown to enter the audience room without an invitation, unless during a public festival or coronation."

"Undaunted, the man, noticing that the king was still reaching for the crown, drove a filthy, worn boot into the nearest guard's midsection and dove for the stairs."

"The king turned, wanting to tell the guards to hold their weapons, but it was too late. Five spears impaled the man before he could advance more than three steps."

Hearing that, Jorann's jaw dropped and a tear formed in his eye, threatening his balance. "They killed him?"

K'Nan seemed about to reprimand him for that tear, then decided against it. "The man's mouth moved wordlessly for a second; then he tumbled over. Dead before he hit the ground, his fingers uncurled and the bag he had been carrying fell onto the floor. An object rolled out of the sack toward the king."

"Everyone gasped. For a full minute or so there was no sound whatsoever in the room. King Toloron, spellbound, slowly descended the remainder of the stairs, and, waving the guards away, picked up the object and raised it high over his head with both hands."

"No one dared to breathe. High above his head was an elegant crown, polished to an impossible luster yet darker than night itself. It seemed to search deep within every onlooker's darkest thought, while simultaneously inspiring awe and comfort. It was at the same time the bleakest and the most illuminating object that perhaps the world had ever seen."

"After what seemed like an eternity, the king slowly ascended back up the steps, turned around to face his subjects, and then placed the crown on his head before sitting on the throne. The room erupted in cheers. King Toloron was happy beyond measure, as what had just happened seemed fated, a fulfillment of some ancient destiny."

Jorann wondered what type of person would accept something under such tragic circumstances. *This 'Lord' Toloron was not really my kind of guy.*

Again K'Nan seemed to sense his thoughts. "The exalted one was not the bastard you're thinking right now, young Jorann," he said. "He immediately commissioned me to find the family of the poor chap and reward them with titles and wealth."

Feeling a bit better hearing that, though shocked at the legendary warrior's use of profanity, Jorann asked, "So you rewarded them?"

"No. I spent many months searching but was never able even to get a region of origin. It seemed as if he'd truly been dropped from the heavens to help the king."

Smiling wistfully, K'Nan shook his head, seemingly unwilling to continue dwelling in the past.

Turning his attention to Jorann again, K'Nan pointed to the wrist which was holding him up in the air. "If I hadn't seen this mark when you returned my sword to me, you would still be a slave to the *Win-Daji*, my young friend. It was divine providence. Now you have a new destiny to fulfill, one that was decided for you even before you were born."

Enraptured, he listened to every word the old paladin was saying as if it were priceless. Who would have thought, from a slave to a young man with a destiny—all in a matter of minutes!

K'Nan continued. "That mark is indeed the Onyx Crown, the symbol of the greatest ruler to ever govern the fourteen, the matchless one, the *Mekuwa Waku*—Toloron of the tribe Taganoh. My former mentor and benefactor...and my friend.

As K'Nan's story ended, the soothing melody began once more. Jorann, whose emotions had been quite affected by the story, became relaxed. '*I wonder how long I have to stay like this?*' he thought.

"You'll be there until I feel like you've learned something, young master. And you'd better learn to mask your thoughts, or not think at all. If you don't, every amateur sorcerer between here and Okonokep will be able to read you as I can. I'm essentially a novice at that."

Jorann was now beginning to realize just how much he had to learn. The thought was sobering.

"Jorann, his grace ascended the throne during a very turbulent time. The tribal lords and provincial warlords were not all content to allow the House of Toloron to rule in perpetuity. Some were secretly still loyal to the young deposed king, Azinna, some were simply jealous of his ascension and believed they would make better rulers themselves."

"From the day he became king until his death twelve moons later, he never knew a moment's peace."

"Why? Whoa....He ruled all fourteen provinces for twelve moons—it must have been God's will. But wait! I thought Toloron only ruled for five moons—the Glorious Five?"

"You're quite correct," K'Nan told him. "But remember Numerian law is very rigid. By our law, a sovereign's reign is not legitimized until he has either sired or appointed an heir, so the first seven or so were unofficially ruled by his grace. This is tradition ever since the age of the seven great kings, as is the tradition that one cannot lawfully rule until the age of twenty-five."

Jorann couldn't help but feel a sense of pity for this king who once had ruled their known world, "What a shame that even kings and queens can be unhappy."

Eyes widening slightly, K'Nan said, "Very astute, young man. However, King Toloron, toward the end of his life, did find happiness. Her name was Aiisha. She was the daughter of a visiting nomadic king who had come to pay tribute to the throne. Blessed Qandisa, never has a finer lady been born under the heavens! Tall for a lady, very slender. Her skin was the deepest brown and flawless, as were her eyes. Mesmerizing eyes, which always seemed to smile long before her lips did." He sighed. "Her lips, that's another tale in itself. Poems could have been written about them. She was witty, yet reserved. She was friendly to all but at the same time appeared aloof, that perfect combination that all men secretly crave in a woman.

"It was mutual love as soon as they laid eyes on each other. My king never stood a chance. Although he was probably a bit too old for her, he by this time being thirty moons—she couldn't have been more than seventeen or eighteen—he looked even older. The worries of the throne had aged him, but he seemed to regain his inner youth whenever she came near." K'Nan laughed, remembering. "And then everything changed."

"Why?" Jorann asked, then inwardly scolded himself for interrupting the story.

"They had a son. A healthy, lively baby boy whom they named Kalaf. This name was was nomadic and of her people's origin. But with a simple thing like that, merely a name, a kingdom was toppled."

Stunned, Jorann waited impatiently for the rest of the story.

"Kalaf," the old warrior continued, "means 'successor' in the Common Tongue. "For the young king and queen, the birth of Kalaf meant that the House of Toloron would continue to rule over the provinces."

"But that was good, right?" Jorann couldn't help himself. "Wouldn't that mean stability for the realm?"

Pala K'Nan shook his head. "Not in this case. Remember as I said, Lord Toloron had never truly succeeded in gaining the complete loyalty of the other provincial lords, most of whom owed some kind of debt to the long-deceased Azoni Azu the Despot, or were incensed about the overthrow of his older son Azinna. Seeing now that Toloron would never bring back the youngest Azu—Zari, from exile, they formulated a plan to combine forces to expel him from the throne."

"However, they weren't powerful enough. At that time, the king could field an army of a hundred thousand men in a day's notice. The combined strength of the four lords who were disloyal to the throne totaled just over sixty thousand. They needed outside help."

"What they decided to do will make their names live forever in the annals of villainous, treacherous, murderous scum. They dispatched spies to the far north, to the land of the Pale Warriors, spreading rumors of the great treasures that were in abundance here, and how we were ruled by a weak and love-stricken tyrant, who would put up little to no resistance to a full-scale invasion."

K'Nan's eyes burned in anger, obviously still angry at how they had been betrayed.

"Well, there has never been a rumor of treasure that the northern pirates did not pursue. King Toloron only received word from his spies at the last moment of the impending invasion. He set forth for the north shore with most of his army, his young queen, and the heir to repel the northern horde." K'Nan clenched his fists in anger, reliving those days.

"I went along with him, of course, even though I could feel that something was seriously wrong. The Great Battle was horrific, Jorann. Thirty thousand warriors, sailors, and knights, clad entirely in some type of crude metal armor, disembarking at the North Port and besieging the *Citadel yo Bolumko* (Enlightened City)."

"Their men, horses, and weapons were all much heavier than ours, and again and again, they hurled themselves into our lines, trying to break out of their position on the port landing. We lost so many men. Good men. Brave warriors."

Despite himself, Jorann became excited. "How many Pale Warriors did you kill?"

At Jorann's words, a frown passed over Pala K'Nan's face. He opened his mouth and just as quickly closed it, a brief laugh escaping.

"Jorann, count to ten backwards and as you do so, try to remove your pinky and then your fourth finger from the dirt. If that feels comfortable, then remove your third finger also."

Jorann didn't think. "10...9..." he removed his pinky finger. "...8...7...." He decided he needed to impress K'Nan once more. Without hesitation, he pulled back all of the other fingers, not including his index.....

....and nothing happened. Amazingly, he, Jorann—slave boy to the Nabii hunters—was levitating upside down, *on one finger.*

"I'm not proud to say that I killed many, and the king even more than I. Many great warriors whose names will never be celebrated fought bravely and were sacrificed on that day." K'Nan acted as if he didn't even notice what his young protégé had just accomplished.

This sobered Jorann up, but his *imoya* remained undiminished. "Sure they will. As soon as we restore the rightful heir."

K'Nan beamed. "The battle actually could have gone wrong so many times for us, yet there was the king, on his famous horse Defender, galloping up and down the front lines, continuing to rally us to hold our positions. Just the sight of him, sitting so tall on his horse, the Onyx Crown on his head, seemed to lend our soldiers inhuman strength. We fought and bled for most of the day, Jorann, but our lines held. The Pale Warriors who disembarked from the ships, not a single one survived. We pushed them all into the Great Sea.

"But at what a cost. We lost two of every three men to repel the northern hordes. It was barely even a semblance of an army that remained. I had sustained several dire injuries, and it was all I could do to stay on my mount. The king had been injured, too, and even the queen had taken up a spear to protect her lord when it was thought all might be lost!"

"Everyone had done well, Jorann. We decided to rest up for a few days and head back to the *khalqaddi* when we were well enough to do so."

Jorann said, "But the treasonous lords were still a threat, right?"

"Just so. We were still ten miles from the *khalqaddi* when we began to see the smoke from a distance. King Toloron sent his scouts ahead to find out what had taken place. They returned with grim news. The citadel had been sacked by the armies of Lords Okon, Mordu, and Zenosh."

"All of the townspeople had been captured and either killed or enslaved. The retainers remaining in the *khalqaddi* had been made to suffer the *shadim shahar.*"

"'Have they returned the youngest Azu to the throne?' his grace asked. 'Yes, Chief,' his scouts replied. 'Lord Okon has taken the Emi Sword and the Tereniuum Crown and declared himself Lord Regent and Protector of the Azu line. The other two lords have sworn allegiance and have been granted the territories of your loyal retainers.'"

"What a treacherous thief, this Okon was!" Jorann said fiercely, anger at what Okon did burning through his veins.

"I was just as indignant," said Pala K'Nan. "I immediately told my liege that we must attack to take back the *khalqaddi.* 'No,' he replied, 'If my guess is correct, we are already surrounded.'"

"He was right, of course, as he usually was. Our approach to the citadel had been carefully monitored, and our position was surrounded. The king had, in error, allowed our vanguard force, the warriors of young Jashu Jasonne, to return to their home province of Suronai. Our remaining ten thousand soldiers were left to face the bulk of the enemy's forces, which now surrounded us. It was a hopeless situation."

"The king then said, 'K'Nan, find me three brave soldiers who are not injured and not married, and bring them to me.'"

"He then said to the Lady Aiisha, 'My queen, have the nurses bring out the *Khuselas* (protectors) as well as our son.' Well, I was puzzled, for I didn't know anything about any *Khuselas*, but like any good soldier, I did what I was told. I went back to the soldiers and found three who had distinguished themselves in battle at the North Port, three who had no families, extraordinary fighters all. I brought them back to King Toloron."

"When I arrived back in the king's tent, there were three newborn babies there, along with the heir, who was around the age of five. They were all dressed in brown, all being held by nursemaids, all with bright shining eyes, and a head full of hair. Very alert, but not crying as most babies would have been after all of the commotion going on. They were without question special children. In addition to that, they all had a curious mark on their wrists. Two parallel rectangles with three cresting points on top. I had only to glance at the top of the High King's head to know what it was."

Barely breathing, Jorann didn't dare move a muscle. He waited as patiently as he could for his new mentor to tell the rest.

"The king told me that on the night of his son's birth, just over four crescent moon's past, a renowned prophetess came to the *khalqaddi* and told him everything that would transpire that day. His fate as king of Numeria was sealed. He said he and the queen would perish there today, along with most of our men. However, it was also foretold that it would not be the end of his line."

"The king then said, 'These three children were all born with this curious mark, all within close proximity to our *khalqaddi*. Their parents were informed of the prophecy then compensated for giving their children in service to the crown. The prophetess foresaw that these three children would one day return the House of Toloron to the rule of the fourteen tribal provinces and serve as *Khuselas* of the heir."

Tears began to form in Jorann's eyes. The mystery he had wanted to solve almost since before he could remember, the circumstances behind his birth and who he truly was, had just been laid before him.

"The attending priestess gave each child a drop of some type of black elixir, which seemed to stain their entire mouth black for the briefest of moments. Seconds later, we could all clearly see the black marks on their wrist begin to glow as if they were aflame!"

Jorann could only think at this point; *if I start crying, he's going to hit me again. Or worse yet, despise me.* He willed himself to remain stoic.

"Even the toughest most hardened warriors in the empire began to cry when they saw, for the first time anywhere, the *Shohamu Taiji*, the mystical mark of the Onyx Crown. Yes, those points and lines right there, Jorann," he assured him with mild amusement."

"The priestess then gave each child to one of the three soldiers and told them, 'You three brave men have been entrusted with a sacred task. Keep these children safe from the Houses of Okon and Azu until they come of age. When that time comes, find Pala K'Nan, son of Loffri, and bring them to him to fulfill their destinies.'"

"Those three warriors accepted the children, saluted the king and queen, and weren't heard from again."

Looking down at Jorann, Pala K'Nan paused. Telling the story had taken most of the night, but it was clear he was not quite finished. "Finally, King Toloron looked at me and spoke. 'Could we have conquered the world, my friend?' he asked me.

'Not according to the prophecy, sire, but we came close.' He laughed then, that full laugh that had always infected everyone around him. Then just as quickly, the laughter stopped. 'Were we wrong to not put young Azinna back on the throne?'

"'How can wanting to preserve the life of yourself and your men be wrong? We did right by the Gods just by not putting a spear through the youngest son, Azzolari.' King Toloron nodded and said to me, 'K'Nan, take my son to where our friends are, east of the Great River. Tell them what has transpired and tell them to keep him safe until the time of his return. Then you must do everything you can to help him ascend to his rightful inheritance. Travel the realm, sew dissension amongst the usurpers, and train the *Khuselas.* I'm sorry I could not let you retire in peace as you've always wanted, my friend.' Without waiting for an answer, he picked up his son, young Kalaf, and handed him to me."

"Unlike the other children, the young prince cried his heart out. I bowed to him and his young wife, the beautiful Queen Aiisha, and galloped away. That was the last I ever saw of them."

Jorann realized that K'Nan had come to the end of his story, without answering the obvious question. "Well?" he asked impatiently.

K'Nan looked at him in surprise. "Well, what?"

"Where is the prince? Is he here now?" He began anxiously looking around the camp, excited to get a glimpse of the boy.

"The prince," said K'Nan absently.

Jorann raised his eyes quizzically at him. "Yes! Can't wait to meet him. Where is he?"

"Somewhere safe." K'Nan's normally confident voice suddenly seemed very reverent, almost hushed. *He obviously has a great deal of respect for this "heir,"* thought Jorann.

"....and the Onyx Crown?" he asked K'Nan. "What happened to that? The last you mentioned, the king was wearing it in battle."

"That," said K'Nan, "is a question that every man, woman, or child in Numeria would kill to know the answer to. It hasn't been seen since that day."

"No one has even laid eyes on the thing?"

"Not a soul. We know for a fact that the great traitor Okon has launched several expeditions west to try and locate it, all ending in failure."

Jorann was crestfallen. *This is not going to be easy.* "So when do we start training?" He asked K'Nan.

Suddenly, he felt the swift spear of K'Nan sweep the lone finger holding him up. Jorann felt he had no choice but to fall backwards but thought better of it and did nothing.

The spear hooked his right leg, and the momentum brought him forward. He did a forward roll and came quickly to his feet. The indomitable spear of K'Nan then thrust towards his front left ankle. Without thinking, Jorann simply raised his foot, keeping his right foot firmly planted this time.

It wasn't much of a counter-move, but he had successfully defended himself against an attack from one of the greatest fighters of all time. He was at this moment completely different from the boy he'd been just ten minutes ago.

"It already began," said K'Nan with a faint smirk.

* *

Hours later, they still sat together, surrounded by the tall viridian grass on all sides, the two of them and at some distance away, K'Nan's men. No, his own men. They sipped cold tea from red grass leaves and wrapped themselves in dried jackal skins to keep warm.

As it was still winter in the drylands, the nights were as un-bearably cold as the days were blanketed with dry warmth. The red grass tea was served cold, but the drink itself contained several herbs that gave a pleasant, warm, almost burning sensation to the internal organs, creating the illusion of sitting by a fire, if nothing else. For many things were permitted in the savannah, but fire was not one of them. Never fire.

"Jorann," said K'Nan thoughtfully as he sipped his tea, "as you've probably surmised by now, you are one of the *Khuselas*, or protectors, of the heir. And from this moment forward, you are destined to do heroic things in your life, for yourself and the four-teen tribal provinces of Numeria.

"When I saw your wrist back at the village, as you reached for Amnesia, I knew it then. However, I couldn't figure out how you could have become a captive." K'Nan shook his head again. "The only thing I could surmise is that your assigned guardian had been ambushed, and you'd been captured and enslaved as a result. He must have been killed."

"But the *Win-Daji*, the women, the children..." Jorann hesitat-ed, not wanting to sound weak.

"I apologize for having to do that, young Jorann, but it was only the gods' will that you hadn't already been found out to be living amongst them by spies of the Lord Regent Okon. The leg-end of the Onyx Crown is well known, and the mark representing it has been on your wrist since birth. They had to be killed."

Jorann was unconvinced but let the matter drop for now.

The wind swayed the leaves of grass both toward and away from the tiny encampment. Jorann looked around him slowly and breathed in deeply, as if savoring not just his new surroundings, but his new life. *Life is such an infinite realm of possibilities*, he thought. Why had he several times in the past chosen not to live it?

"We must begin the search for your other two counterparts, immediately. The empire has fallen into calamity, and the heir will need to be restored sooner rather than later. The prophecy clearly states that only the three of you together will be able to 'restore the rightful prince to his throne.'"

"Why sooner rather than later?" Jorann asked. This was all starting to sound a bit rushed to him. *Mother Qandisa!* He thought. He hadn't even learned how to properly hold a sword or spear yet.

"Finally you're asking the important questions," said K'Nan as he nodded his head. "Because.....we only have a short time before the Toloron-Taganoh line can never be restored again."

Jorann nodded, but he knew there was more.

"Once the youngest son of the Azu the Despot, Azzolari, officially becomes age twenty-five, all of the tribal leaders of Numeria will kneel before him and swear allegiance. When this happens, The House of Toloron's current claim to fidelity of the other tribes becomes void." K'Nan swiped at an imaginary mosquito as to not betray his anxiety at the thought.

"Who are the other two *Khuselas*?" he asked him, curious about the kids he would soon be working and training with, and who were, in a sense, the siblings he never had.

"They were children ordained by the heavens just like you. The three of you together are Chaos, Conflict, and Calm. Each of you are to be highly skilled warriors and possess certain mental abilities. You will all be great leaders of men as well as achieve many individual merits."

You sound so certain, though Jorann. *What if we fail?*

As if sensing his thoughts, K'Nan patted his shoulder. "Don't worry.... your friends are out there. We have a general idea of where, but there will be a great deal of luck involved in finding them, just as there was in finding you. I have a feeling that you are the 'Calm' of the three, and if that's true, 'Chaos' and 'Conflict' will likely show themselves soon."

"Excellent," he responded. "When do we begin looking for them?"

"Tomorrow."

5

Isolated Wisdom

"When the past wanes to oblivion, true destiny is liberated." —
Numerian proverb

Your name is Jorann, his inner voice repeated.

For what seemed the hundredth time, he closed his eyes and
willed himself to concentrate on his new most prized possession,
the name he had been given not long ago, as the venomous kokara
snakes once again rushed toward the dark and damp hell of a pit
into which he had been lowered.

He quickly willed his heart and lungs to come to a stop and
calmly opened his eyes. The strange sight that greeted him was a
lot less terrifying now than it had been the first time he'd experi-
enced this particular training ritual just over two months ago.

About sixty to seventy slithery creatures, forest-green except
for the bright red and orange-flecked scales on the backs of their
heads, all moved quickly down to the center of the pit floor as if
drawn by some magnetic force, and in truth, there was one of
sorts.

These snakes, the kokara, were chosen by Pala K'Nan because
they did not feed on the flesh of humans, guaranteeing some level
of safety to the warrior in training.

Despite this, the venom they released during their strikes
caused violent shivering, hallucinations, and in extreme cases,
long-term paralysis of the entire body.

Their movement toward him was slower now, as if sensing
some prey was there but not sure if it were a dead or a living
thing.

Pala K'Nan had chosen this training with these particular species for another reason—although most snakes can see, the kokara

cannot, yet their hearing is almost supernatural (whereas most snakes are actually deaf). In fact, their level of hearing is so acute that they can hear the heartbeat of most warmbloods.

So sinister Pala K'Nan can be when it comes to my training, Jorann thought grimly. The ultimate method of training yourself to always remain calm is to face the kokara. One who didn't want to feel the painful effects of their venom needed only to slow their heart rate. More accurately, they needed to almost stop their heart rate altogether.

Only by using this method could you fool them into thinking you were a dead organism, and therefore not worth them wasting their venom.

The first time K'Nan had loosed the detesting snakes on him, it was all he could do not to jump up and run. He wished controlling that particular urge had been enough—however, his heartbeat had been palpable, his entire body had become quickly soaked in perspiration.

The kokara found him all too easily—and all too quickly. As the first few of them slithered up his torso and began biting, he screamed, a loud primal wail that contained both agony and disbelief. For not the first time, he'd asked himself was this, all of this, really necessary? However, the old paladin had been insistent.

"When doing battle, young man, you must learn to completely detach yourself from emotion. The sword and spear are cold and unfeeling objects, meant only for death, and so to wield them effectively, you must make yourself just as emotionless. For what good is a merciless weapon when wielded by one who's merciful?"

Jorann couldn't argue. He'd once promised himself while in captivity that if he became free, he would never show mercy to those who'd tortured him. In the end, he'd felt pity for them as they were slaughtered in the valley, and he was more ashamed that he'd been unable to be pitiless than anything else.

He knew if he were ever going to be the perfect guardian, he would have to find a way to detach his naturally benevolent instincts from the tasks at hand, particularly when they involved dispatching enemies of the heir. So if training with the dreaded kokara would help him accomplish that, then all the better.

He'd been "incapacitated" for several days following that initial test—literally his entire nervous system had stalled, and he'd been quite unable to move out of the bed he had slowly come to consciousness in.

Also, he recalled that he'd been far more ashamed of his own "cowardly" scream than of actually failing in the pit. He could never forget the probing look that Pala K'Nan had given him after the massacre of the Nabii hunters, the *Win-Daji*, the one where his manhood, indeed his level of humanity itself, had been questioned.

Thinking about that day and his lack of resolve—and thinking also about the days when he'd wanted his life to end, he knew he had to go back into the pit again, no matter the difficulty.

Days came and went with ease. The kokara trials became gradually easier from that point on, evolving from taxing physical and mental tests of his will to the point where they presented no challenge to him at all. Jorann had reached the level where he could almost entirely stop his breathing and heartbeat to fool them, no small feat for a boy of his age.

But today...

Today, something was very different. The kokara did not stop coming. Although Jorann did try to slow his vital functions, his thoughts began to wander to a time not far gone, a time when he could not move freely as he wished or do as he wanted. Most damaging, though, was that he could not think freely. As a slave, any independent thoughts or expressions are reflected in your moods and one's visage. As such, a slave had to be extremely careful never to entertain thoughts of freedom or independence.

Why couldn't he overcome these memories?

Thinking about his previous life at this particular time and in this situation was not a wise choice. The lead kokara quizzingly emitted its signature hiss and began slowly climbing the length of his sparingly clad frame toward his heart. The other snakes followed suit.

In a last-ditch effort to spare himself from the pain that being cluster-bitten would inevitably cause, Jorann began to recite a verse from an ancient manuscript on meditation that K'Nan had given him soon after starting his training.

Originally written in the ancient language of the *doyenne*, the descendants of the Lightbringers, these verses were discovered within a tattered manuscript by retainers of King Toloron and hidden before the first invasion of the Pale Warriors.

K'Nan himself was not only a warrior and trainer of warriors, but one of the true scholars of the "Forgotten Age" (so termed because of the forced burning of all historical records of the Toloron reign). He had been able to painstakingly transcribe and arrange the manuscript in such a manner that it became an invaluable training tool for countless warriors who had served under the High King.

There were three main premises of the manuscripts, which had been discovered with no titles and had been re-named the *Zakku-Dalla* or "The Classics" by Pala K'Nan.

The first was a profound lecture on meditation and breathing as a means to both bolster your health and increase your strength. This was the section that he had already begun studying, and though he had merely scratched the surface with his lessons, the benefits to his health and mental capacity had already been enormous.

He no longer felt the blazing midday heat or the late evening cold nearly as much as he once had. He didn't feel particularly sleepy or even fatigued as often. He rarely even felt hungry!

However, Pala K'Nan had informed him that these were the most fragmented sections of the *Zakku-Dalla*, and so it was these sections that he'd had the toughest time translating. The old paladin had warned him that as a result, he was unaware of possible adverse physical effects of studying these methods.

That had worried him a bit.

Presently, though, Jorann was more concerned about the kokara bites, as the first three of the serpents had already sunk their fangs deep into his right wrist.

He waited for the usual numbing feeling to wash over him—the arrival of that familiar sensation meant he had successfully sealed off his nervous system from the venom.

By this time, the meditation techniques usually worked, and the pain of the bite and the poison would have subsided. All night, however, he had dreamt of horrific memories from his captive childhood, the beatings, the forced starving's, the degradation, and insults.

For weeks now, K'Nan had been telling him that for him to truly become one of the *Khuselas*, and to maximize his abilities, he would have to forget about his entire life up to now. This included the lowlife soldier who'd protected him as an infant only to sell him later, the sadistic family that had both raised and tortured him, the childhood that he'd lost because of them, and, of course, not being able to seek justice.

But that's indeed the hard part to reconcile, isn't it? Jorann thought to himself. That he would never be able to make them pay, pay for what they'd tried to turn him into. An animal. A lifetime serv—

"Arrrrrrrgggghhhhhhh!!!!!!!!"

The horrific pain of the kokara venom snapped him abruptly from his reverie. *By the heavens*, he thought, *how could I be so careless?* The stinging, paralyzing sensation was now so intense that he could barely breathe, but Jorann knew that if he didn't soon get help, things would quickly become even worse.

As carefully as he could, he managed to extract the rest of the snakes that had been resting on his upper waist without triggering more venom.

With great difficulty, he rose from the floor of the pit, straddled both sides of the cave walls, and with one last major breath to calm himself began half-walking, half-skipping up the wall, using a lung-capacity technique he had been taught by some of K'Nan's band of soldiers.

He knew he had to hurry to reach the opening before he lost consciousness. When he initially began training with the kokara, K'Nan had never left the pit, but as time went by, and Jorann became more adept at controlling the snake attacks, the old warrior had monitored him with much less anxiety and eventually stopped coming by to check on his safety altogether.

If he didn't make it out of this cave opening, it was possible no one would find Jorann until the venom had done real damage to his internal organs.

As these thoughts ran through his mind, he forgot a cardinal rule of climbing smooth surfaces: never let your mind wander. Still four *rods* from the top, his hand lost hold of a small break in the wall, and overcompensating for the mistake, he moved his left boot up entirely too fast to the next foothold, missing another barely visible crack in favor of one that was much too small for his boot to enter.

Cursing his stupidity, Jorann let himself continue to fall downward thirty or so rods—into the shallow hell of the kokara.

When he awoke it wasn't to the darkness he'd expected, but to intense light—the brightest sun that he'd ever seen, so brilliant that he couldn't completely open his eyes.

In his dim consciousness, he heard several voices behind him, none of which he recognized. What was obvious, though, from the volume and urgency of the voices, was that they were in deep disagreement.

Forcing himself to open his eyes wider, he saw that he was lying on his back in a dry salt pool, raised over the surface by a bed of cloven cypress branches. Other than his very unusual bed there was no other living plants, trees, or animals of any kind as far as he could see. His feet were wrapped in silvery white strips of cloth of some sort...no, the more he looked he could see that he was entirely covered with those strips of fabric.

Am I dead? He thought with a start.

Strangely enough, the thought didn't make him panic or alarm him even. He attempted to sit up on the bed of cloven cypress but couldn't. Only in his mind could he move. However, just the attempt seemed to get the attention of those people behind him, because all at once, several firm but gentle hands grabbed him and held him still. Before he lost consciousness again, the last thing he could see was a long thin metal object being inserted into his neck.

* *

This time it was the sound of music that awakened him. He could hear the melody even as his eyes remained closed, a sweet beckoning whisper that seemed to hold a desolate sadness and hint of promise in each note.

Listening to it, he felt as if his mind were a vast chasm with no bottom and endless space, yet the tune being played was lifting him farther and farther out of it. The sound seemed to at once strengthen and embolden him to the point where he no longer felt the fear of death or pain.

He feared only that this divine aria that had apparently saved him from eternal sleep would soon end. The anxiety caused by that thought forced him to open his eyes.

Again, the almost blinding light. What exactly was it? The desert sun? A reflection of the surrounding salt beds, perhaps? Whatever it was, it forced him to close his eyelids abruptly. Right after that, he heard a more hesitant note in the song, which only a few seconds earlier he wouldn't even have thought conceivable.

He now recognized the instrument, an *oude*, an ancient instrument requiring immense dexterity of the mind and refinement of the senses. He had only heard it played once before, by one of the traveling *diobas* who'd encountered the *Win-Daji* sometime before.

That unkempt, travel-weary *dioba* would probably have given his left hand for the ability to play half this well. The thought itself instantly warmed his heart. The man had been a sniveling sycophant and dismissive of him as nothing more than a slave to be ignored.

He'd been happy to see him leave, away from the caravan and into the wilderness, probably to certain death. Involuntarily, he smiled, then tried to open his eyes again. This time the music completely stopped. "Wait," a voice told him. It was the voice of a young lady, as soft a tone as he had ever heard, and ten times as soothing as the *oude* had been.

Immediately, he felt something being placed over his eyes, an extremely cold cloth or compress of some kind, with a strong herbal scent surrounding it. The urge to open his eyes disappeared, and in fact, he felt as if he were better off with them closed...more aware.

Though he couldn't figure out why, he was beginning to feel as if he were no longer in control of his emotions or feelings at all. *Goddess Janeen, what is going on here?* He asked himself, both angry and alarmed now.

"Who are you?" he asked the girl, much more harshly than he'd intended.

"I was assigned to look after you," was the simple reply.

"Assigned? Assigned by who?" he asked, half to her and half to himself.

Then he remembered something. "I fell in the *kokara* pit," he mumbled aloud.

"Several days ago. One of the Elders found you and brought you here."

"Several days?" Worry creased his brow. It was obvious that he had been found and taken away from the pit before K'Nan or his men could locate him.

"Where is here...where am I?" Everything his senses picked up was different from the wilderness and the savannah—the humidity, the light, the smell, the quiet. He was certainly somewhere that he'd never been and perhaps even never heard about before.

Silence. Jorann got the feeling he had asked the wrong question. His anger began to rise. "I asked where—"

"I'm sorry, brave hero. I was told not to give you any information about who we are or your whereabouts. I imagine now that you've regained consciousness, they will be explaining all of those things to you in briefness of time."

Well, at least that's an answer, he thought, somewhat mollified. He then realized he might have seemed a bit ungrateful. Even though they took him, they did at least save him from the kokara.

"*Masiti*," he began earnestly, using the Tandish term for 'Miss,' "it's enough to know that you've given me back my life. I promise to repay your kindness someday, even at the cost of my own life. And I am no hero, but many thanks for your courtesy." He smiled weakly.

There was another awkward silence before she finally spoke, and he could sense her looking down at his wrist in awe.

"You are wrong. We already know you to be a great hero. To be truthful... it's not accurate to say that I've saved your life, your injuries were seen to by the Elders as soon as you arrived. I merely fed you some liquid herbs to help you keep your strength up and played a few meaningless notes to help you refocus your inner radial energy. The *kokara* did much damage there, but even without my help, you would have survived.

"Besides," the tranquil voice said, a bit timidly, "I asked them if I could help. I wanted to do whatever I could to help you."

"Many thanks for your concern, *masiti*," he told her, though he wondered why she sounded so admiring of him when they had never met before. "So how much longer until I'm fully recovered? How long must I remain here?"

"Only until your eyesight returns. And now...I'm afraid...I can never again speak with you."

* *

Jorann sat staring into the brightness. His vision was slowly beginning to return, though he could not yet identify any specific objects.

Even without his full vision, somehow, he could discern the physical make up of everyone and everything immediately around him. He couldn't explain how; he just saw them, almost as if their souls were visible as shapes of energy. There was something different about him now; something in the pit had forever changed him.

Sitting around him in a neat formation were six seemingly gaunt old men. They were tall. They would be considered giants among even the most imposing of warriors. Yet there was not the slightest menacing quality about them, only the aura of total wisdom.

Sitting amongst them, Jorann felt as if all the mysteries of every known object, living or dead, were known to these men surrounding him.

The Elders, he thought. The name was apt. He had recently believed that Pala K'Nan was, without doubt, the wisest man who had ever lived, yet just being in the presence of these men, he realized that had been an error.

"I am honored to meet you all," he said to the group, trying to sound firm and confident. Pala K'Nan had taught him that Numerian men followed only strength and decisiveness, and because he didn't know who these Elders were, or why they had taken him in, he thought it best to portray himself as someone worth saving, rather than a former slave.

"Are you?" a very old, deep, and measured voice asked from directly in front of him.

"Why would you be honored?" Silence.

"I...because I...." Honestly, why should he be? He barely even knew who these people were. It had just seemed like the right thing to say.

He blurted, "I was told it takes extraordinary skill to cure the kokara venom, particularly after such a long time in the body. My own teacher expends quite a bit of energy when he must do so. I was fortunate that you happened upon me. It is indeed an honor to meet gentlemen with such medicinal artistry."

More silence.

"The young hero is quite perceptive," the ancient voice said. "Healing is indeed an art and not a science as most people think. Art relates to the mind, but science relates to the physical body. Art is for things which are known yet cannot be explained. Science is for things that can be explained yet are not known.

However, your injuries were of both mind and body. Your body was injured due to the *kokara*; your mind has been injured for quite some time. Without the mind, the body cannot exist. This is a lesson for you, my son."

Jorann was spellbound. In just a few words, the elder had summed up his past, present, and future. His last encounter with the *kokara* had ended so badly because his mind had betrayed the needs of his body.

"Many thanks for your teaching, Elders," he said, meaning it.

None of the shapes facing him appeared to move or even breathe. He decided that he would forget about impressing them and concentrate on learning as much as he could about himself before he had to leave—if they allowed him to leave.

"The young hero is too modest. What is your purpose in this world?"

A strange question. He thought for a second; then he remembered something the girl had said to him quite casually.

"This, of course, you would already know."

There was a barely audible gasp of disbelief from a couple of the Elders. "Naturally," said the voice of the spokesman. "You have figured out who we are by some method of divination we would not have thought possible. Clearly, your aptitude is exceptional."

"Not really." Jorann shrugged. "But it's obvious that you have aided me despite some regulations your honorable order has against doing so. Also, you healed me and are even now speaking to me despite those same rules of your order forbidding you to do so."

"I gather that a group of truly learned gentlemen such as yourselves would never risk as much as you are now doing unless you have discerned who I truly am."

Again, there was silence. Not for the first time he became frustrated at his inability to see and wondered again when his sight might return. However, he could still feel the rest of them looking at each other, as if they all shared the same sense of...fear. Yes, fear was the emotion he could now feel in the room, palpable now. He tilted his head to the side quizzically, amazed that he somehow seemed able to feel emotions as easily as he once could see them.

"Young hero," said the ancient voice, calmly, "there is much you understand, and yet there is much you do not yet understand. We are indeed an ancient order—you were most astute in that; however, we are one that has been and must remain unknown to your people."

You're doing a great job of it, Jorann said to himself. *I've never even heard of any old men as weird as the six of you.*

The ancient voice, who was apparently their chief, continued.

"The difficulties in healing you were two-fold; we would be required to make ourselves known to you, which we pledged long ago never to do again, and also we were forced to transfer some of the life essence of our civilization to you, to heal you. So, to be perfectly accurate, you are both an outsider, and yet you are still one of us. Hence, the conflict that you sense."

Life essence, he thought. *Man, these guys truly are full of themselves.*

"I see," he said, wanting to ask more but aware that doing so would only stop the flow of information, which at this point seemed necessary to his survival.

"We are the order of the *Pajadin de Hekeemah,* once known simply as the Silent Order, young master. Tell us, have you ever heard of this name?"

"I'm ashamed to say that I'm unfamiliar with your illustrious order, sir." This was the most non-offensive thing he could muster. He had long since despaired of ever understanding the intricate hierarchical machinations of Numeria, which were steeped in thousands of years of tradition, and, as far as he could tell, only served to confine most of its citizens to a life of poverty from birth until death.

A Numerian was born into a *family,* which could be small or extended—with hundreds of members. A large group of families with a common origin, language, and purpose formed a *tribe*—which was headed by a tribal chieftain, but which also contained many elders or *Pajadin*, responsible for making the laws and decisions and recording the history of its members.

The many tribes living under the same commonalities and within a large, partitioned area formed a chiefdom, usually called a *province*. In many cases, the head of a tribe could also be the ruler of a province. Lords Jashu Jasonne and the powerful Sankofa Norna were two of the most famous current examples of this in the empire.

The Numerian feudal system flourished in this way for many years, until these tribal warlords became powerful enough to begin subjugating rival tribes and provinces. The first to attempt to do it was the bumbling Victo Ngeppu, followed by the Azu clan and finally the young Lord Toloron. They were the first Numerians in history to take for themselves the title of King, which in the Common Tongue was pronounced as *Mekuwa Waku,* literally 'Chief of Chiefs.'

This system confused him to no end; perhaps it always would.

He could hear a smile in the old man's voice.

"The young hero shows us far too much propriety," he continued, "As we ceased most communication with the outside world long ago, it would have been quite odd for you actually to have heard of our insignificant tribe. As the wind blows, the dust will gather. As it continues, dust will scatter."

The words jolted Jorann. He recognized them from a passage in the *Zakku-Dalla* Classics. *As the winds blow, the dust will gather, and as it continues, the dust will scatter.*

The passage spoke of sharpening your senses via disassociation from all things earthly—that the identification of all physical matter is based on prerecorded vision, sound, and other sensory-based memories of these objects.

However, because of how similar two or more things can be to the eyes, ears, and nose, most humans have long lost the true sharpness of their senses. Forgetting the familiarity of sights, sounds, and scents make it much easier to recognize their presence. In short, you must forget in order to identify.

He now knew that this order, the *Pajadin de Hekeemah*, had to have some association with those ancient manuscripts he had been studying. He decided to test whether this was true by reciting another verse from the passages.

"That is so," he told them, "and for knowledge to have substance, the dust must become void."

At once there was a great commotion in the meeting. Several voices began to speak, some urgently, most incredulously, a few of them in awe.

"How—how can he know this, this, he...?"

"...not possible...even if he is..."

"...we must thoroughly ascertain this young hero's background."

To Jorann, these men were all beginning to sound a bit nonsensical.

"Wait a minute!" shouted one of the men, a man whose imoya had struck him as being much colder than those of his brethren. The room calmed down immediately, which told Jorann how much they valued this new person's opinion.

The man continued, "How do we know this kid is the real thing? He could just be some unlucky imp who fell into the wrong pit and needed rescuing. Should we truly be revealing our secrets to him?"

"Seema Selah!" spat one of the other Pajadin, "Are you worried that he'll someday be able to curb those future ambitions of yours? What are you afraid of, he's just a boy." Some of the others chuckled in agreement.

There was a long pause, then Jorann heard Seema Selah's voice say with conviction:

"All evil has a beginning."

Jorann was at a loss when he heard this, as the logic was irrefutable.

"Young hero," the old man spoke, much more carefully this time. "Fate is a strange thing. It at once separates us from each other yet binds us together.

Look at the *tegra* birds, which blaze a path across the desert sky, yet can be found nowhere on land or sea. During the night, they travel many *en-yawo*, to a location and for a reason that no one knows, yet it is morning, and again they are overhead."

He continued, "Are our lives not like those of the *tegra* birds? We once lived in harmony with your people, yet became disenchanted with the unnecessary violence and wastefulness of these times and chose to isolate ourselves. However, now, with your presence here, an ancient prophecy that guides the fate of all who follow our order has been revealed, and the moment has come for us to reintroduce ourselves to the world."

"So..." Jorann said, "You're certain you know who I am?"

There was a pleasant sound of muted laughter from the group. When the wise old man spoke again, amusement was still clear in his voice.

"That is certain. If not by the mark on your wrist, then definitely from your *imoya*, that inner spirit which guides us all, illuminates us all, and identifies us all. You are the last among the prophesied three, but the first to seek redemption. You are one of the gifted who will bring peace to the savannah, the *chakkha*, and the wilderness—the ones who wear the mark of the Onyx Crown, the immortal *Shohamu Taiji*.

"Many will follow you, some with highborn names, some with names of low birth, and many with no identity at all, but be certain of this, the entire world will soon know your name. May we have the pleasure of knowing that illustrious name, young master?"

The men around him waited patiently, expectantly, excitement barely containable in their eyes.

He allowed himself a smile, for it was a short time ago that he had no name to give. But no longer.

"My name is Jorann."

* *

Several weeks passed, and his vision hadn't returned. Spring left, autumn arrived. New warriors, guised as helpless infants, were born, while old heroes, whose names once shook the kingdoms, aptly died.

Eventually, he set out to find Pala K'Nan, thinking that by now he was either worried sick or had resigned him to the dead. He looked different than he had when he'd entered the *kokara* pit quite some time ago. His face was still as solemn, deathly so to those who passed him on the official roads, but his eyes now held many emotions.

He'd lost a lot of the muscle that had been built up during Pala K'Nan's rigorous training exercises, but he'd never felt stronger. His hair had once been a jet-black curly mass of tangled beads but had turned almost completely white. It was a combination of the life-force he'd received from the *Pajadin de Hekeemah* combined with his advanced study of the Zakku-Dalla which had caused this dramatic change in appearance, although his face was still youthful.

"You there! Stop!" His thoughts were interrupted by the shouting of a woman's voice. Turning to the right, he saw her. At least, he assumed it was a she. She did not quite resemble a person.

Emaciated and frail, she looked more like a living skeleton than a human. Across her stilted framework of a figure, a dust-covered brown tunic hung unceremoniously from her shoulders to just below her knees. Her feet were filthy and covered by a pair of makeshift sage reed sandals. Her clothes had likely been taken from someone else.

Her eyes, large and brown, were sunk a couple of inches deep into the sockets of her skull. She looked as if she hadn't eaten a meal in weeks.

Mindful that he was on a mission to find Pala K'Nan, he felt nevertheless compelled to stop. "What can I do for you, *miss*?" Though his voice was calm, inside he felt rage building; he wanted to kill whoever had brought her to this state.

"Do? For me...?" Tilting her head, she stared at him for a moment and then began to laugh hysterically. "Ha, ha, ha! Oh my! You poor child, you think I need your help? Oh, how great, how wonderful! It looks as if I were right to come to you now after all! Ha, ha!"

Her laugh, which had sounded somewhat unnatural at first, now bordered on the edge of insanity.

Then just as quickly as it had begun, the laughter stopped, and she was staring up at him with those hollow brown eyes.

"Young man, I have no need of your help. I'm here to save *you!*"

Jorann gasped. Had the *Win-Daji's* relatives somehow tracked him down after all?

The woman continued. "I've been waiting here for days to give this to you and to stop you from following your current path of destruction."

"Destruction?" he asked? "Who was I to destroy?"

"Yourself, for one," she replied. "The whole of Numeria, quite possibly."

He barely stopped himself from rolling his eyes. He was just a boy, almost thirteen moons, not to mention a recently freed slave. Did he truly have that much destructive potential in him? He contrasted this with the prophecy of the *Pajadin de Hekeemah* that he would instead save the world. Yup, he was sure of it now. This old hag was insane.

Before he could utter a protest, she dropped a small cloth bag into his hands, raised a long, bony finger, and pointed it down the narrow road in the direction that he had been heading. His eyes followed her finger but saw nothing that should command his attention.

"Down that road, doth not traverse. Reverse your course, forestall the curse."

She spoke as if another person had control of her voice. Having said the last word, she suddenly dropped into a lifeless heap at his feet.

6

Sania's Chaos

The melody could be heard throughout the various rooms of the house, as it usually was in the evenings. It was always preceded by the busy and excited sounds of the personal attendants, cooks, servers, and companion girls, all preparing for another night of fantastic fun and opulence at Mistress Jayda's Winery, or *Dukka-Vinyo*.

After all the sumptuous meals had been cooked for the evening's guests, the entertainment rooms cleaned, and the discretionary rooms had been prepared, the ritual hour to begin accepting the evening's honored (and usually quite esteemed) guests arrived.

Yet absolutely no one was allowed to enter or begin welcoming until Little Asha had finished singing the unofficial poem of Mistress Jayda's *Dukka-Vinyo*. No one knew the origin of the song, but it was most likely a tune originating in the southern *Kumaz-we*, and spoken in the formal dialect of that region, *khajudic*. Translated loosely into the common tongue, the poem was titled "No Regrets."

Little wildflower,
Blooming in the desert sands, you did not choose to be carried here.
Little wildflower,
Scattered cross the foreign lands, destined to be sought far and near.
Lovely wanderer of the desert, you can never go home again,
For home is now here.

While "No Regrets" was being sung each evening, time always seemed to stand still. The customers could imagine they were gallant heroes, and the ladies were exotic yet attainable. It was the perfect beginning to what would usually be an exciting yet relaxing evening.

"You stole my purse! You little thief!"

With an angry shout, the warm blanket of serenity that had settled like a cloud over Mistress Jayda's *Dukka-Vinyo* instantly vanished. Not long after was heard a ridiculously loud crashing of seemingly every object imaginable.

Irritated and utterly incapable of creating a single melodic note by now, Sullen Peacock, one of the lovely guest entertainers, ceased playing her casseen.

She once had a "real" name, all of the ladies there did, but having arrived at the *Dukka-Vinyo* at the young age of twelve, she was promptly given another one by the winery's talent coordinator, Mohann.

Sullen Peacock, so named because of her sad, almond-shaped eyes combined with a colorful wardrobe and absolutely mesmerizing smile, had been identified as a musical prodigy almost instantly by Mohann. Whoever came up with the name probably couldn't be bothered with the minor detail that the colorful gender of that particular species were actually the males.

She had already learned most of the contemporary instruments of her home province, Jemobha, her father having been a personal musician of the duke of that region for many months. When that particular nobleman fell into disfavor with Regent Okon, the fortunes of his personal staff promptly turned also.

Unable to feed his family, he and his wife finally decided to contract their youngest and favorite daughter to Mistress Jayda's *Dukka-Vinyo* for what amounted to about three moons of food for the rest of the family.

"We will return for you when you come of age, little petal, I promise. Until then, obey Master Mohann. Time will fly by, you'll see," said her daddy, blowing her a soft kiss.

Sullen Peacock had not answered. Perhaps even then she saw flaws in her father's character that no one else seemed to. Predictably, but unbeknownst to her, he gambled and lost every copper of the money Mohann had given him for her contract.

Sullen Peacock never regretted being sold to the winery. She had learned a lot growing up there and had scarcely remembered calling another place home. When her age of emancipation came, and no one came to collect her, she and Mohann, who had grown to love her almost as a daughter, decided she would continue to work there as a paid artist.

So everything was as before except she was now free to go and come as she pleased. She had grown dependent on the predictable daily routine of the wine house; it was something that she appreciated and needed.

Which was why the tumultuous sounds coming from the other rooms were really starting to anger her. As gracefully as possible in case any of her past or future clients were watching her, she scurried down the hall to a large circular room made from saturated willow reeds and vented every six *en-yawo* or so with nine-inch cylinders of *panabo*—large bamboo-like tubes of a dark color.

This was the room for smoking the fashionable *shukko* pipes that had become an almost indispensable part of upper-society life in the days following the Usurpation.

Normally one of the busiest areas of the *Dukka-Vinyo*, currently only two people were in the *shukko* room. One was a middle-aged, heavyset but muscular man standing in the center of the room looking up. Sullen Peacock's eyes followed this man's toward that direction.

Following his eyes, Sullen Peacock saw a what appeared to be a skinny long-coiffed little boy sitting on one of the beams about thirty rods high in the air with a smirk on his face, seemingly in no hurry to come down to face the wrath of the man standing beneath him.

Sullen Peacock winced. The man looking up was Magistrate Dioni, in charge of collecting taxes for a good part of the region, and a personal friend of the tribal lord's most trusted lieutenant, Solmin.

Due to his position, he was almost certainly NOT one of Mistress Jayda's high-paying customers or favorite people, but one certainly did not want to upset a patron of his importance. She knew she had to find a way to diffuse this situation in an amicable way, and quickly.

"Come down here this instant boy, and give me back my purse," the magistrate shouted in halting *khajudic* at the amused youth once again. "If you don't, I'll set fire to this room, and you'll slide down those beams in a pile of ashes instead!"

Standing precariously on his toes in the center of the room, his silken robe dirty and extremely wet, his face drained of color, the magistrate looked quite a sight. It was obvious that he had been chasing this young boy around for quite some time and was worse off for doing it.

"What happened to your clothes, Magistrate?" Sullen Peacock asked him, holding up a delicate silk sleeve in a somewhat vain attempt to cover her eyes.

Upon hearing that, the large man became even more irate.

"Why...this little thief tried to take them...he... dumped a pot of hot tea over my head just as I got my hands on him. The little..." He took another futile jump in the direction of the boy.

Sullen Peacock could not be particularly sure whether his feet actually left the floor with this most recent attempt. She noticed a red, splotchy mark on the back of his neck and shoulders, lending truth to his claim of the tea attack. Despite herself, she felt the overwhelming urge to stifle a laugh.

The boy ducked quickly as the magistrate pulled off one of his peacock slippers and hurled it up. It fell a few *en-yawo* short and fell limply to the floor. The boy laughed for all he was worth, nearly falling from the beam.

"Is that the best you can do, Tubby-strate! Here, try one of mine on for size!"

In one smooth and lightning-quick motion, the little boy slipped off one of his shoes and fired it down on the buffoonish tax man. It landed directly between his eyes, leaving a red mark.

The magistrate fell over onto his backside, seemingly angrier now than he had ever been in his entire life.

In a total rush to get up, he tried jumping quickly to both feet, but being barefoot now, he landed in some of the tea that had been dripping from his robe. Naturally, his feet went out from under him, and he fell again, this time bumping his head on a strategically placed marble figurine.

He passed out immediately.

Sullen Peacock was mortified.

"Oh, gods, now there'll be plenty of trouble. This isn't going to end well at all."

She looked down at the unfortunate magistrate, then quickly averted her eyes. The poor man's rather large belly was sticking out of his robe rather conspicuously in the air and rose and fell to match his peaceful breathing.

Sullen Peacock contemplated leaving him like that for a second, then covered him with another robe before turning her attention to the youngster, who was still laughing hysterically on top of the beam.

"Sania!" she said, in a voice mixed with sternness and amusement, "Come down from there immediately, young lady. I'll have to report this to Mistress Jayda."

*   *

About an hour later, all three of them were sitting in Mistress Jayda's private office. She sat, expressionless as Sania told her a "version" of the past hour's events. Occasionally she would pause and look over at the unfortunate magistrate as if waiting for him to interrupt.

Why she did this, no one knew; the man was unconscious, though propped upright in a chair the same as they all were. He had awakened a couple of times in fits of gasping and coughing but would faint again in rage every time his eyes fell upon the smug Sania.

For assaulting a government official, Sania could legally be apprehended and sold and could even be required to marry the slovenly wretch whom she'd just insulted, once it was discovered she was a girl.

Sullen Peacock batted a lovely eyelash at Mistress Jayda. "My lady," she began, "I know that our young apprentice lately seems to have an affinity for trouble and mischief..." She paused, seeming to think on her next words. Mistress Jayda was not one to trifle with. "It's obvious that she's had a rather *rough* upbringing."

There was no response from Mistress Jayda.

"She both looks and behaves like a young boy, in fact."

Still no response. The look on Mistress Jayda's face had changed from distress to irritation to boredom with every additional word from her.

"However, I can tell that she has certain, er, pleasant features, and talents, that could be quite useful to our business here. My little sister is well beyond the age of apprenticeship training. She should have been assigned to a lady long ago, in fact. To make sure she doesn't get into any more mischief, I would be honored to take her on as my apprentice."

Sania sighed. The last thing she wanted to do was to spend the rest of her remaining youth in big, frilly dresses, wearing her hair in some ridiculous fashion, and generally resembling a fancy-dressed bird.

At Sullen Peacock's words, Mistress Jayda looked up. Eyes as lovely and dark as the rarest mahogany bored into Sullen Peacock angrily for a few seconds before turning to Sania. Immediately her face softened, taking on a look of wistfulness, mixed with some resignation.

Sania wondered why Mistress Jayda was so upset. Sounded like a reasonable enough proposition to her, and she appreciated that her big sister at the *Dukka-Vinyo* was trying to save her neck.

Glancing over at the magistrate to make sure he was still unconscious, Mistress Jayda leaned closer. "Young lady," she half-whispered to Sullen Peacock, "one day you will take over proprietorship of this *Dukka-Vinyo*. However you still have much to learn."

Eyes wide, Sullen Peacock could only stare back.

"Is it so hard to believe?" Mistress Jayda asked. "You've been here a long time. Mr. Mohann thinks the world of you. You are the only one of the ladies that I've ever actually allowed in my office." She waited for Sullen Peacock to reflect on her words.

"I suppose that's true," her protégé admitted.

"But you're not quite ready to take on the responsibility yet, my dear. You are not only extremely talented; you have the rare gift of understanding both trade and hospitality. To have one of those talents is valuable. To have both of them is invaluable. However, the one thing you don't have is perception. You've said yourself many times that we shouldn't dress Sania as a boy, and yet we always do."

Sullen Peacock slowly nodded. "That's true."

Sania herself wondered why that was true, although it was no secret that she rather liked being dressed like a boy.

Mistress Jayda continued. "You just mentioned that she's several moons past apprenticeship. She could easily be working profitably as a musician or courtesy girl now, and yet she isn't."

This detail was undeniably perplexing. Favored child of the proprietor or no, the one thing *Dukka-Vinyo*s never did under any circumstance was turn away a profit, and keeping a woman just coming of age in the *Dukka-Vinyo* without giving her an apprenticeship and assigning her a trade was akin to throwing money into the Great River.

"Sania was not intended to be a normal servant of the *Dukka-Vinyo*," the older girl said finally. "But, but...I always assumed it was because of her propensity for creating disturbances wherever she goes. On-once she gets older, and calms down somew—"

Mistress Jayda interrupted Sullen Peacock harshly.

"Sania was not meant to be *calm*. She was meant to be *chaos*."

Hearing those words, both Sania and her *Dukka-Vinyo* sister's blood ran frigidly cold. What on earth did Mistress Jayda mean by those words? What did she know about her young charge that no one else did?

A little perturbed now that both of them were talking about her as if she were out of the room, Sania said, "I feel like I should be involved in this conversation somehow..."

"Quiet!" both of the ladies said in unison.

"Sullen Peacock," Mistress Jayda said in her most patient voice, "there are two kinds of girls that we never accept as servants here at the Winery. Who are they?"

It took Sullen Peacock no time at all to answer this one. "Those who are proven to be dishonest...."

"Correct, and?"

"Those who have disfiguring or decorative marks on their bodies."

At this, Sania looked down at her hand, which was covered as usual by a white silk serving glove. Sliding the glove off, she raised her hand in the air so the two other ladies could see.

"This," Sania said matter-of-factly, "is what you two are referring to?" All too soon, she was beginning to feel like a freak attraction.

Looking up at her hand, Mistress Jayda and Sullen Peacock gazed upon what they'd naturally seen many times before, but never addressed.

Just below the crest of her right wrist was a tattooed likeness of two black rectangles with three sharp points pointing toward the peak. The way it stood out against her already dark-browned skin, made it look that much more mysterious.

The mark had always seemed almost alive, resting so prominently on her small wrist, but now more than ever it seemed to be glowing.

In ancient Numeria, the quickest way to be ostracized was to have a visibly disfiguring mark or tattoo. Native tribal men who were marked in such a way were usually current or former prisoners of some ordinary lord of the times, invariably convicted of thievery, cowardice, or rape.

They were marked in some prominent location, such as their face or hands so that even commoners would know they were to be reviled and shunned. A woman with any physical blemishes, ink, or piercings, especially on the face, could never expect marriage or even kindness from most men.

Only the *Lifeless Ones*, the *Mejeedi*, decorated their faces in that way. No one outside of their tribes knew why, and the Mejeedi refused to divulge. But hatred for these newcomers and their customs was part of the reason why the "natural-born" Numerians shunned body markings.

It's with these sorts of social misgivings in mind that the two women stared in awe and fascination at the object on Sania's slender wrist.

Slightly embarrassed, Sania hastily slipped her arm back inside the long glove. "Lately it doesn't seem as noticeable as it used to," she offered feebly. "Mistress Jayda, what does that mark mean?" asked Sullen Peacock. "Has she always had it?"

"I'm not at liberty to say, my child," the older woman sighed. "Just know that her tattoo means she can never work in this house as a Leisure Girl."

Excitedly, Sania jumped off of the wheat-woven chair on which she'd been cross-leggedly perched and over Mistress Jayda's desk, excitedly grabbing the old lady by her very round shoulders—it was commonly known around the *Dukka-Vinyo* and surrounding village that Mistress Jayda rarely missed a good meal.

She had quite forgotten that she was disregarding all employer-servant protocol and that she was usually scared to death of the stern old woman. Hearing Mistress Jayda tell her this now was the equivalent of being pardoned by a lord or chieftain.

Of course, there were the true desires of her heart to consider.

It's true, Sania had always been a rebellious and mischievous ward of the *Dukka-Vinyo*, in trouble often and as long as she could remember. She'd endured her share of punishments because of that, scrubbing floors, washing endless dishes, even cleaning stables for some of the most harmful pranks she'd pulled on the comfort girls, whom she detested.

However, she knew deep down that she'd never been rebellious just for the sake of itself; rather, she had rare inner energy and zest for action that couldn't be assuaged by the activities of the *Dukka-Vinyo.*

Everyone knew this. It was no secret to the ladies or Mohann that the only guests Sania ever paid any attention to were the famous warriors and hunters who had from time to time made their way into Mistress Jayda's *Dukka-Vinyo.*

To Sania, these were exciting folk! Some of them carried large bejeweled sabers, hanging disinterestedly from their waists; some had huge maces and axes weighing more than fifty *dan* each.

There were young sons of wealthy noblemen, bored with citadel life and eager to go out to make a name for themselves by slaying some villainous outlaw or other. There were wizened old veterans of the Coastal Wars, full of stories of valor and days when "real men bled salt, and fake heroes perished in anonymity."

Whenever these gentlemen came around and started weaving their tales, true or contrived, Sania had always found a way to escape her chores and make her way to where they were regaling their audiences.

Almost all of the stories were fascinating, but it was the ones regarding the Coastal Wars, the Pale Warriors, and the Usurpation that always sent such a thrill through her. She could never get enough of hearing about the warring tribal chieftains during the Diamond Age, the tyrannical Azu's, elder and younger, the majestic though ill-fated Toloron, and his lovely and virtuous Queen Aiisha.

Even the tales of that jackal's end usurper, the Regent Okon, and his fat overbearing family brought enough excitement and fascination to keep her awake for days on end.

Was Queen Aiisha really that beautiful? Were there warriors as brave and powerful as Pala K'Nan Urmandu, Son of Loffri?

Did soldiers with skin as pale as rare ivory who traveled from northern seas and fought like demons really exist?

Alas, for Sania, all of these brave (and not-so-brave) warriors had only one common element: in the end, they all left the *Dukka-Vinyo*.

In doing so, each one of them had taken a few of her hopes for her own future with them, a future of life and adventure far outside of the small world currently known to her.

They would get to go out and experience the world, fight battles, claim victories; she wouldn't.

It demoralized her almost daily to think of it.

Also, this curious bit; she never understood why and couldn't explain this to either her brothers or sisters at Mistress Jayda's or even to those warriors, but...

She always seemed to *know* what to do with all of their weapons, just after taking one glance at them.

She knew instantly what the strengths and limitations of each weapon were.

She knew if it could be wielded comfortably by a short person or a tall person, a man or a woman, a frail or hardy person.

She also knew, quite quickly, which of those warriors was deadly with the weapon he was carrying, and which ones had never even used theirs before. She could tell by their walk if they had spent too much time on horseback, or if they'd never had any combat training.

How did she know all of these things? She'd asked herself this time and again, angrily, for it seemed as if the gods were toying with her. So what if she ever managed to buy a sword? She would be the only sword-wielding wine maiden in the lower *Kumaz-we*. It was all such a waste.

"Sania!" Mistress Jayda's stern voice jolted her from her thoughts. "What are you daydreaming of now?" Looking up, she saw both Sullen Peacock and the shop owner staring intently at her.

"I'm sorry, Mistress Jayda." Ashamed, she bowed her head— *What a time to drift away.* "I was just wondering," she queried, "What...what about...this?" Sania pointed hesitantly towards her neck.

Completely encircling her neck was a thin copper band, perhaps a thumb's diameter in width. It was both conspicuous and inconspicuous, in that it was in a visible place yet wasn't adorned with any ornate patterns or gemstones. It was her *sharafta-lei*, her band of honor.

This was what warned the Numerian world that she was a contractually-obligated ward of a guild-sanctioned *Dukka-Vinyo* of the empire. In essence, the *sharafta-lei* protected her from harm when she traveled away from the *Dukka-Vinyo*—something that happened far too infrequently.

Of course, wearing it had its detractions as well; she had been forced to ignore many disgusted glances from the oh-so-pious townspeople during her years encountering them as a ward.

Mistress Jayda waved her hand dismissively. "Of course it will be removed, and the sooner the better. That's a concern for later. For now, Mr. Mohann has called a porter to the front of the *Dukka-Vinyo*.

You must help Sullen Peacock escort the magistrate to his carriage, along with this package of our commiseration for his difficulties this evening." She handed a small bundle to Sania.

Sania bit back her protest.

"Make sure the two of you take the service routes only to the front. You must not be seen by anyone. All of our guests have left, but it's still quite early. It's important that the magistrate doesn't remember—"

"Come outside now! Everyone inside this house, come out!" A thunderous voice boomed from outside of the *Dukka-Vinyo*.

The three of them glanced uneasily at each other. Is it possible that word had gotten into the nearby village about the magistrate's plight that quickly?

"Mistress Jayda! Mistress Jayda!" One of the *Dukka-Vinyo*'s attendants breathlessly ran to the entrance of the office. Eyes wild, she looked quite out of breath. "Three soldiers are out front, Mistress Jayda. They're asking everyone to come out onto the verandah." She paused, hands on her sides. "I think they're threatening to burn down the *Dukka-Vinyo*!"

Forgetting their predicament with the magistrate, Mistress Jayda, Sullen Peacock, and Sania all sprang from the room to deal with this potentially disastrous situation.

Standing outside in front of the group that had gathered were three of the largest, ugliest men Sania had ever seen. They all wore green-gray tunics lined with jackal's mane, covering thin brown-tinted armor battle robes and flat sandals.

The insignia on their cloaks represented a tribe unfamiliar to any of them, a three-headed jackal, all three of which were impaled by a crooked spear. Even stranger than their uniforms were their faces, which were identical and identically hideous. Triplets, they were indeed, but each one of their faces was twisted in a completely different way from the other two. One of them seemed frozen in a perpetually leering smile; the other stuck in a hideous snarl. The third's facial expression was tough to fathom at first glance, initially seeming to exist in some realm between the visages worn by his two brothers, but upon closer inspection, it seemed to be an expression of profound sadness. He looked ready to burst into tears any second.

Scars covered their entire bodies from scalp to foot, doing nothing to enhance their looks. Altogether, they presented a shocking and overwhelming sight, and Sania could hear the sounds of several women retching upon seeing them.

There were four other soldiers, uniformed the same as these three, mounted on horseback in the streets and waiting, hands on their swords. Apparently, they were here in support of the other three and did not want to (or were under orders not to) interfere with the business at hand.

Sania was amused. *What kinds of freaks are these?* She thought. In her mind, she named them "Mr. Angry," "Mr. Happy," and "Mr. Sad" to mirror the expressions their faces seemed to be perpetually stuck in.

"It has been determined that the inhabitants of Mistress Jayda's *Dukka-Vinyo* have been harboring Numerian scum, including a known pro-Toloron supporter, a rebel against the tribe Azu," said "Mr. Sad."

Several around her gasped. Who were they speaking of? Sania had heard that a few thousand en-yawo to the northwest there was a young boy who'd managed to defeat and kill the great paladin Jorell Boro, in fair and lawful combat. Some had even said that the same boy had managed to win the Emi Sword in the duel.

However, most people dismissed that as just a fanciful legend, something that sounded good in the *Dukka-Vinyo*s but could never happen in the real world.

Sania wasn't so sure.

Mr. Angry followed. "By divine order of the twelfth chieftain Lord Demetri Otu, Head of the House of the Doomed Jackal, and our revered liege, you are ordered to immediately hand over the insurrectionist to our custody, to be placed under the supervision of Chieftain Otu until he can be remanded over to the Regent Lord Okon for judgment!"

Sania looked around at the others; they seemed to be just as confused. Most of their expressions were a mixture of fear and disbelief. What "insurrectionist" was in Mistress Jayda's *Dukka-Vinyo*, of all places?

"Any refusal or delay in doing so will bring dire consequences. We have a sealed warrant giving us the absolute authority to torch this *Dukka-Vinyo* and put every man and woman here to the sword."

"Any children remaining will promptly be sold to the *Mejeedi* (Lifeless Ones). Hear these words and obey," Mr. Happy said.

As "Mr. Happy" finished his speech, a decrepit old man appeared from the entrance of the *Dukka-Vinyo*. No one remembered seeing him enter, and he most likely would've been denied entry, as he looked like a destitute beggar. With dirty hair and soiled clothes, he slowly made his way off the verandah and exited the premises, carrying nothing except for an exquisite bag casually slung across his shoulder.

For an instant, everyone's mouths draped open as they tried to imagine how this ancient, down-on-his-luck elder obtained such a possession. They continued looking as he slowly ambled off into the distance.

Somehow unaware of the old man, the three soldiers closed their scrolls in unison, making one large snapping sound. Saying no more, they stood motionlessly and haughtily stared at all of the *Dukka-Vinyo*'s inhabitants. Hands resting on their crescent hilts, they seemed impatient to begin killing.

Silence ensued—painful, awkward silence. No one knew what to make of these men. What they were saying sounded a bit outlandish. Supporters of Toloron? Were there any left? And especially far from the western provinces, in the lower kumaze-we, for goddesses sake?

In the Common Tongue, *kumaz* or *kumaze* meant land, and so the two major regions of Numeria were named the *kumaz-i*, literally dry land or desert, and the *kumaze-we*, or riverlands. The third minor region was the *kumaz-ulasa* or the grasslands, but was more commonly known as the savannah.

Breaking the silence, Sania's chirping voice penetrated the cold morning air, incongruous with the solemnity of the moment. "Hey, Jack-asses... Umm... Jackals... There are no more Toloron supporters! Are you too blind to know that or just too ugl—"

"Sania, please!" The voice of Mohann came from behind them all. He was dressed elegantly as always in a long white *borokk* shirt and silk blue trousers. He slowly descended the steps of the verandah and walked toward the triplets, who were noticeably brimming with anger.

"We have never had any quarrel with the esteemed Lord Otu, or any of his men—" began Mohann.

"—or you homely part-time warriors, either," Sania interrupted.

"Silence, child." Simple and direct. Mistress Jayda was not to be trifled with, and Sania willed herself to calm down. She averted her eyes toward the verandah and frowned, transferring her gaze from there to where the soldier's horses were tethered. Her frown slowly morphed into a slight smile, which she immediately suppressed.

Mohann stepped deliberately out of the throng of workers and walked respectfully, palms pressed together, toward the three detestable soldiers. "I must apologize for her ignorance, respected envoys."

"She has not been with us very long and has yet to be taught the correct way to treat revered men of authority such as yourselves." He stopped and smiled reassuringly at the soldiers.

Sania believed that unlike her, Mohann was too blind to see that the enemy soldiers were quite simply there to start a fight. She could tell by the tone in which they read the proclamation, and even by the dark aura that surrounded them.

It was partially for this reason that she wanted to agitate them, to further find out what they wanted from Mistress Jayda.

"Oh, so she's a bad learner, is she?" Mr. Angry shouted. In two swift moves, he had grabbed Mohann by the back of his collar. "Bad student, bad teacher!" he shouted, striking the man on the back of his head three times.

Mr. Angry's two brothers roared in laughter at the scene.

The staff of the *Dukka-Vinyo* was aghast. Mr. Mohann was indeed something of a tyrant to them at times, and when it came to business he was unyielding in his desire to turn a profit, but he never treated them harshly and was always more than fair when it came time to pay wages.

To see him attacked like this was almost as if a family member of their own was in trouble. Many of the women screamed, the children started crying, and one or two of the braver men scowled in anger and began shouting insults.

"You see, big brother?" Mr. Sad chuckled. "A couple of good ones to the back of that lazy pimp's neck, and now all of a sudden everyone here wants to start speaking!"

"Curious," Mr. Happy said.

The sound of Mr. Sad's sword being pulled from its sheath rang throughout the verandah. "Let's see just how much talking these good folks can do with the right amount of motivation, brothers."

These idiots are going way too far, she thought, anger starting to envelop her entire *imoya.*

Amidst more screaming, Mr. Happy and Mr. Angry lifted Mohann in the air by his *borokk* and held him there, arms outstretched.

Mohann was no small man; this was truly a feat of rare strength. The protests from the staff members continued, Sullen Peacock's legs gave way, and Mistress Jayda sent one of the serving girls inside, to fetch her purse for bribes most likely.

A gentle shove turned the serving girl in the other direction and standing behind her was a man. "Stop!" the man shouted. Over a hundred pairs of eyes turned to the entrance to the verandah.

"Magistrate Dioni," Mistress Jayda said, walking toward him. In a lowered hush, she continued, far more tenderly than Sania was used to hearing her speak to people. "We will always appreciate your concern, but it's best not to get involved with these soldiers. They are not under your jurisdiction."

Upon hearing the shout, the three envoys dropped Mr. Mohann back to the ground. Mohann rolled ungracefully, and then, brushing himself off with as much dignity as he could manage, scurried quickly away from the Uglies.

"To hear your concern for me, I feel I could face any danger right now," said the magistrate, who all of a sudden didn't look quite as slovenly as when Sania was toying with him earlier.

With one lingering glance toward Mistress Jayda, he walked head aloft directly toward the three men. "I am the person you seek!" he yelled.

7

Light As A Feather

With the exception of Mistress Jayda and Mohann, everyone was shocked. Not only were there actually pro-Toloron supporters still in the lower *Kumaz-we*, but the lawfully-appointed magistrate of the region was one of them.

Still twenty en-yawo away from the soldiers, the magistrate noticed Sania out of the corner of his eye and stepped deliberately in her direction. Instantly, she felt cold and nervous, wondering if he was finally going to make her pay for having a bit of fun with him back in the *Dukka-Vinyo* earlier.

It had seemed like such fun at the time.

As he quietly looked down at her for a second, a tear formed in his eye.

A tear?

"Whatever happens to me, young mistress, I want to reassure you that my lifetime wish was fulfilled in being humiliated by you this evening." He smiled, a transforming smile, so full of contained joy that instantly all of Sania's reservations evaporated.

"Wh-what do you mean, my lord?" she said in her most humble voice, confused by his demeanor.

"You must not call me that," he spoke to her sternly. "Soon you will know that only one was ever worthy to be called 'Lord,' if you don't already. Do not disappoint me." He reached down and grabbed her hands.

"Remember this, young mistress—*you are the glue that binds.* Seek the man Nank to fulfill the prophecy." With that, he turned away and continued his stroll toward the envoys. Finally reaching them, he turned back to the throng of people.

A lump formed in Sania's throat.

"I am the traitor these so-called soldiers have been seeking," he proclaimed loudly. "And yet, what is a traitor? Is it someone who refuses to swear allegiance to a false house, one that was consummated through treachery, collaboration with foreign armies, and lies? Is it treachery to brazenly torture your sworn tribal lord and brutalize his lovely queen, to slaughter them and their entire clan, and claim their throne as your own under the pretense of regency for a lawfully deposed tyrant's son?"

It took her a while to understand what he was saying, but soon she was nodding her head along with all the others.

He stared at the group defiantly, holding as many of their gazes with his as he could before his eyes stopped to rest on Sania's. All of those watching him averted their eyes and some shed tears.

"The House of Azu no longer exists! I bear witness before you all that this so-called Lord Regent Okon's only concern is for the unlawful ascendance of—" A sword flashed down mid-sentence.

The magistrate's head had been brutally separated from his neck. His life was no more.

Intense silence followed and within it, some peetka birds could be heard nesting a few en-yawo away. The warm winter breeze enveloped the acacia trees nearby, causing a few of the leaves to sway.

Somewhere in the midst of the group, a young child began crying, which served to ignite the emotions of everyone else. All of the children started bawling in unison, along with the ladies. The oppressed sentiment that had begun to heat up with the mistreatment of Mohann now threatened to boil over.

Before anyone could see what was happening, Sania had run to where the magistrate fell, reached down to grab his sword, and sprang toward his three murderers.

Amusedly, Mr. Happy raised an eyebrow and began to redraw the same cutlass that was now soaked in the magistrate's blood. Yet before his cutlass cleared his waistband, Sania swung down, separating his arm from his body at the elbow.

Shock overtook the faces of all who watched. Sania included. She stared at the sword in her hand, amazed that she had so easily crippled a man more than twice her size.

"BROTHER!" Mr. Sad and Mr. Angry shouted in unison as they ran to Mr. Happy, who stood in shock, seemingly trying to figure out why his cutlass was lying in the dirt, still connected to his right arm, no less.

"W-who did this to...me?"

Disbelieving, they all turned toward Sania. "It was the boy," Mr. Angry said.

Reaching up, Sania pulled off the sallow-colored turban that Mohann had made her wear forever, presumably to hide her braids from others. "I'm not a boy, you half-wits," she said as her long black braided hair tumbled down to her shoulders.

Grasping the magistrate's sword again in both hands, she gave the three of them the best "get ready" face she could.

"How does it feel to be made a cripple by 'merely' a girl?" she asked through clenched teeth.

"KILL THEM ALL!" shouted the three Uglies in unison. They each drew their cutlasses, Mr. Happy awkwardly prying his from his former right hand with his left, and ran toward her.

Spears raised, the four soldiers on horseback inched towards the fracas, then halted. In another move that surprised even herself, she parried the first swing from Mr. Sad while whirling around and sweeping her sword toward the not-so-fortunate Mr. Happy's leg, which she chopped off above his knee.

Crying, he fell to the ground in a heap.

Immediately she jumped onto his chest, using it as a spring-board toward Mr. Angry, whose cutlass was aimed straight for her stomach. Scared out of her wits, all she could manage to do was stab with her sword in a clumsy attempt to block it.

Miraculously, the sword fell from his hands.

Sania was now feeling like this was all too easy. Thinking it a good time to show off what she'd learned from some of the guests of the *Dukka-Vinyo*, she decided to play with them a bit.

Unfortunately, just as she was preparing to launch one of the more complicated and showy moves she'd been taught, someone grabbed her.

"Got you, you little—" Mr. Sad had maneuvered around her somehow and had wrapped his slimy arms tightly around her neck.

Without thinking, she rotated the sword grip in her left hand and swiftly jabbed it backwards, impaling it through his midsection.

Mr. Sad's grip instantly released. Not sure if he was finished, she swung the blade in a circular arc upwards, fatally puncturing his heart.

As he fell, she launched herself at Mr. Angry, decapitating him with one blow so quickly that he had no time to block.

Breathing heavily, she dropped the now blood-drenched sword and stared at her hands.

The entire fight had taken about fifteen seconds and had left Mr. Angry and Mr. Sad quite dead. Mr. Happy fared little better; he was lying pathetically in shock and bleeding to death.

Was this what fighting was really like? She thought to herself. *Why didn't it take forever like in the stories at the Dukka-Vinyo?*

Mr. Happy moaned, obviously in much pain.

Finding her sword once again, she picked it up and walked over to him, reaching down and removing the large dagger that was hanging from his waist belt.

He came out of shock just enough to murmur, "No...help...d-don't—"

"I would spare your worthless life," Sania whispered in his ear so that only he could hear, "but it would be letting down the magistrate if I did."

Angrily, she swept the dagger across his neck and watched the life drain out of him.

"Someone help me carry in the magistrate. He'll need a proper cremation," she said to no one in particular as she rushed to the magistrate's side. It was only then that she noticed her arms and legs were covered with minor cuts and bruises.

Trying to lift the magistrate's arm, Sania suddenly found that all her muscles were useless. Annoyed, she turned her head around to yell at the others.

"I said I need some hel—" She froze mid-sentence.

All of them, people who were essentially her adopted family and friends, were looking at her as if she'd just landed on Earth from the heavens. Even Mohann, still injured from his earlier scuffle with the now-deceased ruffians, had his mouth open in wonder.

Of course, Mistress Jayda was the one exception.

It seemed nothing ever surprised or impressed that woman. *Absolutely nothing*, Sania thought.

Before she could say anything to them, the four soldiers who had accompanied the envoys finally rode up. Once they saw how quickly the brothers had been dispatched, and by a girl no less, they had lost quite a bit of their original aggressive behavior.

Slowing his mare, the leader looked haughtily down at Sania and said, "You, girl, have unjustly assassinated three legally commissioned envoys of Numerian Conclave of Regents. You will immediately surrender yourself to our custody and be transported to the citadel for sentencing."

Getting the sense that he was trying to save face in front of his men and didn't actually want to pick a fight with her, Sania said, "Or maybe I'll just give you some of the same treatment those three uglies got," Sania said, reaching down to pick back up the sword.

In satisfaction, she watched him pull his horse back a step, though he didn't run off, as she imagined some men would have.

Maybe he's not so bad.

All the same, she couldn't just turn herself over to them and leave Mistress Jayda's *Dukka-Vinyo* at the mercy of whoever would come investigating the death of the three unfortunate envoys.

Suddenly she remembered something that had caught her attention earlier. "Unfortunately, I can't do that. I'll be a bit too busy arresting you and your fellow soldiers here for killing the envoys yourselves."

The lead rider blanched. "How dare you say such a thing? We just witnessed you slaughter these men. In fact, this place is crawling with witnesses! Come with us, and I will put in a word personally on your behalf."

She smiled indulgently at him. "The markings on your horses, they are that of the Winged Lion, are they not?" She waited for him to reply, although the answer was evident to all.

"That is correct," the leader swelled with pride, sitting up a bit straighter on his mare. "We are all under the jurisdiction of the young Chief Xalamon Ainu, protector of the eastern sands and important ally to the Conclave of Regents! Of what importance are details like these to an insignificant servant girl?"

The crowd bristled slightly at the insult, particularly the "insignificant servant girls" who were watching them. On top of that, they'd all seen with their own eyes how Sania had had just defeated their three champion envoys while barely breaking a sweat and were feeling a little protective of her at the moment.

Unwilling to let them implicate themselves on her behalf, she waved her hand at them, and they reluctantly quieted down.

"Well it should be obvious, then, you were sent on a fool's errand." Without waiting for him to get any angrier, she continued. "This is the first time the four of you have ever been commissioned on an assignment in this area of the *Kumaze-we*, correct?"

The soldiers looked at each other uneasily. "This is...true," the lead rider said.

"Did the Chief Regent or one of his direct subordinates send you on this mission personally?"

"Err, umm that is...no. We were told to accompany the envoys to the *Dukka-Vinyo* after meeting them at the tri-forks area of the *Kumaz-we*. Then, to root out all rebellion from this establishment and return to the Chief Otu as soon as humanly possible."

"No mention from Chief Ainu as to why four of his youngest soldiers would need to accompany three hardened and extremely dangerous warriors from the house of Lord Otu? Don't you think that would be an important detail?"

All four men tugged on their beards at the same time. Apparently, this didn't make sense to them either.

Not only were the House of the Doomed Jackal and the House of Ainu not long removed from being bitter enemies, but it was also well known that Otu was one of the few remaining overlords who wielded the necessary power to actually challenge the dominion of Lord Ainu, the master of the *Kumaze-we.*

One of the other riders, his tone impatient, asked, "Just what point are you trying to get to, miss? Make it simple for us common soldiers."

Surprised by his deferential tone, Sania decided it was okay to spring the trap now. "You and your men were sent here by a retainer of the Conclave, not only to falsely imprison and kill any suspected Toloron loyalists you most likely would *not* have found, but you were then supposed to die quite publicly on the trip back to Okonokep, at the hands of the three ugl—er, envoys."

Though her voice was even and emotionless, inside, she was furious that people could be so conniving and ruthless.

"Your deaths would have, of course, been blamed on these non-existent insurrectionists. Lord Okon and the Regents would have declared a false rebellion, and they would have free reign to purge the kingdom of all tribesmen they declared to be in rebellion against the Azu."

There was another round of laughter, but this time it sounded a bit forced. "Okay," said another mounted soldier, "let's suppose this is all true and not just some cooked up fantasy of yours to scare us into letting you go—"

Not wanting to give them time to come up with any holes in her theory, Sania decided to forge ahead. "It's obvious that they are Crooked Jackals, that's the crest on their uniforms and their saber handles. "But did any of you happen to notice the saddle insignia those three dead idiots were traveling with?"

Everyone's gazes shifted to the three riderless horses. The saddle insignia definitely should have been that of Lord Otu's, since the men were supposedly from that House. Instead, they were white flowers circling the yellow sun.

"The Clan of Lady Tash!" one soldier exclaimed in wonderment and disbelief.

Happy that she somehow knew much more than these supposedly worldly warriors, Sania laughed loudly.

"Yes it's the insignia of Lady Tash and the Deadly Willow tribe, and yes it's engraved on their saddlebags. The question is why and by whom? It's pretty obvious that you guys were going to be murdered and the Willow tribe would take the blame."

Pausing, she looked at them for effect. They seemed devastated at what they heard, but it also appeared that she was starting to convince them that they had indeed avoided a trap.

"To go back to East Rhydor would be suicide for you. If I were you, I'd head to the coastal regions. Chief Otu, Lord Regent Okon, and the First Prince control everything to the east now, and their spies cast a wide net." Sania looked up at him, feeling sorry for the predicament he was in; he was now a young man without a country.

"Young *masiti*, it seems..." repeated their leader, his voice now containing a bit more gratitude. "It seems we were wrong to accuse you of murdering those treacherous dogs. On the contrary, you've saved our lives instead." His voice trailed off, and he touched two fingers to his forehead in a gesture of politeness toward her and the *Dukka-Vinyo* folk. "We'd best be off."

As he motioned his group to turn around and head east, he paused abruptly and tilted his head down from the horse.

"*Masiti*," he whispered. "How did you gain the ability to fight so well?"

Unsure what to say, she just shrugged her shoulders. He gave her a knowing look, most likely assuming she was being evasive, but she honestly had no idea. Again he turned to leave.

Before he could fully turn around, Sania called out, "Wait!" Startled, he jerked the reins back around toward her. "Isn't it impolite to not give your name to someone who's just saved your ass?"

"Sania!" Mohann shouted, but she studiously ignored him.

The soldier stared at her for a second or two, quite coldly. "Although you will forever be in my prayers, we shall never see each other again. Let us part nameless, but please take this."

He handed her a finely embroidered yellow silk handkerchief, then turned and left without another word.

A few minutes had passed before she could take her eyes away from them.

The sun was now almost completely set. In another hour or so, it would again be time to begin the evening ritual with the *Dukka-Vinyo* song:

Little wildflower,
   blooming in the desert sands, you did not choose to be carried here.
Little wildflower,
   scattered cross the foreign lands, destined to be sought far and near.
   Lovely wanderer of the desert, you can never go home again,
   for home is now here.

Sania turned and looked at Mistress Jayda and Mohann, who were both staring at her intently, as if seeing her for the first time.

Was there something different about her?

Mohann whispered something in Mistress Jayda's ear. She looked back at him and then nodded. Mohann disappeared again inside the *Dukka-Vinyo.*

"Sania, my dear. Please come here."

"Yes, ma'am." Even after the amount of havoc she'd just wreaked on three hardened Numerian warriors, she still felt like a young girl in Mistress Jayda's presence. She suspected that she always would. Hands clasped behind her back, she walked over to her and stood awkwardly.

"The rest of you, back inside. Time to prepare for our guests."

With not another word, the men, women, and children all smiled at Sania and walked into the *Dukka-Vinyo.* A couple of the braver ones even walked by to give her a pat on the shoulder, or the head, if they were old enough.

One old goat of a pastry chef, who had often taken pleasure at scolding her for stealing cookies from the oven, tried to give her a weak smile. Sania snarled at her, and she scurried inside like a desert mouse.

Soon after they were all inside, Mohann came running out with a large bag in his hands. He whistled twice, and the stable keepers went to tether the horses that had belonged to the ruffian envoys.

"Put new saddles on two of them and take the other one to the market in the morning," he told them. "Then bring me the sharas to remove her *sharafta-lei*."

"No!" Sania shrieked. "I'm never taking this off. This is who I am." Upon hearing that, Mistress Jayda and Mohann shared a glance of puzzlement, then gradual understanding.

"No—it isn't," said Mistress Jayda. "But you can do that when you're ready. Mohann, make sure the horses are well fed before you take them out."

"Oh, that's great, Mohann, are you going somewhere?" Sania asked him, knowing he rarely ever left the *Dukka-Vinyo*.

"No, my dear," said Mistress Jayda, "you are."

Sania's feet turned cold. "What do you mean, Mistress Jayda?" she asked. "If it's about the fight..."

"It's definitely about the fight, Sania, but not in the way you think." She took the bag from Mohann, the one she'd sent him inside to retrieve. It looked old and extremely worn. Opening it, Mistress Jayda pulled out several contents. There was a book, a sword, and a strange device Sania didn't recognize.

"The only man I ever loved was a warrior who fought in King Toloron's army during the Usurpation—even back to the Coastal Wars. His name was Perdil Taraz, an apt name for him, meaning strong and brave. However, when he came to me, he was a broken man."

"I'd just inherited the *Dukka-Vinyo* from my mother, who had died months earlier. I didn't even know how to run the business yet; it was something that I'd never wanted to do. One night, in the midst of the drinking and revelry, I was sitting in my study and was interrupted by the sound of a baby crying."

"A baby crying?" Sania said, "Babies cry all the time in the *Dukka-Vinyo.*"

"True, but this crying was coming from outside. It was a stranger's child. The cry was different, too, it wasn't the kind of crying you normally hear from babies. The baby was screaming for help, not for itself but someone else. I felt this, as clear as the *Kumazi* sky."

"I ran outside to look around and just there at the Gate of Spring was a lovely baby girl. She was lying over her father, who was unshaven, wearing tattered rags, and covered in blood. I thought he was dead."

Mistress Jayda stared off in the distance. A frightened look crept into her normally emotionless eyes.

"I called Mohann, who had worked at the *Dukka-Vinyo* since the days when my mother operated it, and asked him to quietly help me bring them in, clean them up, and get them fed and rested. I had to find out who this man was who had created such a feeling of love in his tiny child."

In the background there was the sound of activity in the *Dukka-Vinyo* as everyone prepared for the day's work, but, entranced by the story she was hearing, Sania scarcely noticed.

"In any event, after I'd given him a couple of days to rest, eat, essentially recover his strength, I sent for him to come to my office with his daughter. I had intended to ask him some questions about how they'd ended up in that state, give them a few coins, and send them on their way. But the two who walked into my office that morning were entirely different people."

She twirled her famous twin phoenix emerald ring around her finger nervously.

"Of course, a baby is still a baby. However, instead of the filthy, haggardly-looking beggar whom I'd discovered outside the gates, the one who carried her was a strong, handsome young man with an unshakeable air of confidence and an aura of wisdom."

Embarrassed by Mistress Jayda's wistful tone, Sania exclaimed, "Mistress Jayda!"

She ignored her. "The child was close to his chest, he carried it with him comfortably and assuredly, as if it'd been born in his arms. An innocent infant girl. As soon as he walked into my office, he bowed solemnly and said to me, 'Lady Sania and I thank you for your generosity and kindness.'"

Sania froze. This story was about *her!* That man who Mistress Jayda fell in love with was *her* father! Her entire body felt weak. She'd long wanted to know both who her parents were and how she came to arrive at the *Dukka-Vinyo* but after this much time she'd convinced herself that she never would.

"And what did you say to him! Why did he leave me?" she asked breathlessly, tears coming to her eyes.

Mistress Jayda sighed. "I'm getting to that part, child." She took a deep breath, as if she was fearful that the recounting of those past events might become too much to bear. Absently wiping a silvery brown braid of hair from her eyes, she glanced at Sania and smiled.

"I then asked him how he came to be in such a state. After all, it was obvious he was a man of warrior origin, well versed in art as well as warfare. Far above my own station, in fact, but I'd seen enough men come through the *Dukka-Vinyo*s to know the measure of them."

Of course, Sania knew that outside the insulated world of the *Dukka-Vinyo*—within the cold reality of Numerian society—there were distinct classes that separated people based on birthright and that mixing with those who were not in your class was usually forbidden.

"The story he told me was astonishing, if not believable. It's probably well known to you by now. The brave king and his gentle bride. Their loyal counselor. A trusted lieutenant's treachery. An invasion by pale-skinned pirates. Yet this brave soldier, Perdil Taraz, assured me that wasn't where the story ends."

Pausing, Mistress Jayda glanced around for any prying ears.

Beside herself, Sania said, "What? What did he say?"

Mistress Jayda took a deep breath. "He told me that Toloron's line did not end with his death after all. Lord Toloron had an heir—and the heir *survived.*"

Hearing this, both Mohann and Sania almost jumped out of their sandals. The news that King Toloron—Toloron *Mekuwa Waku*, the man who had almost single-handedly willed the many ragged independent tribes of the coast, the savannah, and the *chakkha* into one unified empire, had sired a child before he died was well known, even to the lowest of the Numerians. If, somehow, this heir was still alive today—this news could not be taken lightly by anyone.

The Usurper Okon himself would most likely behead anyone he suspected of even entertaining such a thought. Still, knowing Mistress Jayda as they did, they knew she'd almost certainly done her best to verify and re-verify the veracity of this claim.

It had to be true.

Then Sania had a sickening thought, dizziness overcoming her.

"Careful, girl!" Reaching out, Mohann steadied her.

"I'm...okay...." she said, weakly waving him away. "Does this mean...? Am I...?"

With a quickly raised hand, Mistress Jayda firmly said, "No. You are not the heir, my dear. However, Lord Toloron knew that he could expect little support from his tribes or his kinsmen after his death. So three noble children of the armies of Toloron, all younger than the heir, were bestowed the task of protecting the heir until he comes of age, and of spearheading the restoration. These three youths were fed specially necromanced herbs, which would bestow gifts of warfare and wisdom onto each of them, and they were anointed with a mandate to seek out and eliminate all enemies of the Tribes of Toloron."

She paused again for a few seconds, then said very slowly, very deliberately. "Sania, you are one of the three *Khuselas* of the House of Toloron."

Sania nodded in a slow stupor. *I guess that's how I was able to kill those three goons so quickly.* "So what do I do now?" she thought aloud, her mind full of questions. *Where are the other*

two Khuselas then? Where is the heir, for that matter? "What became of my father after that day?"

Instead of answering, Mistress Jayda glanced sideways at Mohann, who lightly shook his head. It was obvious they didn't want
her to know where he had gone.

"No," Mistress Jayda said to Mohann after a few seconds. "I
will tell her. Sania, I do not believe the man who brought you to
us was your true father, but your *muzuri* (adoptive father). As I
mentioned earlier to you, after this point Perdil Taraz and I fell
deeply in love. For months, the two of us, no—the three of us,
were inseparable."

The three of us, she thought. *Mistress Jayda, no wonder you
treated me more like a daughter than anyone else.*

"Then all of that changed. At that time, Regent Okon and his
soldiers were still looking for Toloron supporters, and the *Dukka-
Vinyo* did not escape their attention. Luckily, your *muzuri* was
not at the *Dukka-Vinyo* at the time. When he heard what happened, he knew that if he'd been here, those soldiers would likely
have discovered you."

A tear came into her eyes, yet they continued to bore into
Sania as she said, "He was an exceptional man with a great sense
of duty, Sania. Although we were in love, he knew that he had a
much bigger task to fulfill for his former king—and that was making sure you became of age. So we decided that although he had to
remain close to you, he could not afford to be so near that it
would complicate matters."

"So what could a man with his talents and intelligence do to
become the eyes and ears of this region, and thus better protect
you? He decided to take up the position of provincial magistrate."

Sania cried aloud, then looked from Mistress Jayda back to
Mohann. They were solemn-faced. No longer could she control
the whirlwind of emotions she was feeling.

"That can't be true. Please tell me it's not true!" She sobbed,
hating herself for being like the weak women of the *Dukka-Vinyo*,
who seemed to cry all day for very little reason. *Or had I been
unfair to them all this time? Was it possible?*

The portly, round-faced man who had come around the *Duk-ka-Vinyo* often enough but had never taken an interest in anything the slightest bit debaucherous, which had seemed odd to all of them. In fact, the only ones he'd ever really spoken to while there had been Mistress Jayda and Mohann.

And you, Sania reminded herself miserably. For some reason, he'd always found the time to seek her out and sternly lecture her on her appearance and apparent laziness, which she'd quickly grown tired of.

It's what had made her decide to have a little fun at his expense during his last visit there. This last thought, she could hardly bear to recall.

"I took pleasure in making a fool out of him...the man who brought me here and took care of me."

"Oh, don't worry about that my child. He would never have let you toy with him like that if he hadn't been trying to determine the full extent of your abilities. Your *muzuri* was a very talented and capable man. Don't let the fact that he added a little weight recently let you believe otherwise."

"Do you really think that a staff officer under the great *Mekuwa Waku* Toloron would have been that easily dispatched by those three messengers, however skilled? It was his plan to die—to continue to hide your presence. Unfortunately, he had no idea as to the true level of your talents."

Mistress Jayda suddenly regained her stern demeanor. "I'm actually a bit surprised that you didn't see through his attempts to hide his ability. You've always been much sharper than that with the other guests."

This was true; she had never been one to be fooled by phony spearmen. This Perdil Taraz, the closest man she would ever have to a father in this life, must have been even more special than Mistress Jayda said.

You knew who he was all this time, and you didn't tell me, she thought unhappily.

Yet no matter how much she may have wanted to, Sania would never say this to Mistress Jayda or Mohann—she still felt greatly indebted to them.

Also, Perdil Taraz seemed to think the arrangement was necessary, and she now trusted him completely. *Odd.*

"So what are these items for then?" she asked, if only to break the silence. The question seemed to cheer both Mistress Jayda and Mohann up considerably.

"These," said Mistress Jayda triumphantly, "are your birthright, my dear. You have been gifted these items from Lord Toloron himself to aid you in restoring his seed to power. Just like you and your two fellow *Khuselas* have been given divine gifts forged from the conjury of the Onyx Crown, so are these three items. The first one is this."

Mohann held up a full broadsword, the same type as those used by the sturdiest warriors. Sania groaned when she looked at it, yet when she grudgingly took it from Mohann, it felt much lighter than she expected.

"*Feather!*" she cried out to both of them. "I'm going to name it *Feather!*"

"Excellent name, *Masiti* Sania," Mohann said approvingly. Mistress Jayda allowed herself a tight-lipped smile.

Elated, she ran through a couple of the sword progressions that she had been taught by one of the warriors who frequented the *Dukka-Vinyo* some moons before.

The sword was exquisite in its own right, of course; the guard was heavily jeweled with diamonds and inlaid with platinum; the blade itself was so brilliant it resembled a mirror. She realized that the greater weight of the hilt contributed somewhat toward the lightness of the sword.

Mistress Jayda pulled a strand of her hair out and dropped it down over the blade. It passed effortlessly over the edge and sliced into two strands. Truly with this sword she could be more than a match for anyone. Exhaling, Sania looked toward the other two items.

"What are these?" Reluctantly placing the sword back in the scabbard, Sania removed the book next. It was large and heavy and simply-bound with papyrus root. On the front of the book, etched in dry quill indigo were two large words—*Lunariis Thoerar*—and below that a few smaller words in a language Sania didn't recognize.

Mistress Jayda had tried to teach her to read and write from time to time, but books gave her a headache. This particular one looked as if it were a thousand moons old, and it felt just as ancient. Slowly opening it and turning a few of the pages, she shook her head. Complete gibberish. She restrained herself from unsheathing *Feather* again.

"I don't suppose you know why he left this for me? I can't understand a single word."

"We have no idea," offered Mohann, "why you were left any of these particular items. However, we can tell you that other than you, they were meant for no one else in our world to possess."

"Sania, a true warrior is just as proficient with the pen as with the sword. It would not be fitting for one of the *Khuselas* of Numeria to be unable to read. Diligently dedicate yourself to that task."

"I will. I promise," she said solemnly. At that moment, at least, she meant it.

The wind was beginning to stir violently around them. Soon it would be dark. With the darkness, the savannah brought death. Soon she would need to leave.

"The last object, you needn't ask about, Sania," said Mistress Jayda. "It is not from our world, that much I can tell you. I cannot tell you what it's made of, who made it, or why. That you will have to discern for yourself."

Taking the last object, Sania thought it was possibly the strangest thing she'd ever laid eyes on. It was comprised mostly of a long cylindrical metal tube. The crescent-shaped wooden handle fit neatly into the palm of her hand, and there was a small hook-like lever protruding from the metal part, which her index finger fit almost perfectly on. On instinct, she pulled the lever back and heard a little click. Other than that, nothing.

There was a transcription in the wooden handle, also completely illegible:

$$\chi \, \rho \, \Delta \, \exists \, \omega \, \vartheta \approx \bullet \, X \, \phi$$
$$\Delta \, \textstyle\sum \, \varsigma \, \Theta \, \forall$$

She had no idea how she was ever going to figure out what this strange device was for. In her rush to begin traveling, she stuck it in her shoulder sack and promptly forgot about it.

"Sania."

Looking up, Sania saw Mistress Jayda in tears. A sight she'd never have thought possible.

"It's been a joy to watch you grow up. In my life I've only cared for two people and, well, I've lost both of them today, so forgive me if it shocks you to see me cry. The last thing your foster father left for you was this letter, which I now give to you. Do not ask anyone to read it to you; it is for your eyes only."

"With that, we must part. Mohann will accompany you as far as the edge of the savannah. Return to us one day." Without another word, Mistress Jayda strode back into the *Dukka-Vinyo*.

Sania began to turn away then shouted, "Wait!" Mistress Jayda hesitated, as if she knew why she was calling her, then slowly turned back. Sania ran about twenty or so steps in her direction, then lowered her voice. "So," she whispered, knowing that Mistress Jayda had already revealed too much at the risk of her life, "who were my real parents?"

Mistress Jayda's eyes shone with a glint of appreciation, then sadness. "No one knows, my dear."

With that, she was gone.

8

Grains of Prophecy

Jorann had been walking west for several days—the exact number he didn't know. That was the power of the wilderness. The *Kumazi* deserts of southern Numeria were famous for a few things, including its unbelievably harsh temperatures, which routinely topped 125 degrees during the hottest months, and the predatory subhuman creatures, often called *Bajallah*, who lurked beneath the sand and waited for days at a time before seeking out animals or humans for food.

In addition to these, the *Kumazi* was known for virtually having no nightfall. There, huge mineral deposits on the desert surface reflect against the lunar sphere so that even as the dominant sun starts to descend from its highest point, the *Kumazi* sky remains ever illuminated.

Because of this, Jorann had only been aware of his own movement. He was walking, moving west. He had to keep walking. He'd set out some time ago after receiving the mysterious warning from that scarecrow of a woman. He'd wondered many times why he had listened to her, particularly over the last few days. She'd given him a sack, which contained an ancient and fragile map. The map had led him to his current desolate location.

The poor creature had obviously been starved and delusional and had happened upon the first person she'd seen, glad to have someone to rave at. He had been the "lucky" individual. Her disappearing into thin air? Okay, that was something he couldn't explain.

Maybe she just turned sideways and was there the whole time, he thought with a grim smile.

After he'd traveled quite far into the region, he realized that he had no idea what he should be looking for, or if he should be looking for anything at all.

He wasn't concerned about food or water; studying the *Zakku-Dalla* had taught him how to shut down his vital organs to conserve energy and moisture—he knew he could survive out here at least another two to three days without nourishment of any kind before the situation started to become a concern.

If this were during the upcoming Great Summer, his situation would undoubtedly be bleak—but that was not the case.

No—the problem was that he hadn't seen anything. Or anyone.

Not a plant, not an animal, nor insect, nor bird had appeared in his path, above, or behind him, since he'd begun his journey. That meant complete silence and complete solitude. He'd never imagined that such a godforsaken place could exist, but lo and behold, here he was...right in its midst.

Jorann sat down for a few seconds to take a rest. A few moments taken to meditate would be enough to clear his anxiety and energize him for the next several hours. With no shade around, not even in the form of a dune, he sat where he was and began to circulate his breathing.

As he pulled his feet into position under him in the sand, his scorched skin stung to the point of annoyance. *Let it all go*, he told himself, *focus on the present. Not where you're going and definitely not where you've been.*

He'd been meditating for at least ten minutes when he'd felt the sand move around him. As he was in a semi-trance, he had trouble at first discerning whether or not it was happening in his mind. Gradually, he became aware of the increasing intensity of the movement—to the point where he considered breaking his posture.

K'Nan had explained to him early in his study of the *Zakku-Dalla* that any interruption of his thoughts could cause a transfer of energy to either his heart, lungs, or kidneys, and thus be fatal. He still remembered all too clearly his experience in the kokara pit. He decided to wait a few moments more before reacting, realizing at the same time that the decision itself was the beginning of the end of his meditation.

However, the sound became more and more pronounced, and the hot winds continued to swirl around him, causing almost unbearable pain. He could now feel the fine grains of sand cutting into his partially-cloaked face. Jorann couldn't wait any longer. With a massive shout to clear his lung passage, he opened his eyes and leapt to his feet.

Looking down, though, he saw that his legs were still locked in the classical meditation position, but he could not feel them. He'd never left the sand. *Stupid kid*, he thought to himself. He wouldn't be going anywhere for a while, at least not by walking. His legs weren't exactly asleep; he'd blocked the flow of blood to his lower extremities, a breathing technique he'd learned from the *Lucenja Classics*—but had forgotten to get it moving again before trying to stand. It would take a couple of minutes.

Meanwhile, he saw that the sandstorm was not a sandstorm at all. Thirty en-yawo in front of him, there seemed to be a combination whirlpool and sinkhole, and every grain of sand in the surrounding area was being drawn to it. Whatever energy source was creating this activity was formidable.

Alarmed, Jorann knew he needed to get his legs working before he got sucked into that thing. He closed his eyes again, but immediately opened them as two strong sets of hands grabbed his arms from either side and began dragging him toward the sand pool. Looking up, he felt instantly sick. Though they were manlike, these creatures could not possibly be men.

White hoods covered most of their faces, but he could see glowing red eyes accentuating exposed bone where there should have been flesh. Their eyes were soulless and unmoving; they did not blink, and they did not look at him. They seemed to be intent only on their goal of delivering him to whatever hell lay ahead of him in the sand pool. The hands gripping him were like iron; he felt as if his shoulders would be torn to shreds at any moment.

Jorann tried to speak. He wanted to ask these hideous creatures all the typical questions asked of their executioners by those who faced imminent death. Who were they, where were they taking him, that sort of thing...yet he sensed that they wouldn't answer him and probably wouldn't even understand.

Then a thought occurred to him—tales the children of the *Win-Daji* used to tell him to try to frighten him when he was very young. He could remember it like yesterday, the song they sang.

We're going to leave you,
Leave you,
Leave you,
Leave you for the Bajallah.

Could these "men" possibly be them—could they be the *Bajallah*? Perhaps the most feared and reviled creatures in Numeria?

If I can just get my blood circulating before we reach wherever they're leading me—at least I'll have a chance, he thought. Once more, he closed his eyes...

...and feebly reopened them. He wasn't yet strong enough mentally to ignore his current predicament. He realized now that he needed a great deal more training if he was going to truly be able to protect the heir, or anyone else. Thinking of his obligations to the kingdom, Toloron's kingdom, he steeled himself mentally.

Whatever lay ahead of him in the sand pool, he had to survive it. He relaxed his mind as he was dragged slowly, agonizingly slowly toward the sand pool. Finally reaching the opening, he closed his eyes to avoid being blinded by the fine grains of sand that sharply swirled. Then the pit of his stomach lurched as he felt himself falling. The fall seemed to take quite a while, but in actuality, he had landed in just over a second.

Water broke his fall. The bottom of the pit was an infernal bog. A rancid, copious liquid that smelled of burnt flesh and animal excrement filled his nostrils. As he started to sink into the bottom of the quagmire, Jorann panicked, but those same two sets of hands grabbed him by the tunic and kept his head above the surface. *If they want me dead, why are they protecting me?* He thought with a sliver of optimism.

Above them, no more than twelve cubits high, was a cavernous roof, illuminated by a shimmery liquid. The ceiling, which spanned the breadth of the underground cave, was adorned with the skeleton of every unfortunate desert creature that had ever lived and attempted to traverse this place.

He was aware that the two men holding him had not glanced down in his direction once. They appeared not to consider him to be a living, breathing person, which disturbed him even more than their appearance.

In the hidden corner of his consciousness, it had dawned on him who they were, but he didn't dare bring it to the forefront. That would make things altogether more real and more terrifying.

Being pulled slowly through the detestable muck in the cavern had occupied his mind for the last few moments, distracting him from their final destination. *What an unfortunate choice of words,* he thought wryly. Now, however, as he looked forward, he could see a clearing in front of them.

Beyond the clearing, the water rushed more violently toward the opposite mouth of the tunnel and amazingly began to flow upward.

Where in the heavens is this going? Jorann wondered. Around the opening, the filth and darkness of the waste-strewn tunnel gave way to a well-lit open dome, perhaps about a hundred square *en-yawo* in area.

Immediately upon entry, the soggy mess continued to flow until it reached a precipice, narrow by now, and fell deeper into the earth. From the sound, it seemed as if the water never actually stopped falling—Jorann could hear no crash below.

He had the feeling that all of this was part of a much bigger puzzle, one he didn't want to solve. Before he had more time to contemplate, he got his first view of the other side of the precipice. Fifty or sixty pairs of eyes were trained on him, completely emotionless. His blood froze. Stepping out of the waste they'd been dragging him through, his captors brought him before the large group, all clothed similarly. In their center was a raised dais molded from fine sand, and on it, a throne made from live *Kumazi* cacti, its thorns razor sharp. Sitting on this was a figure, also shrouded like the rest of them, although in a slightly darker color fabric.

This figure was nothing more than a set of bright reddish-brown eyes peering beneath a hood. It resembled an angular heap of cloth supported by a framework of bones lying beneath. It did not move an inch but just stared in his direction, waiting for him to move or speak. In fact, none of these beings spoke or moved. The cavernous dome was completely quiet.

There was something familiar about those eyes.

Jorann, for his part, resolved not to speak; he realized immediately that he was being appraised. For what purpose, he didn't know—but the silence and the fact that he hadn't been harmed spoke volumes. Moments, minutes, even hours passed. Jorann had regained the feeling in his legs some time ago. His breathing had stabilized, and he'd been able to use the time to meditate.

Freed from the intense glare of the *Kumazi* sun, he'd also regained most of his once-depleted energy, thanks to the otherworldly training he'd received from Pala K'Nan and the Zakku-Dalla. Still, he resolved not to be the first to break the silence, inwardly sensing that doing so would give the advantage of negotiating to his adversary. He laughed inwardly at how similar this situation was to him meeting the *Pajadin de Hakeemah*.

If he asked them where he was, they'd know he was an outsider. If he asked why he had been taken captive, it could be taken as a sign of fear. If he asked who they were, they would know he was an imbecile. No, he wasn't about to open his mouth for these savages.

Another few moments passed, and he saw the figure on the throne slightly nod its head in acknowledgement. On some unseen signal, the other hooded figures in the room sat as one, cross-legged, on the cavern floor.

Though he relaxed inwardly, Jorann still didn't avert his gaze from the leader or move even slightly. "Very impressive," said the faction leader. "I wanted to see if the self-restraint I witnessed earlier was merely an act or your true personality. I'm very pleased to see that I was correct." Jorann said nothing, but his mind was churning. *When did you see me earlier?*

"Why have you come to us?" The faction leader asked.

The question unsettled him. He hadn't traveled all the way to this region to see this group. Had he?

"I...I didn't," he began clumsily.

"You mean you don't recognize me?" the person interrupted with a tone of mock disappointment. With one movement, it removed its cloak. The figure was now clearly a woman, just as emaciated and frightening, but now with features all too distinguishable. It was the same woman who'd sent him on his mission to this desert, the one who'd given him the mysterious warning:

"Down that road, doth not traverse,
reverse your course, forestall the curse."

He stood before her now in complete shock. For one thing, she'd dropped into a lifeless heap at his feet, after warning him. There had been nothing, not even a body, left in the rags to give him a clue as to who she was or what she'd been referring to. He had decided that the only way to find out was to obey her and follow the course she'd given him. So he had, he'd started in a westerly direction from the savannah and continued walking, past the lakes, the ponds, the streams, into complete barrenness.

At first he'd been curious to see where he would end up, nothing more, but eventually, he began to wonder if he hadn't read more into what the obviously insane woman had told him than he should have. He'd asked himself many times if she'd given him a useless map.

Days of wandering in the endless desert had turned into weeks, and he'd convinced himself that he would find nothing in his search. Soon after that moment of resignation, he'd happened upon the sandstorm and the two creatures who'd brought him to his present location.

So the question of why they'd brought him before this woman had now been answered, at least partially. But why had she led him here, and how had she arrived before him?

"You have some information for me," he guessed aloud.

"The young master is very perceptive," she replied. "I do indeed have things of which to inform you, as well as the other *Khuselas.*"

"Do you know who the other two are?" he asked her excitedly.

"It has not been made clear to us yet," she said firmly. Jorann's disappointment was evident. *Does anyone know anything in this crazy place?* He shook that topic out of his mind.

"If this information is so urgent, why didn't you tell me in the savannah?" Jorann asked. "Surely, the information would have had the same meaning? Why drag me out to these wastelands just for a message? And why aren't you dead?"

There was some noticeable bristling in the room amongst the creatures, who he now was almost sure were the loathsome *Bajallah,* the much-hated and feared flesh-eaters of the Kumazi. He cautioned himself to be careful.

"You would be wise to hold your tongue, young Lord Jorann. It is a myth that my men eat the flesh of humans, but they are very protective of me, as you can see." Her meaning was clear: what doesn't eat you can still kill.

"I meant no disrespect to you or your loyal retainers, my lady," he continued, "it's just that I have many things to accomplish, as I assume you already know. Traveling many thousand enyawo on foot to hear a message has caused major delays in my plans."

He decided that if they realized he had only been impertinent because of his other affairs, they'd be more apt to forgive his insults. From what he'd heard of the *Bajallah,* they were an extremely proud and unforgiving species. He would need to be a bit less careless when speaking to them.

The woman sneered. "Your respect means little to us, young hero. It is our respect that you should be concerned with. Not just because of what we have the power to do to you, but because of what we can do to your empire—either as ally or adversary."

The skeleton woman dismounted from the throne and waved away the two guards who still had their arms around Jorann. Reluctantly, they let go of him and took several steps back, menacingly ready to protect their leader if the need so arose. Unconcerned, she looked down at Jorann and motioned him up. At this point, he was indeed able to stand, although his shoulders throbbed with pain.

However, he motioned to his legs in a gesture of helplessness. With a smile, she extended a thin grainy white-gloved hand to him. Not knowing what else to do, he grasped hers. Amazingly, complete normalcy immediately returned to his legs and shoulders.

What type of woman is this, he wondered, *to have miraculous powers of healing and be able to lead a faction as formidable as the* Bajallah? Clearly, he had underestimated her in the savannah.

As if understanding the questions in his mind, she nodded. "We haven't been formally introduced. I am Daphni of the Sands." She waited for some sort of reply, expectantly, from him.

Jorann had already surmised that she must be a woman of grave importance to be able to wield power over the army of the *Bajallah*, but he'd never heard of her before and couldn't help himself from silently uttering, "And?"

K'Nan had taught him that upon first meeting with a nobleman or warrior, always make it seem as if you've long heard of their fame. He explained to Jorann that although the other person knows you're lying, it's a way of maintaining honor.

"Hudumo luhamba fambili." *Your fame is unmatched.* This was the common saying, but Jorann was quite irritated at the moment and didn't feel like being so nice.

"It is a pleasure to finally meet you, for a second time. My name is Jorann." This he said in his most sarcastic voice. She seemed slightly more satisfied with this reaction, and he could somewhat feel a general loosening of tension amongst her minions, as well.

"No need to be so polite," she said. "We *Kumazis*, the people of the Sands, long ago withdrew from the affairs of Numeria. Although we are still more powerful than you can imagine, we voluntarily gave up all claims to the royal houses of the Numerian Empire many, many moons ago. And so, it would be very odd if you'd actually heard my name before. That aside, your journey here to find me is much appreciated."

Jorann blinked. This was a great house of Numeria? In what fantasy was this poor woman living?

"I would like to show you something, young hero," she said. She took off one of her white gloves, revealing an extremely old and withered dark hand. It seemed more like the hand belonging to a skeleton than to a real person. With it, she reached down in front of Jorann and grabbed a fistful of the sand in front of him.

"Every living thing on this planet has a future, some shorter than others, some longer. I knew instantly from hearing about you and then upon seeing you that you were meant to alter the destiny of the *Kumazi* tribes in some way."

Again, he was confused. "How did you hear about me?"

"Spies," she said simply. "How else? We have them everywhere, but I deploy them to watch the movements of one person in particular."

Spies, he thought. *What else.*

"Despite knowing your worth," she continued, "only by reading the sands of this *Mamera Cuvva*—this Cavern of Memories—can I fully see into your future. This is why you were brought here." She paused as if trying to make up her mind. "Would you like to see your destiny? One warning...once seen, it cannot be shifted or altered."

Was it really worth it to see into the future if, once seen, you lose all ability to change it?

He decided that it was. "Yes," he answered. At once, she gently tossed the handful of sand up into the air. The sands swirled, looking merely like disorganized particles floating in the sky.

This is real magic, he thought in awe.

With her gloved hand, Daphni made several random motions in the sand particles. The patterns of sands swirled, came together, separated, and then, suddenly, three recognizable scenes began to form.

"Your sands tell much more about you than any normal human," Daphni muttered, puzzled. "It appears they are projecting your past and present, as well as your future." Jorann was no longer listening to her. Leaning forward, he craned his neck closer to the grains of sand to see the images. His heartbeat slowed to a standstill.

Daphni was correct. There were three distinct moving images before them—like moving mosaics of silica; the sand itself helped to form the images by shifting positions constantly. Hues and patterns were formed by the darker grains contrasting against the lighter.

A few months ago, Jorann would have thought what he was viewing right now was rather astonishing, but since then he'd seen some pretty amazing things.

This was pretty impressive, nonetheless.

The first moving image was easily the most recognizable—he as a young child of only five moons, doing the laborious job of cleaning the stables of the hunt animals. His hands and feet were bloody from the exertion.

Some of the animals were hostile at the smell of blood and the scent of a human, but they were chained. His tiny arms and feet moved slowly from one messy pen to the other. He was covered in excrement from his hair to his sandals. In the background, the children of the *Win-Daji* played and sang happily outside the stables.

He swallowed past the lump in his throat as he reviewed and relived the scene.

Jorann had gone through somewhat of a metamorphosis in thinking since he'd first been liberated from those Nabii hunters some time ago.

Part of him had always, and would always, continue to have a serve-first mentality, because of the many moons he'd been conditioned to think, act, and even breathe like a slave.

He knew this, and inwardly hated himself for it, for it meant that he'd allowed the independent *imoya* that he'd come into this world with as an infant, that all humans are inherently born with, to be quelled by the filthy *Win-Daji* and their brood.

However, since then he'd been studying the *Zakku-Dalla* and training to think as a leader would think and accomplish things that most humans, even Numerians, couldn't even begin to dream of. He no longer doubted that he was an exceptional, even prodigious child.

Because of this, he was able to look back on those times with less shame and almost no hostility now. He even found himself wistfully missing some of the less cruel children who he recognized from the vision but had perished with all of the rest of the *Win-Daiji* months ago.

The second image was much clearer in Jorann's memory, having occurred just months ago. The scene was of him and Pala K'Nan, training in the sword arts. K'Nan had told him many times that his fighting skills would always be a level below the other two *Khuselas*, that it was not where his real gifts would lie. Yet they still needed to train.

On this particular day, they were standing in the swift river currents, one of the tributaries of the Great River, him wielding a sword that was perhaps the same weight of a small child and about the same length. Pala K'Nan had taught him in the beginning that the foundation of swordplay, and combat in general, was in balance and leg strength.

"Only the fighter who is immovable like a mountain can resist the wind, Jorann," he had often shouted in his ear during their many sessions. Jorann initially had been dubious.

Pala K'Nan, patient as ever, had asked him, "Who is the best swordsman of your men, young master Jorann?" Jorann had thought about it for a second—his men rarely fought each other. At first thought, he wanted to say it was Bost, the muscle-bound and extremely volatile captain of his guard. Upon a bit more reflection, though, he decided it was probably Genn'tah, the slight of build, quiet, almost invisible scout guide.

Whenever the men did spar or train in one-on-one combat, Genn'tah always seemed the calmest and most effortless with his swordplay. Analyzing a bit further, Jorann replied out loud. "Genn'tah is the best because his moves are more economical. It's harder to get him out of position."

K'Nan had smiled. "And why are his moves so economical?"

"Because of his leg strength. He can parry and evade without completely changing his position, because of the strength of his legs."

Pala K'Nan nodded. "So?"

"I think I'd better focus a little harder on currents training."

And he had. He'd waded out to the roughest part of the river, in the dead of night, K'Nan and one of his guards standing nearby with a lantern. At first, he hadn't been able to be steady on his feet for more than five seconds holding the curiously heavy spear. The blasted currents always seemed to sweep him away.

"It's your breathing," said Pala K'Nan. "Remember the lines in the fourth stanza?"

"Y-y-yes," Jorann had replied, shivering from the cold night air after taking several river baths.

The *Zakku-Dalla*, as mentioned previously, focused heavily on breathing. However, in addition to the meditational applications of breath training, there were several more physical benefits.

One was the ability to build a level of endurance that couldn't be easily matched, even by people of seemingly greater physical ability. The other was the application of "rhythmic speech," which was a method of reciting cadence to swordplay.

The cadences forced the swordfighter to inhale and exhale on certain words, and thus one could exert maximum strength and self-control by only having to memorize and recite the lyrics to a song. An example was the song he sang that night, *The Ballad of the Doomed Warrior,* which translated into the common tongue read:

Three mile abyss in the rivulet,
Task'd my sword and sole singlet.
Drop't my spear and sent to hell,
Tell baba that I died well.

Essentially, every "T" in the song corresponds to a spear thrust, with the final words in each refrain corresponding to a withdrawal of the blade. Once mastered, this technique made it very difficult for the swordsman to become fatigued. Jorann had practiced diligently and had eventually been able to remain stable in the rough river waters, even while swinging the spear at full strength.

He still wasn't sure if he was a match for Genn'tah, or Bost either, but his fighting ability became much less reliant on speed and strength. He looked up from the vision. Daphni shrugged. "Great teachers produce great students," she said simply. However, there was a menacing tone to her voice, which made him feel a bit uncomfortable.

He shrugged it off. It was time for him to view the third scene, the one presumably showing his future. Looking away from Daphni, he glanced toward the hologram of sand. Immediately, he felt the entire essence of his consciousness leave the cave.

He was part of the vision.

The vision was a hill...no. It was a dune. A large dune, in the midst of the hottest desert, in the midst of the hottest day. He was wearing all white, adorned from head to toe in white linen, a white cloth headdress fastened by a solid gold band around his forehead.

His sandals were white, also, and made from the finest leather. Jorann swallowed. Hung from an ivory-white sack behind his shoulder was a spear.

And what a spear it was! All white from scabbard to handle, the handle adorned with diamonds and two strips of white silk hanging down from it.

It looked like a dream. *Wait,* he thought, *it is a dream.*

Jorann had never even heard of an object as beautiful as this weapon. He felt as if he could almost touch it. Was he actually touching it? He could no longer tell what was real and what was part of the vision. He *did* feel his fingers wrap around the handle. What could possibly be more real than that? A loud earth-shaking roar startled him, and his fingers left the weapon. He looked down the slope of the dune.

As far as one could see, soldiers clad in white stretched across the horizon. No, they weren't an ordinary army, they were *Bajal-lah.* There were thousands, no hundreds of thousands of them. Did that many *Bajallah* even exist?

Their voices shouted in unison. Their axes were pointed up in the air. An endless number of axes, all of them pointed toward the six moons of Numeria. It was a majestic sight, and Jorann felt himself being moved to tears by it. Was it tears in the vision, or were his tears being shed in the cave?

What was reality to him now? Did he know and would he ever know again? Did he truly care? For the first time he felt like an actual leader, not an imposter any longer.

He was a young man with dark brown skin, soft brown eyes, and almost completely white hair. Those were the prominent colors in the vision, the ones that stood out to him. Jorann realized that the loud roar was for him, but at the same time, it wasn't for him. It was because he had touched the ivory spear.

Why had that excited the army? Or had it?

He looked down at his left hand resting on the ivory spear. A third color was visible, one that outshone the ivory of the sword, the brown of his skin, and the tan of the desert. The color was black, and it was a deep, almost soulless black.

Once looked at, this black could absorb any other hue around it. The black came from the tattoo on this wrist—a tattoo of two horizontal rectangles with three points on top.

The Onyx Crown.

He finally actualized what his army was shouting. *Shohamu Taiji!*

All too soon, Jorann was back in the cave, staring up at Daphni. He felt as if the carpet of the universe had been abruptly pulled out from under him, as if there was no safe place he could set his feet on. What was he supposed to do now? Everyone in the cave was staring at him. He could feel it more than see it. Even the robotic *Bajallah*, who normally didn't seem to be looking at anything, all seemed to be turned toward his direction. He felt as if the door to his future had been blasted open. What would he do?

Then, all at once, it came to him. This was his rightful place. He was home, and if he was going to lead the fight to restore Toloron's heir to the throne of Numeria, he would need an army.

Perhaps he would need this army.

"How can I be of service to the *Kumazis*?" he asked Daphni, knowing how high the price would be.

The briefest of smiles crossed her face. "I'm happy to see I was not wrong about you, young Lord Jorann." She rose from the sand dais. "Come walk with me." She reached for his hand, an emaciated branch stretching out to grasp him firmly. He didn't really have a choice. This was her territory, and in strange surroundings, old rules give way to the new.

"Certainly," he said, following her behind the dais, down a set of solid sand stairs, and out of the cavern opening. In no time at all, the *Bajallah* were completely out of sight.

Daphni led him silently through a small winding path of turns, seemingly with no direction or pattern. It was deathly black—he could only tell that they were moving slightly downward—and eerily quiet. It seemed as if the entire cave had suddenly become mute.

After about ten more minutes of walking, their steps got shorter and shorter. Eventually, he realized that they had now begun to move upward in a steep incline. The cavern tunnels, which had been illuminated by the mineral formations lining them, became darker the farther they traveled. It was getting harder to breathe.

Normally never one to speak unnecessarily, Jorann was about to question when, without warning, Daphni made a sudden left turn behind an unseen cavern wall. She then turned again.

One more turn, then they entered it.

Paradise.

In front of his eyes, Jorann now observed an exquisite scene of tall, fruit-bearing trees, pristine streams and waterfalls, lush grass, and the blackest sands he'd ever thought possible. Birds of several species flew and perched happily on branches and swooped without worry over the bustling waters.

"How?" was all he could ask.

Daphni did not answer immediately, instead taking a few moments to let him further take in his new surroundings. At the sound of his voice, the birds and animals, which had been oblivious to them as they arrived, now stopped and looked inquisitively in their direction.

In a feeble apology, he raised his hand to Daphni, but she shook her head to dismiss it. Still, she did not speak. Jorann turned his attention back to his surroundings: the mist rising from the waterfall, the squawking of the condors circling overhead, the setting of the artificial sunlight encompassing everything else. He understood why Daphni did not speak; this was almost a religious experience.

"I almost never come here anymore," she finally said. He didn't know how to reply; he just nodded.

Before he knew what had happened, a knife was at his throat. He froze instantly and looked up to see Daphni's hauntingly beautiful face staring at him, apparently hurt and furious.

"Did you think you could fool all of us?" she said, pressing the knife into his skin. Jorann was bewildered by now. The hot-cold style of this *Kumazi* noblewoman's dialogue was beginning to annoy him. "What now?" he said.

"Don't play the innocent," she spat back. "You've received the life force of those bastard miscreants—the *Pajadin de Heekemah.* How did you meet them? Have they given you a seat on their council? Are you not aware that their entire order is the sworn enemy of my clan unto death?" Her voice had shrunk to an indignant whisper, and her eyes looked ready to explode.

Jorann was stunned. "If I explain everything honestly to you, will you remove the knife?" he asked her.

"One word of untruth," she whispered eerily, "and your body will be sent back to them without a head. Do you understand? I'll make sure you die without so much as a burial place."

Jorann's blood ran cold when he realized the extent of this woman's ruthlessness. "I have no need or intention of lying," he managed to choke out. She nodded, lowering the knife. He told her the entire story of what had occurred between him and the Pajadin, from the pit to the point where he'd first met her.

Surprisingly, she seemed more than satisfied with his rendition of the events and apologized. "If this story is true, you can certainly be made use of," she said cheerily. Not for the first time, Jorann began to wonder about the mental state of this powerful woman of the *Kumazi*.

A few moments later, she took him by the hand and led him back to the cavern entrance. In his disorientation, he hardly noticed them following the same confusing trail a second time.

Again, he forgot about all worldly matters as his eyes and ears processed the wondrous sounds and sights of this underground oasis.

Questions swirled in his young brain.

How was that even possible? Who else knows about this? Why did she choose to show me?

If Jorann indeed wanted to ask Daphni these questions, he had no time to do so. They soon heard a drum signal coming from the cavern opening, signaling their arrival to the *Bajallah*.

The signal was quite unnecessary—it was obvious that these creatures hadn't moved even an inch. Their discipline was extraordinary. Jorann thought it even surpassed that of his and K'Nan's men, which was no small feat.

As soon as Daphni took the seat on the strange dais, the drums ceased. The room became silent again. Jorann felt the atmosphere was now similar to that of a funeral. *Hopefully not mine*, he thought.

On a signal from Daphni, he sat directly across from her, about two *en-yawo* lower. He was comfortable but uneasy. He knew there had to be some deep reason she had just shown him the secret paradise, and she'd already acknowledged that she needed his help....

"Young hero, let me tell you a story. It may take a while, so please indulge me. This story isn't about battles, or conquests, or glory. It's a story about a man. Not just any man. The most handsome, wisest, noblest man the provinces of Numeria have ever seen."

"The High Chieftain *Mekuwa Waku* Toloron," Jorann interjected.

For a few seconds, the cavern was filled with laughter. It was only Daphni, but the sincerity and richness of it filled the cavern. It almost seemed for a moment as if the *Bajallah* joined in, but when he looked more closely, they appeared their usual stoic selves.

Jorann was surprised. It was the first time he had ever seen anyone disrespect the departed ruler in any way.

A few more chuckles and Daphni seemed ready to continue.

"Forgive my lack of composure, young hero. The *Kumazi* sand, as you know it currently, is an accursed land. Mammals, birds, reptiles, insects, even the smallest most insignificant life forms—none of them can exist within these borders."

"The venomous winds that cross over the Western Isles and ignore the coastal lands touch down upon these sands and create the world's most fearsome spectacle, the sandstorms of *Kumazi*, destroying all vegetation—every tree, every plant, and every leaf. This is an unchangeable fact of our existence. Tell me, have you ever thought why this came about?" She looked at Jorann as if expecting an answer.

He shook his head, more interested in hearing her telling of the story than actually coming up with a theory.

"About thirty moons ago, there was a kingdom—an enlightened, thriving, prosperous land that was admired by the powerful and rich, the powerless and poor alike. It had wonderfully majestic libraries, built entirely out of the most precious materials."

"These libraries housed the books containing the history of this world and especially of Numeria from the beginning of time. There were monuments in the *Kumazi* that stretched thousands of rods high, into the clouds, celebrating the ancient deeds and wonders of the almost-forgotten-now *Kumazi* immortals, from the era of Janeen Lightgiver, the founding mother of Numeria to the days before the first celestial beings settled here from the heavens."

"Here there were some of the greatest agricultural and botanical minds ever accumulated. Those great minds devised and implemented a sprawling network of irrigation channels that spanned the length of its borders and carried much-needed water to the crops that fed most of the empire. Every fruit or vegetable ever imagined was reared from those irrigation channels and distributed all over the fourteen tribal provinces for little to no profit for our own *Kumazis.*"

"There was a thriving market for livestock; cattle, wild game, antelope, goat—all raised using the purest methods and never exposed to disease or illness."

"The *Win-Daji*, who so famously ventured into the chakkha many moons later to hunt wild and exotic game, in those days traveled instead to the *Kumazi* and were able to feed most of their families for many months at a time."

"And who ruled over all of this? An old, proud clan; a tribe existing from the earliest days of the empire, who had inherited this land from the celestials themselves generations before; they were known as the *Bello* tribe. Its ruler at that time may have been the world's wisest and most handsome man; he counted every chief of Numeria as his trusted friend."

"His wife did not have an official title. Their marriage had been arranged as an alliance between the Bello tribe and a very minor tribe far to the southern territories. This was done so that no jealous lords could accuse the *Bello's* of ambition to annex the rest of the provinces of Numeria, to rule for themselves.

"To further dispel any similar notions, the chief of the *Bello* tribe refused to keep a standing army of more than five hundred men. He completely counted on all of the goodwill and fortune he had shared with the other provinces to ensure the protection of his family and his tribe."

"A bit naive, wasn't it?" Jorann couldn't help saying out loud. She ignored him.

"One day, this ruler of the *Kumazi* and chief of the Bello tribe went away to the savannah for a diplomatic mission. When he returned, he wasn't alone. He had been entreated by a lord of that region to bring his son with him, to mentor him, groom him, and also to use him as not more than a personal servant—not a small gesture for a lord of a Numerian province, mind you."

"The leader of the *Bello* was impressed, even touched. He considered it a very thoughtful suggestion from that savannah lord—a concession to the fact that he didn't have a son to inherit his lands. What the *Bello* did have was a daughter, about thirteen moons old, who was very impressionable and had misguided romantic notions of her own of marrying a prince from a faraway land."

Uh oh, he thought.

"From the time this young girl laid eyes on the prince, she had eyes for nothing and no one else. He was nothing like anyone in the girl's tribe—he dressed in a splendid brown cloaked robe with gold leaves decorating it on the sleeves and back. In contrast, she felt inferior in her plain white gown with gray sash, and braided hair tucked away in a neat bun, her simple sandals, and her skin without makeup."

"And yet, this young prince did not seem to mind at all. He was tall and charismatic, though only about fourteen at that time. Even at fourteen, his hair was speckled gray, which made him look all the more handsome."

"His hunting skills were extraordinary, he was even better than the big game *Equinox Hunters* who only came to the region once a year, and his combat skills were formidable. A week after he arrived, he had intervened to save a young farm girl from being humiliated by four drunk channelers. Allegedly, he had incapacitated them all within seconds, without even drawing his weapon. The legend of Lord Bello's newest protégé began growing like wildfire, and so did the feeling inside the young girl."

"Can we just call her Daphni?" Jorann interjected.

He had a vague idea of where the story was going, and all of the indirect references to real people were making the story unnecessarily complex.

Daphni was unfazed.

"As you wish. Daphni had fallen in love with this young man. The prince knew it, and Daphni's father knew it. Soon the prince's father would know it also, and he sent instructions via carrier pigeon to his son. Within a—"

Impatiently, Jorann interrupted her. "You asked me to indulge you, not encourage you, milady."

"Would you like the short version of the story?" she asked him, teeth clenched. "Within a month, I, Daphni of the Sands, the most revered woman among the *Kumazis*, had been repeatedly drugged and dishonored and was with child by the age of thirteen."

"What...what did your father do? Surely your tribe wouldn't tolerate such a crime?" he said.

She sneered.

"My father, heartbroken and scandalized, ordered an immediate marriage and entreated the Lord of the Savannah to attend personally for a great show of power and solidarity. Invitations were sent to every great lord and lady of every tribe in Numeria. Soon my father became happy; he would finally get the elusive son he'd never had and ensure security for the *Kumazi* people."

Jorann never imagined that a parent could be so cold-blooded toward their child. *If it were me, he'd still be suffering in a gorilla pit to this day.*

"But I wasn't happy, young hero. Far from it. I'd intercepted a message via carrier pigeon from this young prince intended for his father. The message was short and simple."

Only 500 men are standing in Kumazi. Send honor guard of 2000 men—Province ours by week's end.

Jorann was even more angry, but not amazed. He'd just had the same thought himself.

"What did you do?" he asked her, amazed that she was still able to hold back tears while recounting the story.

"I did what any honorable person would do," she said. "I killed the child while it was inside me, I informed my parents, and we awaited the arrival of the foreign army of the savannah."

Jorann shook his head even more incredulously. *Did she kill the child?*

"Killing your unborn? Isn't that too big a sin?" he asked, more to himself than to her.

"*That's* the big sin in this to you?" she blared at him. "You're feeling sorry for that *accursed* seed of his that grew within me? Perhaps you're not as bright as I thought, young man! What are the odds that a child born of deceit, rape, and treachery could ever become a just rule? I did it a favor."

Jorann was not convinced that what she did was the right thing. He began to consider whether or not she was deranged.

"But," she said after taking a few seconds to cool down. "I wasn't done. My parents made arrangements to flee to the southern isles with all of our belongings. The plan was to go down there, regroup, recruit allies, and then head back to retake the province. I had other ideas." She shivered, remembering everything at once.

"What?" said Jorann, knowing that she was holding something back.

"I destroyed it," Daphni said.

"Destroyed...it...?"

"Yes," she said, "all of it. I incinerated the irrigation channels, the statues, the buildings, the libraries, the skyscrapers, the crops. I killed the livestock, all of the plants and trees...and..."

"What?" Jorann said, mouth open.

"I killed them. I killed my parents."

Jorann was aghast. "You *what?*"

"I killed them. Both of them. You see, Jorann, I had to. I could see the looks in their eyes, the looks of disappointment, of fear, of resignation. They were not the same people they had been a few days before. They had been changed."

"I understand, but..." Jorann tried to speak but had no words. He felt as if he was in the presence of pure evil or pure madness. Either way, it was unsettling. What else could she possibly have to tell him? She had destroyed an entire tribe.

"I did this so that I could be free to exact my revenge. And I did," she continued, "only a few months after that verminous lord arrived to find this land in ruins, I arranged to gain work as a comfort girl at his favorite *Dukka-Vinyo* a few hundred miles east of here. I dismembered him in his sleep. His son was not so easy to kill."

She frowned, a murderous look in her eyes.

"His son's political ambition was not finished, by a long shot. He became a very important man in Numeria. For many moons, I tried to catch up with him, to get him to make a mistake so that I could exact my revenge."

"I got very close a couple of times, but not close enough. Then a couple of months ago, on one of my many trips to the savannah, the best opportunity to avenge my parents I will ever have presented itself to me."

Avenge your parents? Jorann thought. *You killed your parents.*

"You're right, young hero," she said, reading his mind. "I plunged the knives into their throats while they slept. Directly, I am responsible, but they were dead as soon as that young prince decided to betray me. Even before that, they were dead as soon as his father connived this scheme to infiltrate the House of Bello. So you see, my parents' murder was an act which I committed, but I alone am not culpable."

Jorann wasn't quite so sure of that, but he let it pass. "So who were they?"

Daphni smiled, a smile that would chill the heart of even the most callous murderer.

"The tribe of the savannah that betrayed our house was *Toytuuni*," she told him in a lowered voice. "Its ruler of that time was the man known as Loffri the Just." Panic rose within him as she slowed her voice down even more and said to him, her eyes burning deep into his soul, "His son's name was and still is K'Nan, and if you want to leave this land, he is the man you must swear me an oath to kill."

* *

At that exact moment, Jorann's mentor and teacher, Pala K'Nan, was disguised as a simple farmer, wandering among various huts in a small village. The village was located centrally in the province of Dago, about a day's journey east of the Great River.

This was originally the most prosperous region of Numeria, a place where farms once stretched for hundreds of thousands of enyawo, as far as the mind could imagine. However, the wars had taken their toll, and many of those who had been farmers and laborers had long since moved into the khalqaddis and the citadels to find work.

K'Nan had left the heir in the care of one of his closest comrades, a man named Bayo, just after the defeat at North Port. At his instructions, they'd taken up residence in Dago Province and begun a life undercover as a farmer and his young son. The arrangement was ideal as there were very few Azu loyalists in Dago—although there weren't many Toloron loyalists either.

The farmers of Dago Province were free-thinking people.

Remembering the instructions Bayo had sent, he slowly made his way on foot through the group of huts, the late evening moons his only source of illumination. Hearing sudden lively activity from a building to his left, he hurriedly halted and crouched down in slight irritation. He wondered if it would have been prudent to bring the twins along with him.

Realizing the sounds were just a family making merriment, he shook his head and kept moving, careful to pick up his feet both to minimize the noise as well as prevent himself from needlessly slipping in the dirt and being discovered. Soon he came to the place he was seeking, the fifth house on the end of the row, closest to the well.

The inside was as dark and quiet as the outside was rundown. With hesitation entering his heart, he opened the flap and prayed that no animals were lying in wait to betray his presence.

No animals were there, but neither were there any people, any furniture, or any sign that anyone had been there for quite some time. K'Nan struck a flint and used it to ignite a candle he'd pulled from his tunic.

He smiled. He could envision that the two of them, Bayo and Kalaf had indeed lived and been happy here and his mind drew a picture of how their lives had been structured within the confines of these tiny walls. Continuing to point the candle towards the corners, he couldn't ascertain if they'd left temporarily or permanently.

"They're gone." A childish voice from the doorway startled him. Frightened, he swung the candle around and saw a young girl of about seven or eight, standing in the door in her evening clothes, staring at him innocently.

"Who's gone?" He asked, hoping that he could get some information from this young child without having to ask much. He knew that even his Tandish accent would be enough to betray him to the far-reaching agents of Lord Okon.

"Symeon....he was my friend—and his dad." She looked sad as she recollected this friend of hers.

Symeon, thought K'Nan hopefully. Maybe he had the wrong house. "What did your friend Symeon call his dad?" he asked the little girl.

"Oyabi."

K'Nan broke out into a cold sweat. They'd both made a game since schoolkids of writing and pronouncing their names inversely. Bayo was Oyab or affectionately Oyabi—just as he had always been Nanki or just *Nank*.

"Where did they go?" he asked the child, desperately moving closer to her with the lamp and kneeling down so he could be closer to her height, and hopefully, less threatening—though she seemed far from frightened.

"Men came for them in the night. I saw Oyabi fighting them. He was good. But there were too many. They killed him."

K'Nan felt the strength leave his legs but knew if he passed out it could mean his death as well.

The heir had been forcibly taken. The very future of Numeria was now in doubt. How could he get him back? Time was running out. The usurper Crown Prince would be anointed ruler of every tribe on the continent in just months.

Then a thought occurred to him. He had no idea where Kalaf was; it might take a year or even several to find him. By then the usurper Azzolari Azu will be cemented on the throne.

But, although his own future *Mekuwa Waku* was missing at the moment, he knew that Azzolari was under heavy guard somewhere in Okonokep. Having a coronation without a Crown Prince would be difficult.

I have no choice at this point. I've got to try and locate the Azu child.

He put the candle down on the floor and sat in front of the girl. "What's your name?" he asked.

"My parents named me *Herri*. It means—"

"—Blessed," finished K'Nan for her.

"Yes!" she shouted joyfully. "You obviously speak the Common Tongue also, not just Tandish."

"Shhh—that has to be a secret between just you and me, ok? You're old enough to keep a secret, right?"

"Of course I can!" she said indignantly. "I'm almost nine years old, you know."

"I can definitely see that," K'Nan exclaimed, "but since you know so many things I have a couple more questions to ask you. Things I don't think anyone other than you could possibly know."

"What's that?" she said, pride causing her cheeks to swell momentarily.

"When did these bad men take your friend Symeon away and do you remember what they looked like?"

"It happened a long time ago. I was very little," Herri told him. "But I think Symeon will come back. We used to have lots of fun picking the apples together. He also taught me how to use a bow. I'm pretty good now." She stared into the room, wistfully.

"I keep it clean in here for when he comes back. He'll be happy when he sees that. Oh—all green!"

K'Nan was snapped out of his melancholy. "Green?" he asked her absently.

"Yes, definitely green. The men who took Symeon all wore green. And they all carried giant crescent spears. They were very scary."

A deadly glint showed in K'Nan's eyes, but only for a second. He smiled as he glanced down at his young helper.

"Little Herri—I think I know where your friend is. When I find him, I'll make sure he comes by someday to visit you. Would that make you happy?"

Her answer was the happiest (and best) hug he'd ever been given—by anyone.

9

Return of the Sword

"The trouble with civilizing societies is...you must commit barbarous acts of cruelty in order to do so."

The tavern's dining area was cramped and full of travelers seeking sustenance during the late winter evening. At a mostly inconspicuous table in the far western corner of the room, three wizened gentlemen sat sharing a pitcher of tepid water.

Two of them were dressed almost exactly the same, in crisp black tunics and gold outer garments, which would normally have stood out in such a place as this, but so secluded was this part of the restaurant that it enabled them to stay discreetly from view.

Their companion, sitting directly across from them, was a bit more conservatively attired—if you could call it attired. He wore little more than a white loincloth, a white half-robe and white-thonged sandals, all impeccably clean.

All three were chatting quietly and inhaling the local medicinal herbs, or *huvukah*. What else except talk of politics could cause men to be this absorbed in conversation at such a public place?

"The heir will inherit," one of the golden- garbed brothers stated determinately. "It is the will of the seven gods." He looked at his two companions with sort of a twisted half smile. "All this talk of legitimacy is for the losing side. In another six months or so, the rightful heir, Azzolari Azu, will be of ruling age and become the Heir Apparent officially, ensuring a peaceful succession. Trust me, my friends...it will happen." Having said this, he looked hesitantly at his similarly-dressed companion, hoping to be affirmed in some way.

That particular person, though similar in garb, looked to be about twenty to thirty moons older. Long reddish brown whiskers, interspersed with the occasional white, adorned his wizened face.

As he stroked them thoughtfully, the casual observer could almost see the considerable wisdom concealed behind his calm yet searching eyes. Although the two men were brothers, at least in the comradery sense of the word, there was not much else the two of them had in common.

Unlike his elder brother, known to the members of the Gilded Fishermen's faction as Rushdi, or "Wise One," the younger of the two had no compunctions about speaking his mind, regardless of immediate or long-term consequences.

It was, to be truthful, a habit that had gotten him into some serious trouble in the past and had certainly kept his status from rising within their clan, but what could he do? To ask a man to change his nature is akin to asking him to change his religion—a virtual impossibility. His brother was cautious by nature and never wanted to discuss politics.

"Saddique." Rushdi thought for a few moments before addressing him. "There have been rumors of things. East Rhydor is arming. The First Prince himself has been seen leaving the citadel to evaluate his outer defenses. The Coastal Region has been stirring for the last few months. And..." He hesitated.

"What?" Saddique said, leaning forward.

Sighing, Rushdi continued on. "There are even rumblings from the *Kumaz-we*. Word has come th-that...Chief Toloron's last remnants of support may be reappearing after so many moons...." With that, he trailed off. There was really not much more that needed to be said after that. Everyone knew the consequences of there being truth to that statement. A return to civil war, blood, and much death were sure to ensue.

"Rumors spread only by lazy peasants," Saddique sneered derisively. "How long have we been hearing these Toloron rumors? Since the day he so unceremoniously got himself and his entire army and bloodline butchered? I'll bet he never thought twice—"

"You silence your damned tongue!" Rushdi shouted at him, looking around the room nervously. To speak the name Toloron was a serious offense, punishable by ignominious death—most likely preceded by agonizing interrogation and torture from agents of the Regent Okon.

Saddique soberly looked around the establishment, but it didn't seem as if people were paying much attention after all.

Two tables to the right were a couple of penniless and depressed-looking *diobas*, or minstrels, possibly distraught that the loud noise and overcapacity of a place like this made it virtually impossible for them to belt out a song or two for a couple of copper pieces.

Saddique despised diobas, having wanted to be one of them as a young boy, the admission of which earned him a week's worth of severe beatings from his father.

Next to them was a holy man, or *abdu-kudus*. Despite the distracting noise around him, he remained extremely focused on a single cup of tea on his table. Although he was abnormally, almost grotesquely large, his manner was extremely slight—something, which combined with the dark brown hood on his head, seemed to make him almost disappear.

Watching him made Saddique's hairs stand up on his arms.

Alarmed now, he surveyed a bit more. Toward the center of the room...yes, he saw them now. There were two more curious individuals sitting there, hands lightly gripping their scimitar hilts. He started to his feet, but a lightning-quick hand on his shoulder from their elderly companion in white forced him back down.

Saddique swallowed hard. This was going to be a brutal fight, judging from the looks of their enemies.

Looking over at Rushdi, he saw that his elder brother's steely-eyed glare seemed to strengthen him. Rushdi's eyes moved down meaningfully to his dagger, which had been carefully placed in front of him on the table.

The blade—the ceremonial and traditional weapon of their tribe. It was always worn in the open, never hidden like what a common criminal would do. Always made from the most precious ivory, a warrior had to prove his valor many times over to even be considered for the honor of carrying one.

Rushdi's message was clear: *We are surrounded. It is now time to fight.*

In a measured, even voice, their companion spoke to both of them.

"It seems like the sins of your tribe have finally caught up to you. At a glance, we seem to be outnumbered by twenty-five or so of the enemy to just the three of us. Perhaps one or two fewer."

"Fortunately, we chose a fortuitous location to make a stand. As such, we don't need to worry about being surrounded and can fight with our backs to the wall. Still, the best we can hope for is to take most of them with us, as to not shame our ancestors." His expression turned peaceful.

"The two of you had best make your final offerings as briefly as you can now. They are merely waiting for me to leave to begin the assault."

"But, but, Uncle," Saddique said desperately, wanting there to be some other alternative to dying in this meaningless place, "aren't you one of the best fighters in the entire *Kumaz-we*? Surely, the three of us are more than a match for—"

"For your average group or tribe of fighters...yes, absolutely. However, there are at least twenty seasoned men, probably hand-picked by the First Prince for this assignment. These are not your average fighters. You had best make your final offerings."

Reluctantly, Saddique and Rushdi obeyed, grabbing a candle from the table. Heads bowed, they both spoke simultaneously in low whispers.

Father of the Sands,
Protect Our Homeland
Cast out the Infidels,
Purify our waters
Accept This Tribute of blood.

In one smooth, swift motion both brothers had swept the knives across a semi-blemishless area of their forearm and initiated a small stream of blood that splashed the candles, causing them to temporarily spark and flicker in the dim light of the restaurant.

Closing their eyes now, they waited until the trickle of blood became not more than a tiny drip, then, deed done, wrapped their arms with bandages always neatly stored within their garments. Grotesque ritual completed, they both felt much calmer.

Without another thought, Saddique grabbed the dagger and began to stand up. At that moment the huge wooden doors to the restaurant opened, and a strange young person strode in, a disinterested look in his eyes as he surveyed the room.

This person's skin was darker than the complexion of most—even in this area north of the savannah.

More so than his skin, his visage and aura appeared dark, accentuated by jet-ebony eyes. He was attired in a ragged hooded black tunic, the hood partially obscuring his braided locks, which one could tell were perhaps a bit too long.

Huge black gloves, obviously meant for an adult, grasped a silver chain-linked belt, to which was attached a long black scabbard, the handle covered by a silken-black cloth. Whatever the weapon was, it looked comical attached to his belt. It was much too large for his slight build to wield effectively.

The youth's build was slight; his face was heavily scarred and wore signs of extreme fatigue and sadness that normally only came with a lifetime full of traumatic events, but this boy couldn't have been more than twelve or thirteen moons. If these things weren't enough to make all of the "customers" curious about his origins, then his companion definitely was.

Accompanying the boy, just like it was any average domesticated animal, was a wild *Mnyama*, standing stiffly silent next to the lad and observing the surroundings in much the same fashion as his young human companion. A *Mnyama* was a huge, nomadic, dog-like animal of the savannah and plains of the African continent, particularly indigenous to Numeria. They were extremely aggressive, carnivorous animals who traveled in packs and hunted big game, in much the same fashion as the fabled *Win-Daiji* who made yearly pilgrimages into the desert lands and the chakkha for fame and fortune.

A pack of three or four Mnyamas could easily take down the strongest of lions. More importantly, being nomadic, it was almost impossible for them to be caught, much less domesticated.

How this one came to be the companion of a young pubescent youth was a mystery unto itself.

"Two plates of food and water."

It was more of a command than a request, and the youth's black eyes bore into those of the adults in the room, ostensibly searching for the proprietor of the tavern. Unbeknownst to him, that particularly cowardly man had sensed the fight which was about to happen—all of the customers had been paying more attention to their weapons than the menu—and had taken the boy's sudden arrival as an opportunity to skulk away to the safety of the stables outside.

At almost the same time, another much older man, with the appearance of a beggar, stood up and began to exit the tavern. This elder looked extremely filthy, but was carrying an exquisite bag over his right shoulder. It appeared to be gold-sequined and adorned with gemstones. It was such an incongruous picture that everyone was too startled to react. Without a word or even a glance at anyone else, he left.

One of the men, who Saddique had noticed earlier and identified as a *dioba*, stood up and spoke to the boy. "A serious matter is about to take place here, young man. I'd advise you to leave soon so as not to get mixed up in it."

The youth had been surveying the room now for almost a minute and seemingly took no notice of the dioba's words. He noticed that there were exactly twenty-seven people total, and that twenty-four of them, though seated, were arrayed in a battle formation meant to surround the remaining three men, who were sitting in the far corner.

Although this was certainly in the midst of the dinner hour, there was no food on the tables. He glanced toward the three men in the corner and found two of them to be moderately good fighters, and the third one to be most likely exceptional.

He knew that if all twenty-four of their enemies combined against those three, they would not be able to survive the battle. He seemed to hesitate a second or two before making up his mind. Apparently, he wanted to avoid conflict but genuinely seemed unable to.

Slowly and deliberately, he motioned the Mnyama to stay and made his way over to the table in the corner, eyes upright and calmly defiant. The men in the restaurant were amused. There were a variety of men here, but they all had one element in common: they were frightening to most people.

Most youths would never be so bold as to actually walk through a gathering of thieves, murderers, and bandits such as this. Reaching the table in the corner, he looked down at the newly-spilled blood on the table and frowned, then glanced at the gentlemen. They were agape in disbelief, but the boy seemingly didn't notice, speaking to them slowly.

"My apologies for interrupting your dinner, gentlemen. Might I take a seat and share a cup of water with you?" Without waiting for a reply, he sat down in the empty chair, poured a cup of water from the wooden pitcher on the table, and drained half of it in one go.

Nodding his head in satisfaction, he reached again for the pitcher to pour himself another cup. Saddique and Rushdi were speechless. In most of Numeria during those times, the highest gesture of respect you could show a person was to share a cup of water with them. It was done widely, not only as a way of greeting but as a symbolic way of choosing sides. This boy's message was clear to all in the tavern—I'm siding with these three.

"Hey, kid!" A booming voice from a few tables away bore down on him. "We have business with those two rascals sitting at the table with you. They're wanted by the First Prince for sedition and rebellion, and this entire room is filled with bounty hunters if you hadn't noticed."

"Two?" said the boy, his forehead wrinkling slightly. "There are three gentlemen sitting here. What are your plans for the third?"

Imperceptibly beneath the table, Rushdi gave Saddique a slight nudge. Saddique was annoyed.

The boy scoffed. "It seems like everyone is a traitor where the First Prince is concerned these days. However, I've no intentions of stopping you all from making your cowardly money. I was merely thirsty and noticed that the only table with anything on it belonged to these three." He picked up his cup of water and drained it again, refilling it immediately.

The spears-for-hire in the tavern all glanced at each other a bit sheepishly, realizing that they weren't being as discreet as they'd thought.

The boy stared morosely down into his cup. For some unexplained reason, an ominous chill filled the entire room.

"But since I've drank two cups of their water, I feel compelled to intercede on their behalf in some way."

In a flash, he flicked the cup about fifteen gaits, toward the man with the booming voice. Startled, the man, a giant of a person, feebly attempted to lift his weapon, a heavy iron mace, which acted as both his sword and shield.

He was trying to cover his face, but the cup was casually flicked with such speed and velocity that he'd barely grasped the mace before it crashed into his forehead, knocking him out and drenching his hair with what remained of the water.

The conflict had begun.

Two of the three men dressed as *diobas* (the ones who didn't address him) threw themselves immediately into the boy's path, their weapons being a couple of heavy ivory flutes equipped with bladed ends. They were exquisite weapons and should have been wielded by expert combatants, but unfortunately, the *diobas* were just as inept with weapons as they were with music.

Before they'd even had the opportunity to enter the fight, the young man had smashed both of the flutes into dozens of pieces without seemingly using his weapon.

It became clear to everyone that this kid was no novice—in fact, he was an amazing young fighter, with a unique combination of skill combined with an almost uncanny sense of anticipation that all of the truly great warriors possessed.

The two men, now without weapons, sheepishly backed away toward the throng of bounty hunters, and when at a safe distance, fled the establishment.

Saddique and Rushdi looked at each other in wonderment. Just as it appeared that their lives were about to expire, providentially they were saved by what had seemed to be a nothing of a boy, an unassuming ragged young man accompanied by a wild animal. Yet it would seem quite cowardly for them not to intervene. Hesitantly, Saddique leaned across the table toward Rushdi.

"Why is he helping us?" he whispered to his older comrade-in-arms.

"I have no idea, I've never seen him before. Best to wait a bit more before combining forces. This entire meeting has been a series of traps within traps. This could be another one." Saddique nodded.

As they debated helping him, the boy was calmly dispatching fighters—still without the full use of his weapon.

One of the more cowardly men, armored from the chest down with some sort of heavy chainmail (almost unheard of in the humidity and heat of this region) and armed with a peculiarly altered black reed, noticed the boy being distracted by more men posturing for position.

He used the opportunity to launch a couple of very small darts that had been tipped with a kind of foreign substance. This action was against the rules of conventional combat of the time, as they were all fighting in close quarters. To use projectiles of this sort was seen as the most *nemaah* of tactics.

Derisively, the boy turned to the sounds of the darts being thrown and sneered. "You seem to have dropped your projectiles. I'll return them to you." He waved one ragged sleeve in the direction of the darts, and almost imperceptibly, the darts flicked back to their original owner.

"Sorcery!" exclaimed several of the hooligans in the tavern as the darts hit their owner.

That unfortunate coward instantly froze, his entire face turning a very dark shade of green. He appeared to try to speak, but no words were audible, and in seconds, he had stopped moving altogether.

Everyone was aghast. Poison was absolutely contrarian to all rules of civilized combat in post-Usurpation Numeria.

Several men hastily moved to the "standing corpse" to warily go through his things.

"Wait." The young boy moved away from the table toward his would-be assassin. The now twenty-or-so bounty hunters surrounding him appeared to pay no attention. Even after the tremendous skills, particularly for his age, that he had just shown, they still seemed to think of him as more lucky than formidable.

They crowded even closer in to look at the body.

A loud, ear-piercing noise caused everyone in the tavern to cover their ears with their hands. The source of the loud noise appeared to be the boy, who had just partially unsheathed his sword, and now grasped it threateningly by the handle.

"Please move away from the body, I would like to take a closer look at it," the boy said quietly.

However, at this point, no one in the tavern was looking at the unfortunate assassin's corpse. Forty-six pairs of eyes were now focused on the weapon protruding from his scabbard. The boy had surreptitiously moved the silken cloth from the handle of the sword before removing it from the sheath.

Now everyone could see clearly the ornate black handle, emblemed with the head of a lion, symbolizing absolute rule. The handle, polished to an impossible luster, extended to a magnificently sharp jet black blade, outlined by the purest platinum edge.

The Emi Sword.

There were incredulous looks all over the tavern. If this was the Emi Sword, then this young punk had to be the same kid who defeated the First Prince's personal paladin, Jorell Boro, the First

Knight. The rumors had been circulating all over the eastern territories about that now-famous incident.

It was now being said that the person who had stolen the Emi Sword had been an extraordinary boy, less than sixteen moons of age, endowed with other-worldly strength and intimidating size, that he had literally squeezed the life out of Pala Jorell with his bare hands around his throat.

There wasn't practically a tavern in all of Numeria where the ballad of Pala Jorell's death hadn't been performed by now.

This was why when they looked at this youngster now, there was a great air of disbelief. This kid was far from being muscular; he was actually quite thin. He looked as if he'd been starved for weeks.

Perhaps he was tall for a boy his age, but certainly, the legendary First Knight would have been able to handle this kid. Wouldn't he?

Just this question was enough to convince all in the tavern that perhaps the tales of this child's combat prowess had been exaggerated, to a great extent.

At first unable to take their eyes off of the legendary weapon, an almost unsurpassed instrument of death that had only been heard of in songs and poetry up to this point but had never been seen by anyone with their own eyes, gradually the looks of disbelief began to be replaced by greedy stares.

They began to whisper amongst themselves.

"He's the one."

"That's the boy the Regent seeks."

"...he killed the First Knight."

"...just capturing the sword alone will make us famous."

"...if we all move at once, there's no way he can stop us."

One of the men, a turncoat *umbali* (spear for hire) called Staxx, took advantage of the commotion to adjust two throwing knives farther down his sleeves. He didn't know exactly how he was going to be able to get the Emi Sword away from everyone else in the restaurant, but at this point, that didn't matter.

What he suspected was that the young boy who carried it was formidable and possibly couldn't be defeated by every fighter in the tavern combined.

Therefore if he were to kill him now, despite using less than heroic methods, the other fighters may, out of appreciation, allow him to be the caretaker of the sword until it was safely returned to the Regent's possession.

Perhaps.

Slowly, he took a step toward the far wall, attempting to gain a clear path to the boy. The boy's attention at that moment was transfixed on the corpse. Although wearing light chain mail around part of his face as well as his body, his features—the sneering expression, the ferret-like eyes, and sallow complexion, were hard to mistake.

It was none other than "Witless," one of his old prison tormentors—the one who had given him the scars, which remained on his face to this day.

*   *

Jorann felt as if he were a God.

Or at the very least, someone extremely important—at long last. For about twelve days he had been leading his "army," about two hundred *Bajallah* warriors gifted to him by Daphni of the Sands, through the unbearably hot wilderness northeast toward the *Kumaz-we*. He had had very little food, water, or rest in that time but had discovered that he no longer seemed to need any of them, and more importantly, neither did his men. He knew from his lessons with K'Nan that one of the biggest worries for any commander of soldiers was how to keep them adequately supplied.

Happily, he did not have this problem with the *Bajallah*.

To his left and right were Znz and Srz, the two whom he had appointed as his lieutenants. On this, he had wisely consulted with Daphni, as he had only gotten to know them hours before leaving for his mission. She had explained to him about the weird language they spoke in, when they even deigned to speak, how there were no vowels or vowel sounds to be found anywhere. So their names sounded like "Zuh" and "Shh," if he ever had the opportunity to introduce them.

He rather doubted that would happen.

In his pack he had been gifted two extraordinary items from Daphni, a chameleon mask that enables the wearer to appear as whomever he imagines, and a unique Kumazi axe—incredibly light, powerful, and made from a metal that she'd explained no longer exists.

He felt even stronger now.

As they continued to move deliberately—him mounted, they on foot—he realized that the destiny that had been chosen for him by King Toloron and that soothsayer long, long ago was not the same destiny he would want for himself. He did not know this mythical Crown Prince, whom he was supposed to be so keen on restoring, had never met the *Mekuwa Waku* Toloron, and plainly didn't care about the Usurpation. His loyalty to K'Nan, if he were proven innocent of Daphni's charges against him, would be enough to compel him to fulfill his role as a *Khusela*, but...

...what he really cared about was the slave trade. He wanted to wipe it off the face of the earth. What if he could put the full weight of the armies of the Wilderness to accomplish just that? Wouldn't his name be remembered for centuries? Wouldn't he finally erase the ghosts of his past life as a cowardly slave?

A single huge vulture flew overhead.

Jorann looked up at it absently, noticing that its path of flight was fairly opposite of what it should be for this time of the day. All living creatures should be taking some kind of shelter as it was just before noon. Quite simply, to not take refuge from the sun and sand at these temperatures meant death.

All of a sudden the *Bajallah* began murmuring amongst themselves. Two hundred left hands simultaneously reached for their axe handles. Surely a simple vulture wouldn't invoke such fear in some of the world's most vicious warriors?

From the top of a cliff four hundred en-yawo to the right, three more vultures glided overhead.

Even Jorann, with his extremely limited knowledge of the wilderness, knew that something was amiss. He needed to take charge fast or risk losing his new army's respect.

Scanning the direction from which the vultures appeared, he began to motion his scouts to move in that direction. Znz and Srz simultaneously shook their heads, then pointed about eighty degrees in the other direction.

He understood immediately. The vultures were running toward something, not away.

Instantly he spurred his camel in the direction of the vultures. After a minute of furious galloping, the scene he came upon nearly caused him to be sick. Lying half-submerged in the slime-filled puddle of a leaking water-skin, a young man wearing Numerian warrior garb was being eaten alive.

One of his eyes had already been removed and was being fought over by two of the six or seven vultures clustered around his torso. The man was either unconscious, or no longer possessed the ability to scream. Jorann was tempted to walk away.

He turned his camel back toward the regiment of *Bajallah*, when a thought suddenly occurred to him. This man is a Numerian warrior, well-provisioned, in the middle of the wilderness. He is unmounted, yet he was able to make it this far. Something was wrong.

Reaching for his bow, he effortlessly shot three arrows into the pack of birds, actually killing four of them with the three bolts. The other two vultures reluctantly flew off into the distance but remained within sight, chastened.

Not really wanting to dismount, Jorann brought his camel to within a few *en-yawo* of the unfortunate man. To his surprise, the man tilted his head slightly in his direction, his one good eye trying to get a good glimpse of his unexpected savior. Hastily, Jorann dismounted from the camel.

"I...I...thought you were them...thought you...finally..." The man's voice trailed off. Jorann looked all around him but could see no one.

"What happened to you?" he asked the man. He still couldn't put his finger on what was so out of place.

"Are you the boy?" asked the man.

"What boy?" said Jorann, thinking to himself, *Of course I'm a boy.*

"The one everyone's so afraid of. The boy they're all after."

"Who's after?" he inquired urgently. He leaned in closer to the poor man, the smell of his exposed entrails increasing his level of queasiness.

The man laughed, highlighting his current state of delirium. He seemed to be trying to swallow. Jorann looked at his water skin and saw that it was empty. After hesitating, he grabbed his own from around his waist and held it over the man's mouth, careful to not do much more than wet his lips. After all, there was not much help he could give him at this point, and there was no need to waste precious water.

The effect, however, was immediate. The man smiled weakly and looked directly at him. Jorann guessed that he was about twenty moons old, had been in excellent physical condition, and was most likely from royal stock. There was nothing distinguishing about his clothing, however on his finger was a ring with three initials:

H.R.M.

"Who are you, sir?" he asked.

"I'm history. That's all that matters in the sands, in the *Kumazi*...whether you will live or die. A person's family name means nothing out here." He seemed to struggle to sit up, which was ridiculous in his current situation.

"You can't be him," the man weakly said. "Y-you don't have the sword."

This man was almost incoherent and kept babbling about a young boy and a sword. Who could he be talking about?

"Okon's...men...are here."

Jorann went numb, thinking he must have misheard.

"Okon?" he repeated. "Lord Regent Okon?" During his lessons with K'Nan, he had learned about all of the elite and powerful men and families of Numeria, and especially the members of the all-powerful Conclave of Regents.

Arguably the most terrifying of them was the man who'd betrayed the *Mekuwa Waku*—Lord Toloron himself. His legs began to feel numb, and he scarcely noticed his *Bajallah* forces arriving at the site.

"You said Okon is here," he continued to probe the poor man, knowing his time was short. "Where is he? Why is he here?"

"He...is...looking...looking for you," came the feeble reply.

Looking for me? How does he even know about me?

"Where is he? Where is Okon?" he said, his rising voice mirroring the increasing tide of fear he felt within.

As if in reply, the dunes surrounding them all began to shake in unison. The vultures returned overhead and were joined by several more, ostensibly appearing out of nowhere.

In panic, Jorann rushed over to his camel while motioning to his men to race toward the high point of the outermost ridge to their east. This would put the sun a bit more behind their backs than the enemy and force their attackers to fight at a disadvantage.

The *Bajallah* were incredible, all flying past him toward the outermost ridge. Well, perhaps not flying, but they were certainly gliding on the surface of the sand. Suddenly, it was all he could do to keep up with them.

Just managing, he saw his lieutenants Znz and Srz motioning instructions to all of their warriors. Brilliantly, they began to form a peak formation, with all two hundred of them separated into two lines forming a vector shape.

Once in formation, they motioned for him to take his place just inside and to the south of the northernmost point in the vector.

The commander's place.

In the distance, they could hear the sound of the enemy. Jorann guessed that they would be right beneath them in about two minutes. He glanced around. The *Bajallah* were both motionless and emotionless.

Is this where I'm finally going to die? He thought.

* *

Still in the tavern, Gesi was using the scabbard of his Emi Sword to pry at Witless's hand, which was greenish-gray and scaly. He was sure that if he poked the skin with his sword's blade, there would be a fair bit of rigidity there, but Numerian custom demanded that a sword should not be withdrawn completely from its scabbard unless in a fight—an oft-broken tradition.

Investigating Witless's tunic and armor turned up a few more items, seemingly unimportant, except for a small pouch of gold coins and a couple of letters, which he carefully extracted, read, then stored away in his breast pocket.

Now seemingly having forgotten or no longer concerned with the reason he'd just been fighting, Gesi wordlessly began walking back toward his companion Mnyama. The bounty hunters and *umbalis* were all agog at his arrogance.

"You think it's that easy to leave?" said one of them as he flung a short spear toward Gesi from about twenty cubits away. Gesi knew just from the sound of the spear that it had been thrown with tremendous velocity, from someone who knew what they were doing.

Not daring to be careless, he pivoted to his left, at the same time drawing the Emi Sword, but two more spears had been launched at him from opposite corners of the tavern.

Aghast, Saddique and Rushdi drew their daggers in the corner, knowing they were too late. They had waited this long to try and discern the young man's true intentions, thinking that this could just have been yet another trap set for them by the bounty hunters who had casually invaded the tavern like so many desert mice in the wilderness.

Only when they saw the viciousness of the first spear that had been launched at the boy unawares, along with the other two, which would almost certainly seal his fate, did they finally realize he couldn't possibly be working in tandem with the filthy *umbalis* surrounding them.

Far too late, they also realized that not only had they lost the chance to assist the boy, who had saved both of their lives by earlier intervening on their behalf, but they had also squandered a real opportunity to extract themselves from this precarious situation.

For almost certainly would the scum of bounty hunters fall upon them as soon as the boy, along with his precious Emi Sword, had been eliminated.

Amazingly, however, the youngster not only dodged the first lethal spear, but hacked down the other two in mid-flight. The combat instincts of this boy, along with the power of the Emi Sword, were astonishing indeed!

Saddique and Rushdi were now encouraged. In a flash, they launched six daggers each, four in the directions of the slower moving spear throwers, and two simultaneously at the individual who had seemed to have almost superhuman force when launching the first spear at the youth.

That individual, the hooded *abdu-kudus* that Saddique had mistaken for a lazy minstrel just a few minutes earlier, had miraculously seemed to rise from his pre-confrontation slumber just in time to cowardly ambush the young boy.

Again Saddique noticed his grotesque facial features, which had been partially obscured by the oversized grayish-brown cleric hood which he and Rushdi were now both certain was being worn to conceal something familiar underneath.

As the two daggers they had launched hurriedly seemed to float languidly toward the *abdu*, he glanced to the two of them. A mouthful of gold teeth split his lips to form a hideous grin; he obviously felt as if he had nothing to fear from the daggers.

Standing up, the *abdu-kudus* made no attempt to move out of the path of the approaching daggers. Time seemed to stand still for all of those viewing in the tavern until amazingly, the daggers passed completely through the body of the *abdu* and into the wall. Was this a man or a demon?

Rushdi and Saddique were frozen. Sure, they held several more daggers ready to hurl in his direction, but was there really going to be a different result if they launched them? Not only had the two brothers stopped their counterattack in apprehension, but even the other *umbalis* who had been around him were cautiously beginning to step away.

Seemingly oblivious to the atmosphere of dread suddenly permeating the tavern, the *abdu* fixed his gaze intently on Gesemni for a few moments.

"I came here hoping to uncover a fraud, and instead I depart having witnessed a rare truth. Such is my good fortune. We shall meet again very soon." With a short nod in Gesemni's direction, and almost without seeming to move, he had departed.

Realizing that the remaining members of the ambush party were not planning on letting him leave without the sword or a fight, Gesemni immediately sprang toward the two nearest *umbalis* (mercenaries) in the room, his Emi Sword pointed high in the air.

* *

Jorann was now wholly convinced that the attacking party had no connection to Okon. Okon would never personally deign to travel to this wilderness to look for a mere boy, any boy—no matter how formidable.

Yes as he watched this "army," which was not really an army but more like a raiding party of about two thousand men, bear down ferociously on him and his *Kumazi* regiment, he couldn't help noticing that they did indeed bear some characteristics of a seasoned professional army.

One, their formation was quite disciplined. There was not a single soldier out of place. Also, they were all wearing the same uniforms.

So were they bandits or did they fight for Okon?

He didn't have time to ponder as the lead riders of the two thousand smashed head first into the *Bajallah*s. All too quickly the sights and sounds of his first real battle completely enveloped him.

Within minutes, it was all over. Jorann, exhausted and covered with blood, felt surprisingly exhilarated as he and his two lieutenants surveyed the scene of the carnage they'd just helped create. Almost every member of the attacking force was dead, save one or two unfortunate survivors who were too injured for him to interrogate.

Jorann took out the handkerchief that he'd found on the unfortunate, now deceased warrior. For some reason, Jorann had thought that Okon was searching for him. Now it didn't appear that way.

He smiled slyly. The way he felt at this moment, even ten Lord Okon's could not touch him.

Let them ALL come, he thought.

10

Mistaken Masiti

Sania and Mohann had ridden through the shallowest reaches of the savannah for two days now, and yet they were still occasionally finding dead bodies. Old and young, male and female, there appeared to be an inexhaustible trail of them—all stricken with the same mysterious affliction, as there were no traces of blood on their bodies, nor any signs of starvation or exposure.

The horses they had taken from the *Dukka-Vinyo* incessantly neighed their disapproval, sensing that they were being led to some foreboding place.

By now, Sania had long stopped crying. Early the previous evening, about three hours west of Mistress Jayda's, they'd seen the first. A family—man and woman and a young boy who looked to be around seven moons or so—lay about ten *en-yawo* from the main road, in a small clearing beneath a few mini-*bardjia* trees, which were looked at as sacred by many of the nomadic tribes of the savannah.

Sania had assumed that they were only sleeping. Fifty *en-yawo* ahead, they spotted a young woman, awkwardly sprawled at the side of the main trail, in a very similar fashion.

This time they'd dismounted and approached the young lady. "*Masiti*," Sania had said, prodding her gently with one of her white-gloved hands. The young woman didn't stir at her voice or touch.

Becoming bothered by the repetitiveness of these discoveries, Sania looked back at Mohann, who shrugged his shoulders. She reached both hands out to turn the young lady over. "No, Sania. Use your sword instead."

She blinked twice but then understood. It could be a contagion. Thinking about that possibility made her break into a cold sweat.

Reaching to her scabbard, she stood up and placed her right boot underneath the lady. Sliding Feather underneath, she used the leverage to roll her over gently. Sania was stunned. This young girl, pecan-complexioned with hazel eyes and dark brown braided hair, bore a great deal of resemblance to her!

Her face was frozen in a quizzical expression. She appeared so young and full of promise, even in death, that Sania couldn't hold back her tears. Mohann, perhaps knowing what thoughts were going through her mind, covered her shoulders with a sympathetic arm.

"Just when we get accustomed to life, comes our turn to die," he quietly told her.

Mohann had seen and done many things and was something of a worldly man; odd considering how long he'd lived in the savannahs of Numeria. That said, he understood the tragedy of lost youth as well or better than most. He'd been responsible for running a business whose operation depended on it.

Sania reached a white glove down and closed the young girl's eyes, no longer caring about what misfortune had befallen her. If they'd had more time, she would've requested that Mohann help her bury the poor girl, but they'd been given strict orders from Mistress Jayda to get out of the savannah.

She began to walk away—then, on impulse turned around and approached this girl again, unable to overcome the strange feeling that their encounter was more than an accident.

Reaching her hands into the young girl's tunic, she found some coins and a couple of letters. Unfolding one of them, she recognized it as a pass to travel as a woman.

Sania understood that among some tribes and particularly in some provinces, females were allowed to move about only with male companionship. Those who broke this custom risked becoming victims of violent travelers, archaic courts, or the notorious slavers guilds of the savannah.

The other letter was just a simple note.

Your clan brothers Saddique and Rushdi are meeting with an abdu-kudus beneath the river. They will need you to attend. Leave immediately.

None of that meant anything to Sania or Mohann, so they left the young girl there. After a few more hours of traveling, they decided to fortify a camp for the night. To prevent themselves from falling prey to the many nocturnal beasts that traversed the grassland, they'd cleared out a decent-sized area, perhaps about twenty *en-yawo* in diameter, and had surrounded it with *jasprine* root, a favorite treat of ninety percent of the grassland herbivores but lethally poisonous to most of the predators.

As it was strictly forbidden to start fires in the savannah, this was their best option.

After Mohann had prepared them a small meal of leopard's milk cheese and sausage along with some graybean stew, he fell asleep almost immediately. Sania watched him, utterly grateful for his companionship.

She had no idea where or even who she was, and even less knowledge about what dangers and challenges lay in front of her. Just the thought of making this journey, including all of the grim discoveries by herself, was scary as hell.

Gods, Mistress Jayda, she thought. *Once again you've proven you know so much more than anyone else.*

She reached inside her tunic as quietly as possible. After some considerable effort, she pulled out what she'd been looking for without making too much noise. The handkerchief that the young warrior had given to her at the *Dukka-Vinyo* rather than giving her his name. She'd kept it close to her all this time without even realizing it. A handkerchief, in her estimation, was much more personal...

...or so she preferred to think. Looking down at it under the candescent moon, she was a little taken aback that she hadn't noticed the craftsmanship and detail when he'd first presented it to her, but of course her mind had been full of other matters then. The handkerchief wasn't silken but was made of some sort of precious threading. In the bottom corner, initialed quite elaborately in radiant indigo lettering, were three initials.

H.R.M.

So those are his initials, she thought. *Perhaps he wanted to tell me his family origins the entire time but knew he had to observe the proper rituals and customs.* At that thought, she perked up considerably and even became oblivious to her macabre surroundings after a while. Before she knew it, she'd fallen asleep with the young soldier's handkerchief still crumpled in her hand.

She awoke a few hours later to the pungent smell of tea. The tea she recognized easily; *Kimbaa* root—it was a staple in the savannah because it could be steeped without heat. Her cup sat in front of her, along with a haunch of stone bread, and some cured quail meat.

Her handkerchief lay beside it, carefully folded and placed next to the cup. A flush stole over Sania's cheeks as she sat up against one of her saddlebags and picked up the cup of tea. Trying his best to appear engrossed in his journal and failing, Mohann suppressed a smile. She fumed. The awkward silence continued for about five minutes—until she'd had enough.

"If you tell a single soul, I'll stab you in the neck!" she hissed. With that, Mohann exploded in laughter, transforming his face entirely from the stern disciplinarian that she'd grown up fearing for most of her almost thirteen moons into that of a warm friend and confidante.

Despite herself, she smiled. Within a few seconds, they were both chucking incessantly.

"Ah...*Masiti* Sania..." He inhaled, trying feebly to stop his laughter. "Mistress Jayda was right about you; you are indeed formidable." Then just as suddenly as his mirthful laughter had begun, it stopped.

"*Masiti*. What you're experiencing right now is quite natural. I would be much more concerned if you had continued showing no interest in boys whatsoever. I would probably even be tempted to blame myself for putting you in these boy's clothes for all of these moons."

He allowed himself another chuckle. "However, I feel I'd be letting you down if I didn't remind you that our empire, our civilization, perhaps even our entire existence depends on your commitment to the cause for which you were anointed."

"Remember that a few days ago, the thing that you wanted most in life was to have a purpose. You wanted adventure; you wanted excitement. Most of all, you wanted to be free from the possibility of ever having to entertain anyone. Do you remember this?"

Tears forming inside the corners of her eyes as she thought again of Magistrate Dioni, Sania nodded. But she thought to herself that Mohann couldn't have been more mistaken. She had always admired men; their bravado and their aggressiveness—and their fearless approach to life. However, her attraction to boys went no further than that; in fact she was sure that girls held more allure for her along those lines.

Mohann looked at her, mistaking her pensiveness for contrition; compassion evident on his face.

"Okay then, my brave young warrior. I believe nothing more needs to be said. Finish your tea; we still have much traveling to do."

*　　*

They continued to see bodies. All told, there were hundreds of them. Under the seven-rod tall blades of grass, it continued to be very difficult for Sania and Mohann to identify them until their horses stumbled. However, the closer they got to the edge of the savannah, where began the majestic lower *Kumaz-we*, the sparser in frequency the bodies appeared. Soon they had completely left the savannah, and the dead, behind.

Sania had never seen a more majestic site than the Great River. How could she have, considering the extent of her sheltered upbringing? In front of her wide, disbelieving eyes stretched mile after mile of bright greenish-blue water, bordered on each side by dark amber patches of soil and long *lyfolia* plants, which provided a natural barrier to the river's edge.

She could not see where the river started or where it ended, nor could she look to the other side of it. She had heard rumors as a child that the Great River was the center of all living things on their planet, and looking at it, she wondered for the first time if that were actually true. "It's big," was the only thing she could tell Mohann. Mohann smiled, perhaps remembering his own experience of visiting the Great River for the first time.

However, the Great River never changed. Along the river line were many moored straw and hemp rafts, lined up as far as the eye could see. Each of them had one or two raftsmen waiting patiently for a traveler to hire their services. Most of the raftsmen were bare-chested but wore long steering pants and hemp sandals.

The clothes were chosen for their durability. Standard attire, like those worn for riding horseback, would be torn to bits when these raftsmen tried to traverse the jagged white-water boulders that could be found about two thousand en-yawo downstream.

They walked past a few rows of the raftsmen, none of them standing out as looking particularly agile or quick, or even interested in making a profit. Most of them were stretched out on their rafts, bamboo woven-hats tilted over their eyes, and trying to catch an afternoon nap.

Some were engrossed in conversation with others, seeming more intent on socializing that preparing for a journey down the river. A few more looked hopefully in their direction, then spotted the *sharafta-lei* around Sania's neck and disgustedly waved her on.

For the first time, Sania was feeling the true consequences of refusing to reject her past affiliation to the *Dukka-Vinyo*; she was finally seeing just how judgmental and unfair other Numerians could be.

She shot Mohann a look as if to say, *how the heck am I supposed to choose from this?* Just after, they approached a raft that was only being monitored by a small child, no more than five moons of age. Sania and Mohann looked around but could see no one else who was operating the raft. They slowly approached the vessel and looked at the boy, preparing to ask him where his parents were.

Seeing them walk toward him, he smiled and reached out his hand. Shrugging, Mohann gave him a ten *dinarra* coin and watched as the boy tucked the coin away in the waistband of his shorts.

Nodding, the boy gestured toward the back center of the raft as both Mohann and Sania looked around for his parents. "Please sit. Please sit. Arrive soon." He spoke to them in halting khajudic.

Sania began to protest, but Mohann silenced her with a wave and motioned her to one of the two seats located toward the back of the raft.

Mohann, you better know what the heck you're doing, she thought.

Without another word to either of them, the young boy untethered the *hempe* ropes that firmly anchored the raft to the temporary wooden mooring. He then reached down, his tiny hands picking up the steering oar. Taking his seat at the front, he thrust his passengers about five en-yawo away from the riverbank in one smooth, natural motion. Sania looked at Mohann, shrugged and smiled, relishing her first water voyage, albeit a small one.

The weather that day was quite warm, particularly for the end of the cold season.

There was, however, a firm breeze blowing against the boat, slowing them all down. One unseen benefit was the periodic respite from the heat it provided.

There weren't many people on the continent whose skin could resist these rays for long periods of time, with the obvious exceptions being the *Mejeedi*, or Lifeless Ones, who had migrated from the northern dry lands to the civilized areas in massive numbers.

Above Sania, several egrets flew from the center of the river toward the bank, searching for nesting places. These reliable egrets were how most travelers were aware that they had reached the *Kumaz-we*, but there had been an effort to drive most of them out by the savannah hunters for the last ten moons or so.

This was due to their propensity to call out at the approach of humans and thus warn the big game of the hunter's arrival.

Most of these efforts had come to naught; the egrets of the *Kumaz-we* were just too numerous and ecologically symbiotic with the Great River to be wholly exterminated.

The young boy steering the boat was a prodigy. Of course, Sania had never been in a boat before, but she was certain that she could not do what the boy did, and at such a young age. The sound of rushing water in the distance could soon be heard, and she felt Mohann stiffen next to her.

Ahead, she could see the drastic texture and color change of the river surface from smooth and dark blue to extremely choppy and more of a whitish-gray tone.

Even the egrets behaved differently around the rapids; they flew faster, closer together and in tighter formations than they did farther up the riverbed, almost as if they were being agitated in some way by the power of this majestic force.

Feeling Mohann glance at her, Sania said, "Relax, Mohann. Do you think he would have taken us out this far if he didn't have a plan for the rapids?"

Mohann didn't have time to respond because they'd already reached the rapids. The boy motioned him and Sania toward the hempe ropes; he wasn't much for speaking, peculiar considering that he was little more than a toddler.

Still, they immediately understood. They were supposed to wrap their arms and waist in the hempe ropes so that they wouldn't be separated from the raft once the water became un-friendly. They hastily complied.

The young boy himself took his steering joist and quickly tied it down to the back of the raft, almost at the same time unfastening another steering joist, this one just as thick in diameter, but nearly a full three *en-yawo* shorter.

A regular seven-rod staff would be challenging for the youth to steer the boat with, for various reasons, not the least of which was the inability of a person small in stature to take it out of the rapidly moving water from stern to mast quickly.

Depending on how the waters were pummeling their vessel, a normal raftsman may need to change ends or sides of the raft to redirect its trajectory at any moment. With this four-rod steering joist, it was indeed possible for the child to do just that.

No sooner had the child readied himself than the first group of breakwaters slammed against the boat. "Aaah!" Mohann called out as the force of that first break sent him slightly airborne.

"What by the heavenly moons are you yelling at?" Sania asked him. Sheepishly, he shrugged. "Just imagine you're on an unbroken horse or something," she yelled at him, "but I hope you're not going to do that for the rest of the trip!"

That Sania could hear him or his scream over the roar of the breakwaters was no small feat. As they were now fully engaged in the rapidly moving waters, the noise was deafening.

After they'd hit the first obstacle, the boy took a long stare at the path they were on and frowned. He then skirted to the back of the raft, joist in tow and thrust it into the water. Sania expected that he would change their trajectory and move them toward the coastline.

To their surprise, the boy didn't raise the steering joist after placing it in the water. Instead, he kept it there, anchoring the boat in place for the briefest of moments. At the last second, he lifted the steering joist, and the force of the breakwaters catapulted them about fifty en-yawo down the rapids. The lad used this technique several times to slingshot them farther and farther down the river.

For Sania, this trip was the culmination of thirteen moons of repression and missed opportunities; it was a much more symbolic start to her new journey than physically leaving the *Dukka-Vinyo* had been.

So far, she was enjoying every second of it. She had entirely forgotten about the revelations of the last two days, the young warrior who'd given her the handkerchief, and even the mystery of all of those poor people dying in the savannah.

All she could think about was the exhilaration of the journey, the rush of the winds past them as they hurtled down the break-waters, the taste of river water in her mouth, and the smell of it on her clothes.

Far too soon for both Sania and Mohann, the breakwaters suddenly began to calm. The boy reattached his augmented joist to the back of the raft and grabbed the normal one. Shaking his head with a smile, Mohann sat back in his seat and turned to Sania.

"I guess the old saying is true, after all," he told her.

"What's that?" she asked. She was not one to care about old sayings, or new.

"That there is one certainty in life. 'The old must inevitably give way to the young.'"

She raised her eyebrows. "How's that? Seems like the thing they have the hardest time doing."

"First, you and the way you fought those soldiers, while all of us adults were powerless, now this child. It looks like there are many able people among our youth."

With that, he relaxed, to enjoy the rest of the journey, not knowing that every en-yawo they traveled was currently being watched.

* *

"You're saying there are two of them?" Kaeyron, the man spying on Sania and Mohann, asked. He had absently been swat-ting away river gnats for the last few moments and never had much interest in what this particular scout, Sei-Sei, ever told him. The man talked too much.

Kaeyron understood that most of that was merely his ultra-awkward way of being friendly, but he just didn't have time for that kind of small talk. The Regency was on edge. Armies that had been inert for moons were now beginning to mobilize. Some of the rumors going around were too fantastical to be believed, but some seemed plausible enough.

Was there actually a surviving heir of Toloron?

Was there a new outbreak of the dreaded "painless death"?

Had K'Nan Urmandu, son of Loffri, actually resurfaced outside of the wilderness to aid the House of Toloron?

Was there still a House of Toloron?

Kaeyron had sighed inwardly upon hearing all of this news. It was too much to process. He had never cared about all of the rumor and innuendo—until today.

Today he had received a confidential dispatch from the House of Azu—under the actual command of Lord Regent Okon—informing him that loyalists to the House of Toloron would begin to traverse the *Kumaz-we*, en masse. Their primary objective was unknown.

He was to be particularly vigilant in making sure that no children under the age of emancipation, about fifteen moons, were able to safely cross through the *Kumaz-we*, whether alone or with adults.

Why he'd been given these particular orders, Kaeyron had no idea. The part about children was especially perplexing to him. What harm could a kid cause? He had three of them himself.

He smiled, thinking of his two daughters, Nia and Habi, as well as his youngest, his son, Jag. His children were innocent, good-natured rascals who spent their entire days playing and learning and could never harm a soul.

Even his son, Jag, all of three moons, who should be showing interest in the sword and spear by now, only wanted to spend his days swimming and playing games in the river.

Kaeyron shook his head.

The fact remained, though, that he had an explicit directive, which could not be altered or disobeyed. Several traps had already been sprung for Toloron loyalists throughout the *Kumaz-we*.

A large ambush had been set up in the tavern just a few thousand en-yawo south for a couple of suspected pro-Toloron loyalists. There were even steps being taken to eliminate everyone traveling through the savannah who might be headed to the coastal regions. What those might possibly be, one could only guess, he thought to himself as he snapped out of his brief reverie. These two travelers, this older man, and a young girl, definitely fit the description though.

Sei-sei nodded. "Two."

"I'm not sure if our orders are meant for children who are traveling alone, or those traveling with adults also," he stated weakly. Kaeyron had no stomach whatsoever for harming children.

"Well, the orders are for you to carry out, my friend. I am merely a scout, but I will say this—these are the kind of instructions that come with an implied threat, if you get my meaning." Sei-sei's jaw was set as he spoke.

Kaeyron knew. Better to be thorough than to see his entire family, including his three beautiful children, burn on a spear. Still, there were some things that a man of honor and conscience absolutely could not do. His mind was made up.

"Make sure when they land, they get an escort to their destination. Through to the tavern keep." He wanted no part of this directive.

He repeated the question to himself once more.

Has K'Nan, son of Loffri, actually resurfaced?

*   *

A few hundred thousand en-yawo away, the answer to that question was apparent, at least to the *Pajadin de Hekeemah*. The famous Toloron loyalist and warrior, K'Nan of Loffri himself, was busy grilling those reclusive wise men.

"I don't understand what I'm hearing," he thundered, "you knew who this boy was, his importance to all of the tribes! You knew, and you still allowed him to leave without so much as a token escort!"

He knew he was becoming quite agitated, something unbecoming his rank and reputation, but for reasons he couldn't quite comprehend, he had allowed himself to get worked up.

The head of the council smiled uneasily. "We do understand your frustration. Guilt and embarrassment are the only two emotions that get worse with the passage of time."

K'Nan had already been irritated at not being received as an honored guest, and now these people seemed to be actually lecturing him.

I should have mowed you all down at Daphni's request moons ago, he thought in disgust.

"How dare you presume to know my thoughts?" he spat. "If I send for my m—"

"You should know the Pajadin de Hekeemah fear not death, Pala *Kuhesi-wa* (honored knight). We would be more interested in you telling us why we sense no affection for the boy within you?"

"None," chimed in another of them.

So you have the boy's best interest at heart now, K'Nan thought sarcastically. *And I'm a baboon's uncle.*

"Lord K'Nan," spoke one of the more diplomatic Pajadin, "do you know precisely who the *Khuselas* are? Not just their identities, but what each of them represents?"

"WELL OF COURSE I DO!" K'Nan thundered. "They are of course Chaos, Conflict, and Calm—"

"Excellent!" The Pajadin interrupted him. "Not only do you know, but you have listed them in order of their greatness. Now, may I ask you, which of the three is most likely to be *Calm*?"

K'Nan froze. Of *course*, he thought. *The other two couldn't possibly be as passive as young Lord Jorann is.* He nodded to the Pajadin council.

"Let's not speak nonsense." He said to them. "I was disappointed when I first met the boy. He seemed to be a child who had accepted that his past life was as it should have been. The *Khu-*

selas must be three of the greatest leaders the world has ever seen. Naturally, I had some doubts."

"But?" the chieftain asked.

K'Nan bristled again. "It's none of your business, but let's say the boy quickly proved himself through his diligence in training and his studies."

The men of the Pajadin looked at each other for a few seconds, then slowly nodded their heads.

"Just so. We also sensed a great deal of submission within him, yet unlike you, viewed it as his greatest asset."

"Asset," K'Nan scoffed. "How can a leader so easily adapt to a life of slavery?"

"He was essentially born into that life; it was not the life he chose. Have you ever asked him why he never tried to run away? You should do that one day."

K'Nan was taken aback. He hadn't bothered to think that there could be an explanation.

The Pajadin Seema Selah pulled out a very ancient-looking scroll from his robe. Casually, he tossed it over to K'Nan, who took one look at it and froze. His lower lip trembled. Opening a page, he noticed that his hands were also shaking uncontrollably.

He looked at the words, but they were blurred. Grimacing, he held the book away some distance from his eyes—and the words gradually came into focus. He didn't know why, but the older he got, the harder it was for him to see things directly in front of his eyes.

There was a legend of a strange device which could fix this malady when placed over the nose, but he'd never seen it firsthand, as it was said to only exist among the Pale tribes of the north.

However, he only needed one glance to know that this book was authentic.

"Just so," Seema Selah said. "This is the original book you know of as the *Zakku-Dalla*, I believe. The boy knew passages from this book and how to apply them to the concepts of life without effort and without flaw."

"We believe that what verses he recited came from remnants of either corrupted or diluted copies that are still out there in the world. Those are not the real thing. This one is."

K'Nan almost couldn't believe his good fortune; the things that could be learned and taught to the *Khuselas*, as well as their armies—just from within these pages could guarantee that the restoration would be made real.

"Thank you." He managed to let escape his lips, wondering why he was being gifted such a treasure from a group who had a reputation for never involving themselves in external affairs.

One of the other Pajadin spoke, more sternly. "Thanks to the *boy*, the young Lord Jorann. He will one day be a great leader of men. Remember, Pala K'Nan; if you want to be a great leader, you must first learn to be a great follower. The young hero is both; that is how his time in servitude helped him."

K'Nan nodded his head, slightly ashamed and slightly annoyed that he was being lectured at this point in his life.

More kindly, a third Pajadin said, "Take care of young Lord Jorann at all costs, brave sir—for it has been foreseen..." He hesitated.

"What?" K'Nan inquired. The man, slightly younger than the rest, looked hesitantly at the others.

"One day, young Lord Jorann will avenge your murder."

11

River Prodigy

In his typical prospecting fashion, Mohann had offered the boy a generous tip and even a job at the *Dukka-Vinyo* once they disembarked. The boy had just shaken his head, smiled, and tipped his cap. He didn't accept either the tip or the offer. At this point, they weren't confident that he could speak at all.

Having been told there were many horses for hire at the river basin, they spent a few minutes looking for people selling them. Unfortunately, this appeared to be a bit of false information. They saw no one selling horses. More accurately, they didn't see any horses at all.

Sania looked at Mohann in a mild panic. They'd done well to get safe passage down the river and quite quickly, but their journey had just come to an abrupt end if they weren't able to get new mounts to take them wherever they were supposed to go. Mohann simply shrugged. "If this is where the horses are supposed to be, this is where they will be."

What a dumb thing to say, Sania thought, liking him in spite of it. No sooner did she think it than she heard the creaking sound of carriage wheels coming through the clearing to the riverbank. She hadn't thought about carriages, but maybe it'd be better than nothing, assuming it was for hire.

A clunky, sprawling box-on-wheels being pulled reluctantly by a pair of rueful disease-ridden mules came into view.

It seemed so out of place in this setting—more like something that would be found in the densely populated regions of the north—that Sania instantly felt apprehensive when she saw it.

"Well, here we are," said Mohann. "There was no need to fret." She shrugged. As the carriage stopped, she noticed a portly, bright-skinned driver.

Everything about his physical appearance suggested someone who was unassuming, but Sania could instantly see that it was intentional. The way he held the whip in his hands, quite effortlessly, the upright manner in which he sat in the carriage, and most haltingly, the alertness of his eyes, instantly told her that she'd better be on her guard.

"Carriage for hire, sir?" The driver asked Mohann, faintly saluting him.

Sania stifled a laugh. "Yes," Mohann said, reaching into his tunic and extracting a small feathery brown purse. He shook out a couple of coins, gave them to the driver, and handed the purse to Sania. "Take the lad wherever he wishes to go." Mohann raised his hand to Sania and helped lift her into the carriage.

"Wait," she said. "You're...not coming?"

With a firm shake of his head, he said, "No." His answer was short but final. "Orders from Mistress Jayda, remember? I'm to accompany you only as far as the river. The remainder of your journey will have to be made without me. To your benefit."

For a moment, Sania was at a loss for words. After all, this was the man who'd provided for and taken care of her for most of her short life. Though she'd known all along that separation from Mohann was inevitable, she still couldn't help feeling sad.

She reached down from the carriage and touched his shoulder tenderly. "Thanks for everything."

"On the contrary, *Masiti* Sania" he whispered to her, "it is I who should be thanking you. The reasons why will perhaps someday be known. May the gods never neglect you." With that, he turned and walked back to the river. Slowly shaking her head, Sania stared after him.

When the man wanted to leave, he didn't fool around. She dismissed him with a shrug of the shoulders and looked at the contents of the purse in her hand. She looked up at the driver.

"What's your name?" He smiled, showing a mouthful of rotten teeth. "My friends all call me Sei-sei. How may I serve the young master?"

"Well, Sei-sei," she blurted, having almost forgotten that she was still dressed as a boy, "take me to a tavern for food and a place to sleep...and make sure it's the biggest and most dangerous place around."

Sei-sei smiled. "We are of the same mind, young master. Relax, we will be there in less than a half hour."

* *

Sania was growing tired of the driver's stupid grin, which he wore all the way from the river. She'd tried several times during the trip to make idle conversation, with little success.

The rustling of the river reeds as the carriage rolled toward the tavern had been the only sound she'd heard for the past twenty minutes, and she just wasn't used to being this quiet, particularly when she was nervous. In addition to that, she was still a bit apprehensive about this man's origins.

She'd thought that maybe she could try and figure out his background by chatting a bit. Unfortunately, he seemed to know what her intentions were. He just shook his head and grinned every time she attempted to ask him a question.

By the gods, she thought, resisting a strong urge to give him a quick stab in his ribcage with her sword.

One less idiot for Numeria to be burdened with, she thought, but suppressed her urge.

A few minutes later, just as she was planning how best to lift Mohann's coins from his purse and ditch the carriage without paying, they suddenly halted. Sania glanced around her and saw a nice marketplace, seemingly located within the village center. Situated within a few *en-yawo* of each other were several trade shops—a cobbler, blacksmith, and swordsmith.

All three were empty. Sania raised an eyebrow in puzzlement. It was the middle of the day, and those weren't even the only abandoned shops. There were another six shops that she could see—all empty. Why was no one here now?

The answer came in the form of a loud outburst from yet another building located directly across from them. This place was much larger than the other three—a bit too small to be an indoor market and maybe a bit large for a tavern, although it was three floors tall, always a telltale sign.

Loud shouts were coming from inside, and it sounded like tons of furniture was being smashed to bits. No sooner did her ears perk up to those sounds than a body flew through one of the windows of the tavern. The unfortunate soul appeared to be a young, well-built man with no hair and exotic markings on his teak-colored robe.

Forgetting about her plans to play a joke on the idiotic carriage driver, Sania ran up to the poor man and turned him over. He appeared to be the unfortunate victim of a sword slash, but the blow had been delivered with such speed and precision that it had barely left a mark on the man's body. Curious, she dropped the man back to the ground, walked up to the window, and peered in.

Chaos was erupting inside the small tavern dining space. There appeared to be a group of about fifteen men surrounding a boy about her age. The boy was handsome. The scars on his face just added character, in her opinion.

He was armed with nothing more than a black sword, an impressive looking weapon, if nothing else—and with it, he was able to keep a group of five of the grown men at bay before pivoting and attacking five more men, and finally moving to the third group. Sania instantly saw that it was a great strategy, but a flawed one.

Being as young as he was, naturally his physical strength would wear out soon, and he would fall helplessly into the hands of the mob threatening him. All they needed to do was play defense, and he would eventually tire. That is, unless his strategy was to unleash the wild beast standing by the door, vicious-looking but disinterested.

Fortunately for the young boy, every once in a while one of the men would stray forward, attempting to end the conflict immediately and take credit for the victory. Every time it happened, the boy's sword struck out quick and fierce, as it most likely had with the chap who'd been unceremoniously ejected through the window of the tavern.

As Sania continued to watch the riveting battle, her eyes eventually focused on three men in the corner of the tavern, neither taking part in the fight nor completely disengaged from it. They stood out to her, not just from the weird clothes they were wearing but also because they seemed to be wary of each other. *That's it*, she thought, *they're not taking part in the fight because they're too busy watching each other.*

Soon though, her eyes turned back to the young boy. The tavern itself was in shambles, which worked to the advantage of the men, since the boy, who was weaker but had an enormous speed advantage, was unable to use his fleetness of foot to outmaneuver his attackers. Sania instantly felt much respect for this kid, as well as a kinship of sorts, remembering the battle against the three "Uglies" that she had fought not too long ago.

At the same time, she thought maybe he was a bit too arrogant; he had an obvious disdain for his assailants, even though he was in a precarious situation. That was a dangerous quality for a fighter to have.

All at once, the remaining group of ten men, who had previously been watching the boy dismantle the last group of five, raised their weapons high and with blood-curdling shouts of "AZU!" they rushed at the young boy. They'd apparently given up on combat etiquette and phony courtesy.

In his haste to move to an unoccupied corner of the tavern, the boy tripped on one of the felled chairs and lost his footing. Sania thought he was as good as dead. Angrily, the cowards moved in for the kill, advancing slowly toward the boy, who was now on one knee holding his black sword in their direction.

This entire time, Sania had been wrestling with whether or not to help the boy. It wasn't that she was scared; on the contrary, this was precisely what she'd been hoping to find when she'd asked to be taken to a "rowdy" tavern.

Her issue was that she wasn't sure who was good or not, and she didn't want to make the same mistake she'd made with her foster father. Perhaps there was some reason why all of the men wanted the boy dead so badly. He was a bit young to be a rapist and didn't really seem to be the murdering type, but perhaps he'd stolen something from a noble?

Deep down she knew even if that were the case, the manpower being used to hunt him down seemed a bit excessive.

While she was wondering this, one of the men walked past the window where she was hiding. Bending down even lower so she couldn't be seen, she grabbed her large dagger from her backpack and stabbed in quickly through a space in the wood panels, hoping to get lucky. The results were instantaneous.

"Arrrgh!" The cry was deafening as the unsuspecting attacker's tendon was severed in two by the sharp blade. He fell to the ground, shrieking. His cohorts nervously looked around but could see no other foes in the tavern.

"*Zosherai!*" Several men started shouting 'witchcraft.' They didn't cease moving toward the young boy but were not nearly in as much haste to attack him now.

Outside, Sania was in stitches. *What imbeciles,* she thought. *They deserve to be wiped out, or else they'll spread their stupidity elsewhere.*

At that instant, the two men in the corner now decided to act. As one, they drew their daggers and flung them impressively at all five men at once. The speed with which they were able to do this astonished Sania—she could see that the men themselves were just slightly above average fighters, but with the daggers, they were extremely formidable.

Mouth agape, she watched as, at the last moment, the fifth man in the group immediately used his own weapon—a three-pronged shepherd's whip—to strike down three of the daggers before they could reach their intended targets, though the fourth dagger succeeded in embedding itself into one of the more fierce-looking men.

Unfortunately, the two in the corner were immediately attacked from behind by the final inhabitant of the tavern, the eccentrically-dressed old man who Sania initially thought to be their ally. As they both reached inside their robes for more daggers, their wrists were caught in a vice grip, surprisingly one from which they were unable to extract themselves, despite considerable attempt.

Calmly, the old man leaned in and whispered something to them.

Quickly, Sania made her way to the tavern entrance. "I've only got one question for all of you," she said. "Why does it take so many heroes to beat up an ugly little kid with a cheap black sword and a scrawny beast for a pet? Surely the First Prince can do better?"

Everyone turned at the sound of her voice.

The two men who were being held in the corner were shouting at her incessantly and winking, then seemed to calm down as she stared at them blankly. Their expression was of complete disappointment.

They seem as if they know me, she thought.

Instead of joining the fight though, Sania casually strolled over to where the other youth's pet was tethered. In awe, she stuck out a gloved hand and poked gently toward the neck of the beast, wondering if this creature she'd only heard stories about in the *Dukka-Vinyo* could actually be a real Mnyama.

"SKAACK!" The indignant shout from the creature almost startled Sania out of her sandals, as well as everyone else in the room, save the young boy. Sania stuck out her tongue to cover up her momentary lapse of bravery. "Hideous creature!" she said scornfully. The beast snorted and paid no further attention to her.

"Young *masiti*," the boy said from his kneeling position. "Please don't provoke my friend."

"*Masiti?*" said the remaining attackers. Everyone in the bar peered at her a bit closer, looking at Sania as if she'd grown two heads.

"How did you know she's a girl?" one of them asked.

The boy ignored them. He instead shifted his weight forward toward his right foot. Unseen by the men but noticed by Sania, he then discreetly reached his left hand toward an opening in the back of his sandal and withdrew two sharp wooden slivers. *Very sneaky*, she thought.

Now, though, the men were more interested in Sania. They were *umbalis*, which naturally meant that their character was not of the highest level. This was never more apparent than in their attitudes toward women.

"She wears the *sharafta-lei*," one of them remarked in a whisper. Sania again wondered if she should have thought more carefully before deciding to keep wearing her copper neck band.

"Not from around here, are you, little girl?" said a smelly runt no more than four *en-yawo* tall. He reached out for Sania's hand, totally turning his back on the boy. "My friends call me 'Stumpy.'"

Sania almost retched. She just realized that she had smelled this man's stench moments before she'd even decided to enter the tavern.

Just the sight of his hand reaching for her gave her the insane urge to pull out Feather and chop it off, but after a lightning moment of reflection, she reached inside her tunic and pulled out a square-shaped object, which she quickly tossed to him. His first instinct was to duck. The object landed harmlessly on the floor next to him.

"Stumpy" seemed taken aback as he looked down at it. "What's this?" he said to her. The other men squinted their eyes toward his hand, wondering what further witchcraft was at hand.

"I thought you wouldn't know," she said. "It's called soap. Using it will help you grow taller, or so I'm told. You should try it some time."

Two of his co-attackers began snorting with laughter. In a rage, Stumpy threw the bar of soap in their direction and rushed toward Sania. "You'll learn manners the hard way, then, little bitch!" he snarled at her.

He reached for her elbow, but all of a sudden realized he seemed to be groping for air. Looking down at his arm, he saw that his hand was no longer attached to his wrist. Instead, it lay on the floor, oozing blood. Puzzled, Stumpy looked down again at his wrist and noticed that it was shockingly spurting blood.

"Are you 'stumped'?" Sania asked him, one corner of her mouth smirkingly curled up.

Hearing the timely, if terrible joke finally jarred his senses and he burst into a loud, ear-piercing scream, then fainted.

"YOU LITTLE BITCH!" shouted the three remaining attackers, seemingly more out of fear at seeing the effortless way the girl had dispatched Stumpy than anger at her for injuring him. They turned their backs on the boy and instantly raised their weapons high to rush at her.

"What?" She smiled innocently at them. "Weren't you all traveling together? I just did you a favor."

Still kneeling on the ground, though, the young boy readied the two wooden slivers. Pulling back his right hand, he stopped immediately as she looked meaningfully into his eyes and shook her head.

Hoping the boy would listen to her, Sania waited calmly as the men rushed at her. They got closer and closer to her neck but oddly were not able to pierce it. She was a small target in comparison to them.

Mere centimeters away from her neck, Sania turned slightly to the side. Both swords crossed with her neck seemingly between them. Any other fighter would have used this opportunity to counterattack, but she reached again for her weapon.

She seemed to be almost inviting the two brigands to chop down at her with their weapons. A bit wary, they looked at each other and instead of swinging their blades down toward her neck again, they thrust them at her sternum instead.

The young boy now appeared to regret listening to her. It seemed inevitable now that the two *umbalis* would take her life; still, he pulled back his arm in an attempt to launch the projectiles.

"Stop!" the voice of the old, strange man from the table in the corner forced them all to freeze; even the *umbalis,* who were mid-attack, did not move. They instead waited with their weapons pointed at Sania's chest, beads of sweat running down their faces, as if waiting for a command.

Still conspicuous in his all-white eccentric garb, the old man released the wrists of the two men he'd been restraining. Turning his back to them unconcernedly, he walked over to the young boy, still kneeling, throwing projectiles ready.

"Such a hero at your age. Rare indeed." He extended a hand to the boy. "You two may wait for me outside." Without another word, the final two spear-hires—who looked more like young nobility than low life cutthroats, lowered their weapons, took a nervous glance back at the old man, and did just that. They left quickly, leaving the tavern keep eerily quiet for a few seconds. "You two could not have defeated all of those men even fighting together, you know," said the old man, raising the boy up from his perched position.

"It was only the combination of their mistrust of each other, lack of discipline, and greed that caused their undoing."

The young boy seemed to think about it for a second, then nodded. By sheer numbers, they should have lost the fight. Sania shrugged her shoulders.

The old man continued, "When confronted by a large force of adversaries, a true hero recognizes the danger they're in. The two of you are excellent young fighters, but you're both far too arrogant—you rely too much on your talents and too little on your instincts, and one day it will cause your defeat. What do you say to that, young lady?" He turned to face Sania.

Deep down, she knew him to be correct, but she was never one to give in that easily. "It's easy for spectators to criticize. Why didn't you join the battle if you thought you could defeat us?" she said scornfully.

"Join the battle?" the old man scoffed. "Do you two have any idea who I am?" he asked them. "Of course," said Gesi. "My foster father made me memorize the names, background, and appearances of all of the great tribal leaders of Numeria. You're the Lord Reverent M—,"

"I am not the exalted one; merely one of his many subordinates," the old man interrupted him, laughing harshly. "How about this? You two come with me now voluntarily, and I will guarantee your safety. No harm will come to either of you."

"So you work for the nut who's responsible for starting the *Kula Selawa*?" Sania asked him incredulously. "Give me one reason why we should trust the word of a lying zealot like him?"

At her words, an evil gleam began to glow in the old man's eyes. He ambled towards her, his age making it seem more laborious than it should have. Brown stained teeth split an unnatural smile as he sneered at her.

"Since when is someone who isn't even old enough to be my great-granddaughter qualified to know whom she can or can't trust? Trust is a complicated thing. Most humans in their foolhardiness completely trust those they shouldn't."

"I don't—," Sania interjected.

"As well you shouldn't. Agent Moh! Come!"

The very moment Sania saw her old friend and mentor, Mr. Mohann walk into the tavern, wearing the military uniform of the conclave warriors instead of the *Dukka-Vinyo* apparel she'd always seen him in, she knew she'd been stabbed in the back.

"TAKE THEM!" The old man shouted as dozens more soldiers surrounded the tavern.

12

Towards Revenge

Opulent.

Only this word could justly describe the private library of Okonokep, the infamous fortress vainly named after the Lord Regent himself, Okon Ashwar.

The absolute center of power in the Numerian world, Okonokep was a monumental achievement in architecture as well as a reminder of the limitless wealth of the gold and diamond mines of Numeria.

To complete the library, nearly twelve tons of the purest Hammazi gold had been shipped in daily from the Petruvian mine barges to provide its flooring. If that weren't enough to justify the word opulent, then one could gaze upon the walls and ceilings. Forming the luxurious walls of the massive entryway were numerous sheets of painstakingly polished ivory, seized from the tusks of the treasured *Jhaida* elephants of the Numerian steppe.

The *Jhaida* elephants were much smaller than traditional elephants in size but had tusks three times the length of traditional pachyderms.

Rumors had always abounded that the walls were not made of ivory but of the skeletons that remained of King Toloron's once great army after it lost at the North Port. People spoke at great length on how the bones had been harvested and polished to a high sheen, a constant self-reminder to the Regent Okon of his prowess at war.

However, there was no truth to that rumor, which may have even been started by Okon himself to strike fear into the hearts of his enemies.

Moreover, forming an almost lurid moulding to the ivory walls were rows of jade and emeralds, looted from the personal fortunes of countless noblemen and soldiers who had dared to challenge the legitimacy of the Lord Regent after his massacre of the Toloron forces.

On the ceiling was painted a massive and vivid mural of some of the famous battles of recent times, including conquests of Azu the Despot, Victo Ngeppu, and those conquests of the Lord Regent Okon himself. Conspicuously absent were victories won by the armies of Toloron and the Loffri tribe. Naturally, this was an exclusion never questioned by spoken word.

At this moment, none of the seven inhabitants of the study were concerned with the plushness of their surroundings. They were instead embroiled in a heated discussion. Holding forth at that particular moment were the famous tribal chieftains—Lords Jashu Jasonne and Muta Mutuofu.

"Lord Jashu, I could not disagree more," Lord Mutuofu injected, "the last thing the provincials need at a time like this is a spectacle. Despite Lord Jasonne's *noble* intentions, a contest of games will do nothing more than waste money and distract the common people from their work."

"What we should do instead is plan a grand celebration of the heir's Ascension Day and invite every loyal citizen of the Numeria to come and kneel before him." Most of the others in the room nodded their approval hearing this.

Lord Mutuofu was the polar opposite of Jasonne in every way imaginable. He was the staunchest of Azu loyalists. He was extremely fond of speaking, whereas Jashu was secretive, in word and thought. His clothes were simple; in fact, he often appeared destitute. Yet his family and lineage were arguably the most ancient and revered in Numeria, being a descendant and currently chief of the venerable *Ashanti* tribe of the coast.

"Why can't we do both?" Lord Jasonne replied. "Could there be a better reason for staging a grand contest of combat than in celebration of a young master's Ascension Day?" He paused for effect.

"It's simple enough to plan. We *invite* all loyal noblemen and their families to visit Okonokep, acknowledge the Crown Prince's twenty-fifth birthday, and kneel before him as a gesture of good-will. After those formalities conclude, what better way to send his loyal subjects home than with a grand feast and tournament as a celebration?"

Mutuofu frowned. Philosophically, he saw nothing wrong with the suggestion, and in fact, it made a great deal of sense. However, he had been appointed to this Conclave by the Regent Okon, despite his wielding considerably less influence than the others, for one purpose—to thwart all suggestions and political actions of Conclave members who were ex-Toloron supporters.

Because of this, he was often called Okon's lapdog behind his back, but in their secret agenda, Mutuofu had so far been quite effective. On the other hand, Lord Jasonne was no fool. He knew what had been happening during the Conclave votes and suspected why, yet despite his impotence within the Conclave, he'd still been able to use his appointment to keep abreast of Lord Okon's activities as well.

They were numerous. Just earlier today he'd heard reports from a spy within Okon's personal cookstaff, a young woman who originally came from the Northern Territories but whose parents had been cruelly tortured by several Okon soldiers just after the Usurpation—Two details which made her the perfect mole. According to her, the Lord Regent's official alchemist had been experimenting with a variety of tasteless and odorless drugs that could be used to alter drinks.

Several ounces of the experimental substances had already killed a dozen prisoners who had tested them in the form of tea. This was extremely alarming to the young nobleman, for poison is renowned for being the only weapon which has no conscience.

Since hearing this, he'd taken extra care to refuse all food and drink offered him in Okonokep. His mind was in confusion. Who was Okon's intended target, and why?

"The name day must take place and must be as extravagant as possible—befitting his young grace," Jashu reaffirmed. "We've all heard these stories coming out of the kumaze-we and the savannah." Everyone nodded.

"Only with the Crown Prince's lawful reaffirmation do we no longer have to consider these false rumors of 'prophecies' and '*Khuselas*.'" He wanted to end any justification Mutuofu had to continue his disagreement. This was his masterstroke.

A third voice, this one sultry and captivating, shocked him with its allure. "Lord Jasonne's reasoning is quite convincing." The person got up from where they had been reclining in a seat behind a tapestry in the far corner of the study. The priceless fabric depicted a mother wolf protecting a cub under twin moons. It was this person's usual place to sit during the Conclave meetings, and the choice was symbolic.

The figure stepped from behind the tapestry, slowly, almost deliberately.

One black sandal became visible; it carried an exquisitely-shaped light bronze foot. Adorning the final toe of that delicate foot was a thinly-cut jade and gold ring, priceless.

The lower peoples often said that if one were only to see the silhouette of this woman, it's possible that they could immediately go to hell completely content. For most, finally seeing such a person after hearing this would invariably result in disappointment, for how could the rumors of such beauty ever be surpassed by the actual appearance?

In at least one woman on the planet, though, there would not be such a letdown.

Lord Jashu, as he always did, willed himself not to stare in the direction of the Lady Ilayna. He himself was certainly no stranger to beautiful women, or men for that matter. However, upon their first meeting, he'd quickly realized that there was something irresistible and maybe even unnatural about her voice and gaze.

Her tone would lull you asleep and then her voice would relieve you of your senses. It was a one-two combination that most mortals could not defend against. He'd had an unnerving feeling since their first meeting that the right words from this woman, whispered into his ears at the wrong time, would make him another one of her pawns in the never-ending game of Numerian ascension.

Currently in the empire, no one held a more significant advantage in that game than this woman, for she was the mother of the heir to the provinces and tribes of Numeria. She was the 'Most Revered,' the widow of the former king Azoni Azu (the Despot) and mother of Azinna Azu, the boy king, and now his younger brother, Azzolari (Zari) Azu, recognized by most in Numeria as the rightful successor to its throne.

Only seen in public on extremely infrequent occasions since the death of her eldest son (at the hands of then Lord Toloron), she had become even more pale and solemn-looking than in her legendary days as queen of the Empire.

These days, when Lady Ilayna spoke, she spoke with the authority of the heir and the Lord Regent Okon through him.

"The realm could never show enough gratitude for your valuable advice and your loyal support of the heir, Lord Jasonne. Although most would agree, as would I, that lavish celebrations and fighting exhibitions are a bit much for a boy who hasn't even acknowledged ascension yet, we must take this opportunity to be more assertive with those who still refuse to recognize my son's birthright as the future ruler of Numeria."

Ilayna cast a surreptitious glance in the direction of Jashu, who held her gaze reluctantly. It was no secret that he'd once been the staunchest of Toloron devotees, a fact that he didn't like to hear mentioned, even suggestively.

"The celebration will be held as discussed, along with the tournament. During the celebration, we may invite some members of the royal tribes to allow their sons and heirs to remain with us in Okonokep and enjoy our hospitality."

She scanned the library, challenging anyone to object further. No one dared. Even Lord Mutuofu, who had taken the opposing viewpoint, had only done so to counter Jashu Jasonne. There was no further debate.

"Good." She was now ready to press on to other matters. She had always abhorred these meetings, thinking that the Conclave was mostly composed of sycophantic ineffectuals. She'd been unable to sleep last night after more disturbing reports reached her from the kumaze-we.

That entire area needs to be incinerated, she thought disdainfully. She had a feeling that the true threat to her son's throne lay out there beyond the savannah and *Kumaz-we,* dormant for now, but ready to return and pounce at any moment.

"What rumors have we from the kumaze-we?" she inquired aloud.

Normally Lord Jashu, whose legendary spynet far outclassed the capabilities of the other regents, and was perhaps only rivaled by that of his own kinsman Prikkar Pax, would have spoken first. Everyone was mildly surprised then when a winded, raspy voice was heard immediately in the library.

"Rumors?" that voice said. "There are no rumors, but there is much news." The voice halted in a fit of violent coughing. Jashu thought amusedly that each cough sounded like a death-whistle. Ostensibly, this person did not have many moons left to dwell among the living.

The coughing ceased. The person wiped away a line of saliva from his chin with a shimmery green ornate sateen cloth. "Bring in the informant," the withering voice managed to command. Without a word, the two iron-wrought doors to the study were opened from the outside.

A pathetic wreck of a man was jerked into the room by a palace guard. He was barely covered by a tattered and filthy cloak, which looked like it may once have been gold. His hair had mostly been burned away; what remained was singed and dark brown. The man's face was grotesquely disfigured from heavy beatings he'd taken. His left eye was swollen shut; his smell was fecal.

"What kind of 'informant' is this?" inquired Lord Ikona, another member of the Conclave. Like Lord Jashu, he descended from an ancient and eminent family and believed true power should be inherited from bloodlines.

However, unlike his more famous counterpart, he also believed in a strict code of honor and etiquette amongst those of the higher classes. Naturally, he looked down upon Lord Jashu's fixation on espionage, torture, and carousing.

The sight of this unfortunate creature being thrown into their midst was at this moment enough to turn his stomach.

"Is he reporting on the squalid living conditions of the *Majeedi*?" He guffawed at his own joke.

The old man spoke again. "Tell them who you are," he commanded. The old man's face had become iron; the coughing had ceased.

"I'm...my...m-m-my lords...your servant is Br-brother Saddique...of... "

Jashu strode up to the man and lifted his head up by the hair, staring harshly into his eyes.

"You've been subjected to *kimozo* venom...who tortured you?"

The others in the Conclave glanced uneasily at each other. *Kimozo* venom, extracted painstakingly from the poison ducts of the *kimozo* sand beast, was one of the more lethal naturally-occurring substances known to the world at that time.

One fraction of an ounce injected into the bloodstream was enough to cause fatality in almost any living organism.

Due to its ability to permanently reduce its victims to a vegetative state, King Toloron once outlawed the use of the venom.

As a proponent of its use and someone who had experimented with it many times, Jashu Jasonne saw the current situation immediately for its implications. Someone had wanted to torture and glean information from the unfortunate wretch, but they didn't want the information to ever be repeated. Lord Jashu knew instantly that they'd be able to extract no "news" from this messenger.

Suddenly, as if by an inner signal, the man's head raised. His eyes looked at the man who had questioned him, first to his person, then to his face, and finally moving to his eyes. Those eyes fixated on Lord Jashu for a long moment. They were suddenly clear and bright.

"Well?" Jasonne repeated.

With difficulty, the lips struggled to release a sound. It sounded like a strained whisper. "Sho...ha..mu...Tai...ji...."

There was total silence. Lady Ilayna placed a hand over her mouth. The sickly old regent's lips parted, revealing a wicked grin, highlighting two rows of completely black teeth.

Jashu stared into the man's eyes. Despite the *kimozo* venom, they seemed aware.

"Why did you say that phrase?" he asked him. The eyes stared back at him.

Coldly. Knowingly.

"*Shohamu Taiji,*" he repeated.

Jashu looked around the room, praying that no one had noticed his automatic reflex had been to kneel upon hearing the words. Eight pairs of eyes were staring back at him, some in shock, some sneering, and one or two looking disgusted. They were all studying his face to see his reaction. Then there was the final pair of eyes. Those he avoided. He grabbed the man by the chin and said slowly, "What did you see? Speak quickly—speak clearly! What's going on in the *kumaze-we?*"

The expression in the eyes changed. No longer full of life and lucid, they had suddenly returned to being black and empty. Jasonne shook him a couple of times, but he knew it was no use. This man was finished.

Jashu went to lower his head and lead him back to the citadel guards, but suddenly blood started flowing from the man's mouth. His body convulsed, and the head drooped down permanently. There was an extremely thin spearhead protruding from his chest, and standing behind him was the old man, dagger in hand.

"LORD REVERENT MORDU! How dare you kill a prisoner of our Crown Prince without permission!" Jashu thundered.

The old man sneered at Lord Jashu's disgusted expression.

"You all saw it," he replied to the Conclave. "He spoke words of treason! The penalty for uttering those words is death by *shad-im shahar.* What I just did for that wretch was merciful. Lord Jashu, have you forgotten?"

"I did not forget," the young nobleman replied quietly. "But if our purpose was to extract information from that..."

"You needn't bother yourself about that," he paused for effect. "I've succeeded in extracting all of the information the heir and the Conclave need regarding the recent events in the *Kumaz-we.*"

"So we're to believe the truth from your own mouth now, secondhand?"

"Isn't that how it usually comes from your spynet, Lord *Jashu?*"

"My sources have never failed the heir and never will, Lord *Mordu.*" The two of them were essentially playing a game of how perverse they could make the other's name sound—the other members of the Conclave thought it hilarious that two of the most powerful men on the planet were reduced to this when at odds with each other.

Mordu had long since ceased warring and carried a dagger, but no sword or spear, which made him virtually the only lord in the fourteen provinces to not do so. His only ornaments were his extremely long and white cloak, made from the thinnest of materials, and combined with the gauntness of his physique—this made him appear skinnier than a reed in the late autumn wind, ready to be whisked away at any given moment.

His face was haunting. Bright grayish-green eyes set deeply within their sockets provided a stark contrast to the blackness of his skin and the pure whiteness of his beard, which was braided like his hair and extended to his chest.

His other ornament, the one he was rarely without, was the abnormally large two square-rod book, which he usually clutched to his person like a branch to a drowning man. Red leather bound, with ornamental lettering in gold casting, there were only three large words across the front:

ƎΟυμΟ τ 8ƎΟυƎη8

Translated from the tongue of the ancients to the common tongue of Numeria, it meant "Way of Daeryon."

Daeryon, known as the Progenitor, was the supreme ruler of the ancient pantheon of Numerian gods and was actually credited with creating the first male and female Numerians.

Reverent Mordu was a staunch zealot who did not tolerate anything less than absolute obedience and worship of the old faith—hence his hatred for anything Toloron-related, especially Lord Jashu—his former reliable spymaster.

"Lord Jasonne believes—" he began, sneering openly at one of the last bitter reminders of his days of persecution by Toloron.

"That's enough." An eerie, high-pitched voice sounded in the room. All sounds, and most of the breathing, in the room halted in the same instant. Another person, who'd been observing unseen in the opposite corner of the study from Lady Ilayna, stood slowly and purposefully.

All eyes moved toward him, shocked at his sudden action. They heard the slow click of his thatch sandals across the marble floor, agonizingly slow, toward both Lord Jasonne and Reverent Mordu.

Of average height, he was less than two rods tall, with angular shoulders, extremely long arms, and springy legs; his presence seemed slight and overpowering—you could either fail to notice him in a room or fail to notice anyone other than he. He dressed in traditional Numerian battle gear, all black with a silver capelet, as he had every single day since the age of fourteen, even on his wedding day. It lent him a sinister air, as did his mask.

The mask. Silver-forged from the rarest metals found in the southern mines, it was an eerie reminder to his enemies that this person could be in their midst at any moment and not be recognized. He often was, to be sure. Some said that was the reason for the exaggerated pitch of his voice; he was trying to disguise it so that he could remain anonymous during his many excursions beyond the gates of *Okonokep.*

This last rumor was false; he never disguised his voice. He also never spoke unless he had to.

Lying beneath his mask was a sprouting tuft of white hair, completely white, extending down to his back but tied together in neat bunches every six or so inches with bands of more silver. His eyes seemed to pierce from the small slits that were cut into the mask, seemingly illuminating the grim guise even further.

Okon had a manner of movement and speech that was more feminine than masculine in nature; this, combined with the fact that he never carried a weapon, sometimes caused men to forget that he was one of the most legendary warriors in the history of Numeria.

However, it was the sheer might of his army—about sixty thousand men strong—which struck fear in the hearts of the other tribal warlords and nobility of Numeria.

And why wouldn't it? Lord Okon's infantry, combined with his five hundred elephants, twenty-thousand cavalry, and numerous tamed *kimozos* meant that he was much more likely to die from the spear of one enemy than from an army of spears.

He had very little reason to fear assassination. Day and night he was attended by his infamous cadre of personal bodyguards, the *Okonomelo*, literally translated as "Eyes of Okon."

If the *Okonomelo* were not enough of a deterrent, Okon himself was said to have attained the highest level of the *Noa Sana*, the ancient Numerian black art of sorcery. Traditionally, warriors and sorcerers distrusted each other and had little respect for each other's abilities. This made it virtually impossible for accomplished warriors to learn spellcasting, or for necromancers to become proficient in combat.

Apparently, the Lord Regent had found a way to bridge this divide. Perhaps these rumored abilities in *Noa Sana* was why he rarely carried a weapon. Perhaps it was his confidence in the *Okonomelo*. No one knew for sure.

"Lord Reverent Mordu," Okon said, his voice a piercing needle, "the young Lord Jasonne is quite correct in this case. Only an agent of this citadel, with the full backing of the Crown Prince, can lawfully conduct a treason inquiry. You overstepped the limits of your authority."

A tone of extreme courtesy was heard, which put everyone in the room on edge. Okon was never as deadly as when he was at his most polite. Reverent Mordu made to kneel, quite a feat at his advanced age, but Okon quickly placed a slender brown hand on his shoulder to stop him, the Lord Regent's long black painted fingernails lending a sinister look to the gesture.

"You were acting in the interests of the young heir, my friend—too much propriety isn't necessary in this case."

Inwardly Mordu exhaled, but his outward veneer was still that a proud, petulant old nobleman. "Thank you, Lord Regent," he replied, somewhat consoled.

"However," Okon said, "since you were fortunate enough to interview with the traitor, before his death, please be kind enough to inform us of your findings." Beneath the silver mask, eyelashes fluttered. Everyone in the room knew the current situation; if Reverent Mordu's recounting of the details were not satisfactory to Lord Okon, he would not leave the study alive.

Lord Jasonne laughed inwardly at his enemy's misfortune. He was perhaps the only man in the room who wasn't in abject fear of Okon, or anyone else for that matter—but he was interested in learning what Mordu's vicious actions had been able to extract from the man.

Despite the outwardly filthy and tattered gold clothes he had been wearing, it was evident to him that the poor man had some combat ability and a proud heritage, perhaps as a member of one of the many warring clans of the *kumaze-we.*

How had he met such a fate?

Mordu began. "As you recall, after receiving multiple reports of treasonous activity, the Conclave authorized a bounty of a thousand silver pieces for the person or persons responsible for the death of the three warrior-emissaries at an unregulated *Dukka-Vinyo* owned by a woman referred to as Mistress Jayda by the locals."

Some of the Conclave nodded, others waited impatiently to hear more.

"Five hundred soldiers were sent to the *Dukka-Vinyo* itself to arrest Mistress Jayda, the patrons, workers, and all others who may have been witness to that treasonous act, for interrogation in

Okonokep to be conducted personally by the Lord Regent and Lord Jashu Jasonne." He seemed to have difficulty getting the last word out.

"Unfortunately, when the soldiers arrived, they found that it had been completely deserted. A couple of squatters who'd been inhabiting the place told the soldiers that Mistress Jayda had released all of the ladies who worked there from their contracts, given them cash gifts, and sent them away. Then they'd taken most of the valuables and headed west, into the sands. The squatters had no information on the murder of the three envoys, but they'd heard rumors, since substantiated, that a girl had killed them all and then fled into the kumaze-we."

"A girl?" interrupted Lord Mutuofu, "are you saying the three soldiers were all killed by a single girl?"

"Precisely," Reverent Mordu confirmed, irritated at being interrupted by the sycophantic noble. He continued.

"The soldiers then killed the squatters and burned the *Dukka-Vinyo* and everything in it. It turned out to be a fatal mistake, as a large cadre of knockout elixir, used to induce 'unwilling' first-time women to have relations with the clients, was left in one of the rooms undetected."

Jashu stifled a laugh, knowing what was coming next. The others were aghast.

"Once the elixir caught flame, the fumes spread for over a thousand *en-yawo* and incapacitated the soldiers sent by Lord Otu under our direction. They were then incinerated by the flames, to the last man."

There was a stunned silence. A story like that couldn't be improvised or conjured up. It was almost poetic.

"I sent about two thousand of my men into the sands to find her, as rumors of a child prodigy in the area had begun to spread for many hundreds of en-yawo. They were all slaughtered. Apparently, our paid adviser, a former captain in the army of Lord Otu, had a change of heart and decided to warn the girl. His body has not been recovered.

"Luckily for all devotees of the young prince, word of the bounty had already spread. Another rumor, which we now know was false, circulated that the girl was an accomplished acolyte of the Gilded Fishermen's clan of thieves and assassins.

Two other acolytes of the faction, including the betrothed of the suspect, were discovered to be in the town of Sidanee on clan affairs. I had one of my agents set up a meeting with these two Gilded Fishermen at a dining hall in a tavern there. I also arranged for around thirty or so of the most capable *umbalis* to be present, in disguise, in the same room."

Jasonne was taken aback—seems he'd underestimated the ruthlessness of his zealot counterpart, though it did seem an excessive amount of men to use for capturing a mere girl.

"The good news is, we are certain that my agent, as well as the bounty hunters, succeeded in locating the girl responsible for the murder of the three warrior-emissaries at the Jayda *Dukka-Vinyo*. The bad news is, none of the bounty hunters survived to collect their silver fortune."

The room inhaled sharply as one. The things Reverent Mordu was saying to them were not only unimaginable, but also unthinkable. What "girl" would have the brazenness to commit treason against the heir and the ability to kill thirty cutthroat *umbalis*?

"This traitor," Reverent Mordu pointed to the motionless heap on the floor, "was one of the two members of the Gilded Fishermen with whom I had my associate arrange a meeting. His name was Saddique. Saddique's elder faction brother, Rushdi, also attended the meeting.

It became evident later that their sister acolyte wasn't, in fact, the same young woman who'd started the disturbances, she was this man's betrothed. The two of them actually bear an uncanny resemblance, which is where the confusion began."

"How did you know this?" interrupted Lady Ilayna.

A grim smile touched Mordu's wrinkled lips.

"All in good time, my lady. Before my subordinate had time to find whereabouts of their tribal sister, the two Gilded Fishermen sniffed out the ambush. A furious fight ensued, and not long after it began, my paid *umbalis* started to get the worst of it."

Lord Mutuofu sighed. "It seems the fighting ability of the Gilded Fishermen's faction is not to be trifled with." The others nodded their heads in silent agreement.

"Maybe so," continued the Lord Reverent, "however, the faction brothers Saddique and Rushdi hadn't even joined the fight yet."

"The girl?" Jashu asked.

"No, at least not yet. Next, a young man, about the same age as the girl we were looking for, had wandered into the tavern before the ambush began and took a personal interest in saving the Gilded Fishermen's lives."

The members of the Conclave shook their collective heads. This story was becoming more and more fantastical with each turn. They wanted Mordu to get to the result of the encounter, but the details were so hard to believe they knew they needed to hear everything.

"This youngster was clothed in all black, from his light armor to his undergarments. His appearance was very dusty, as if he'd just wandered into the *Kumaz-we* from the savannah. Perhaps this is the case; after all, he was accompanied by his wild pet *Mnya-ma*."

He glanced at the faces of the Conclave; all of them seemed astonished, save for Lords Jasonne and Okon. Lord Jasonne's expression was more of rapturous excitement; he couldn't wait to hear more. Okon was never impressed by anything.

Mordu decided the time had come to impress Lord Okon.

"If you think that's interesting..." he began.

They waited.

"...the boy was carrying a weapon on him. A jet black sword, ebony blade and all—completely black except for its platinum edge." He paused for dramatic effect.

No one in the study moved. They could feel the cauldron of rage boiling inside Okon. Lord Mutuofu coughed discreetly; Jashu Jasonne took the opportunity to innocently admire an antique set of paintings hanging from the ceiling that he'd never noticed before.

To his credit, Okon ostensibly was only slightly trembling. Inside, however, he most likely was about to lose control.

The others expected him to fly into a rage and demand to know the whereabouts of the young boy. They'd all heard the inflated tales originating from East Rhydor—how the mysterious son of a royal *avaremba* had defeated the First Knight, Jorell Boro, in single combat and had the audacity to steal the First Prince's legendary *Emi* Sword.

As the First Prince and Okon were brothers by marriage, Okon—as well as all of Numeria, saw this as a direct affront against himself.

To their surprise, Okon's slight tremble stopped. He calmly glanced over at Reverent Mordu, nothing visible through his silver mask.

"What happened next?" was his only reply. Their respect for him increased; even Jashu Jasonne applauded inwardly. Self-control and patience were perhaps two of the most valued virtues in Numeria. Other than Okon, who else could have reigned their emotions in so quickly?

"An *abdu-kudus* (holy man) who had taken no interest in the proceedings up to this point, launched a vicious sneak attack on the boy while he was mid-combat."

"According to our deceased friend here, the attack would have killed ninety-nine percent of most seasoned warriors, but somehow this kid managed to avoid it. The *abdu-kudus* then vanished.

"Then the girl appeared. THE girl. With her own unique sword, dressed as a boy. She began helping the boy, Gesemni, I believe. After about two minutes or so, they had managed to defeat the entire lot of *umbalis*, including...." Mordu's voice trailed off with hesitation.

"Including who?" Jashu almost hissed.

"The natural and adopted sons of Lord Norna of Ikiye, Jacub and Symeon, were in the tavern—they were mistaken for umbalis as well and also killed by that young criminal." Mordu's face was full of contrition at the news.

Okon stood up slowly and walked to a table in the center of the room. Leaning against it, and not trusting his legs, he pondered for what seemed an eternity. No one made a sound.

"You're quite certain that *both* heirs of the Ikiye province, the only heirs of Sankofa Norna are dead?" His high pitched voice could barely be heard now.

"Quite sure, Lord Regent." Reverent Mordu said.

The Conclave was stunned. In their minds, these two youths, a boy and girl had just become the two gravest enemies of the empire. An heir was the most valuable asset in Numeria. How were they ever going to account to Lord Ikiye for his?

Reverent Mordu continued, oblivious to the consternation in the room, "Fortunately, this conclave doesn't rely upon *umbalis* for the preservation of the realm. On a prearranged signal from my agent, as well as an informant we planted in Mistress Jayda's *Dukka-Vinyo* many moons ago, the soldiers of Namir Solla surrounded the tavern and demanded that they come out alive or else the entire building would be set ablaze."

"Of course they refused?" Lord Jasonne inquired.

"Most certainly, for children are quite stubborn and have no sense of misfortune. They did not surrender, but my agent took advantage of everyone's distraction to toss a capsule of *sonagrass* into the tavern hall. In a few seconds, all save him had been incapacitated."

"A knockout drug?" Jashu asked, his disgust apparent.

"I assume you have no objection with Reverent Mordu's methods, Lord Jasonne?" Lord Okon said, too politely. News of the death of the Norna boys had removed the last vestige of sympathy in him for the other two children.

Jashu shook his head very slowly, knowing that now was not the time but wishing he could unsheathe his sword and bathe the entire study in Okon's wretched blood. *A curse on you and the next seven generations of your descendants,* he thought bitterly.

"Wonderful. Please continue, Lord Reverent," Okon encouraged, without enthusiasm.

Mordu said, "The soldiers all claim to have seen, simultaneously, on both youths a tattoo of a black crown on the left wrist—three sharp points of black underscored by two rectangles of black. Same tattoo markings; same location; on two different youths."

"*Shohamu Taiji,*" said one of the noblemen in the room.

No sooner had he began speaking did an unseen dagger thrown by Lord Okon impale his throat.

Blood, which before today had never before been shed in the inner sanctum of this Okonokep study, splattered a few priceless art pieces in the room. Lady Ilayna gasped. Reverent Mordu made a sign of blessing and tightly grasped the talisman on his necklace. Lord Jashu winced outwardly but inside felt completely aglow, maybe for the first time in moons.

Okon looked at the rest of them, terrifying as ever behind his silver mask.

"The penalty for treason is death. *Lihlala yinlalifa!* Long live the heir!!"

"LIHLALA YINLALIFA!"

Once the cheering died down and the members of the Conclave fell silent, Okon took a seat, right next to Jashu Jasonne.

"Now," he said calmly. "Now that these traitors are in the custody of the Regency, we will deal with this soon enough. More importantly for the moment—arrangements must be made for those *Kumazi* seeking shelter from the Great Summer; also, I have some ideas on how to deal with this 'Painless Death' plague."

In shock, the other nobles looked at him with a mixture of trepidation and awe. They had all partially suspected that Okon dealt in the black arts of witchcraft and the supernatural, but could even he cure the plague that had recently been ravaging the savannah and kumaze-we?

The solution, he explained calmly, was to intensify the *Kula Selawa*, the Toloron treason tribunals, focusing these latest trials primarily on the new immigrants. Despite the lack of coherence in his reasoning, no one objected.

Those parasites could use a little cleansing, he thought to himself in disgust.

Epilogue

Water.

There is no water, the voice in his head, the only one he'd heard from in days, told him.

He was hurting. His eyes hurt. They always did. They hurt when he opened them; they hurt from the light. They hurt whenever he closed them shut. They were full of sand, and insects, and grass.

So much grass around here.

He'd been crawling for days. He couldn't walk. He wanted to, and his legs were there. He'd checked several times, just to make sure. But he couldn't move them. It's a truly horrific feeling to know that parts of your body which used to function no longer do. Your brain has to be retrained to cease asking things of that body part. The retraining process is long and arduous, and he was currently mid-stream in his own personal journey.

And so, because he had lost the capacity to walk, he crawled.

Crawling was significant for him. He had once as a child made his nanny crawl on her hands and knees in the latrine because he had become bored. The poor woman had tried to leave his family household to find work somewhere else.

He'd then accused her to her face, in front of his parents of stealing his own personal golden figurine collection, knowing that he had thrown them down a well months earlier in a childish tantrum.

The unfortunate nanny had been brought back and put to death, protesting her innocence until the very end.

Yes, crawling had always been significant in his life. When his inheritance had been usurped, and he'd been effectively disowned by his parents, he had gotten on his knees in his father's study, pleading with him to change his mind. His father had not relented, and for months afterward, his biggest shame had been in the crawling and groveling, not in the rejection.

Now here he was, Jacub Norna, once proud heir to the Tribe of Ikiye, crawling on his hands, his face and clothes caked in mud.

He was crawling because he had refused to stand up when it mattered.

He was now fighting for survival because he had forgotten how to fight for himself.

But those days were over.

He didn't know when and certainly wasn't sure how, but he knew that his crawling days were finished, and the time had finally come for him to stand. Or make a stand, at least.

He would find his father and kill him.

He would find the scourge of Numeria, the Lord Reverent Mordu and kill him.

Finally, he would locate his treacherous, murderous cousin, Symeon Norna.

Cousin.

At the thought of the word, he wanted to spit, but he lacked the moisture. His "cousin's" death would undoubtedly be the most horrific of all.

But first, he had to survive the savannah.

Thank you, Father Daeryon for my preceptors. I hated them, but they taught me how to survive all different types of hell. Help me find my way to revenge; he prayed silently.

He had lasted this long from the insects that he had come across, some of which he knew were high in protein while trying to avoid the poisonous ones, which he had been told were usually adorned with colorful markings.

He'd managed to not die of thirst by sucking on the tallest blades early every morning and swallowing as much of the dew as he could, but by late afternoon, he was always parched and miserable again.

He'd been taught that when lost, particularly in the savannah, the only time you should travel is during the day, but that was not possible because the temperatures were far too hot for someone in his condition to travel under the sun.

And so, he covered the majority of ground under the moonlight instead, praying to his ancestors for the forbearance of the savannah's loathsome predators.

He raised his head, something that took considerable effort. Looking into the distance, he could see nothing but the dreaded grass for many *en-yawo*. Still, he knew the direction he needed to travel in, the direction that would take him to his father's domain, towards the tribal provinces of *Ikiye*, *Goza*, and *Elesaa*, towards revenge.

Acknowledgements

Journey's this long are impossible to make without the help of friends, family, and collaborators—whether official or informal. *The Onyx Crown* began five years ago, as I found myself watching fantasy after fantasy on television and wondering why the characters of color all seemed to be slaves, former slaves, or pirates. This is not representative of our glorious past, and hopefully the words of this newest generation of Black, Asian, and Latino authors will ignite a desire in our youth to research our true history, not that which has been given to us.

I would like to begin by thanking my mom, my brothers and my sister Cindy for their many years of allowing me to be the black sheep. Thanks also to my children for continuing to inspire me to want to achieve new goals.

My fondest indebtedness to my wife Alexis and also to Stephanie for your years of support.

To Nick—I'm proud of you, nephew.

To my best friends Everett, Wes, Dre, Michele, Cwam, Stacey, Ray, Kevin, Carylton, JJ, Daryl, Bruce, Kelley, and Wole—thanks for always being there.

I especially need to give thanks and much appreciation for all of the long hours of editing to Melissa and Parisa. You both helped me turn rambling words and aimless ideas into something that resembles a fantasy novel in miraculous fashion.

To Natasha, without whose initial encouragement this book may have just remained an idea—thanks for everything.

To Dawn, your guidance and advice have been invaluable. Go Hawks!

A special thanks to various establishments in the DMV where I allowed to write and focus when it was impossible to do so at home. Busboys and Poets, Tryst, Wegmans, Starbucks—you all played a role, but there were so many other places as well.

To the great independent bookstores of the DMV, including Politics and Prose, Kramerbooks, Mahogany Books, Upshur Street Books, Second Story Books, Capitol Hill Books, the Potter's House, and many others. I have browsed your shelves and enjoyed your conversation. Just know that you will always have my admiration and support.

I would like to express my fondest appreciation for the writing communities on Wattpad, Goodreads, Bookbub, Instagram, and Reedsy for your timely encouragement and feedback.

Follow your dreams.

—Alan Hurst

About the Author

Alan Hurst has been a fantasy fiction enthusiast since his first reading of J.R.R. Tolkien's "The Hobbit" at age nine. He considers legendary wuxia authors Gu Long and Jin Yong as his biggest influences. Mr. Hurst began writing The Onyx Crown in 2014, after noticing a lack of Pan-African themes in medieval fiction. Additionally, he wanted to create ethnic fiction that could be embraced by all descendants of the African Diaspora. He currently resides with his family in Maryland, USA.

Made in the USA
Middletown, DE
18 February 2019